T0196860

# One Thing Leads to a Lover

# Also by Susanna Craig

*The Love & Let Spy Series*
Who's that Earl

*The Runaway Desires Series*
To Kiss a Thief
To Tempt an Heiress
To Seduce a Stranger

*The Rogues & Rebels Series*
The Companion's Secret
The Duke's Suspicion
The Lady's Deception

# One Thing Leads to a Lover

*A Love & Let Spy Romance*

## Susanna Craig

**LYRICAL PRESS**
Kensington Publishing Corp.
www.kensingtonbooks.com

LYRICAL PRESS BOOKS are published by

Kensington Publishing Corp.
119 West 40th Street
New York, NY 10018

All Kensington titles, imprints, and distributed lines are available at special quantity discounts for bulk purchases for sales promotion, premiums, fund-raising, educational, or institutional use.

Special book excerpts or customized printings can also be created to fit specific needs. For details, write or phone the office of the Kensington Sales Manager: Kensington Publishing Corp., 119 West 40th Street, New York, NY 10018. Attn. Sales Department. Phone: 1-800-221-2647.

Lyrical Press and Lyrical Press logo Reg. U.S. Pat. & TM Off.

First Electronic Edition: April 2021
ISBN-13: 978-1-5161-1059-9 (ebook)
ISBN-10: 1-5161-1059-5 (ebook)

First Print Edition: April 2021
ISBN-13: 978-1-5161-1060-5
ISBN-10: 1-5161-1060-9

Printed in the United States of America

*To Melissa,*

*for helping to make the 80s so much fun the first time,*

*I couldn't wait to revisit them*

# Acknowledgments

As always, I'm grateful to the people who've supported me and my work: my agent, Jill Marsal; Esi Sogah and the team at Kensington; the lovely ladies of the Drawing Room; my university colleagues and administrators, who have been not just generous but genuinely encouraging; Amy, who always knows what to say; my mom, who encouraged the habit to begin with; my patient and loving husband, to whom I fully intend to keep my promise not to procrastinate...someday; my daughter, who still thinks it's cool to have a mom who writes books; and all my readers. Thank you!

# Chapter 1

For as many of her thirty-two years as Amanda could remember, her mother had been urging her to mind her step.

Not that Amanda was particularly clumsy—barring the summer of her twelfth birthday, when she had grown several inches taller in mere weeks and both the dressmaker and the dancing master had thrown up their hands in despair over her ungainliness.

No, the wrong-footedness Mama fretted over was primarily of the social variety. Did Amanda comport herself properly? Did she say the right things to the right people? Did she attract neither too much notice, nor too little?

Amanda had always been a little too curious, a little too bold to suit her mother.

One might have hoped—Amanda certainly had—that her mother would relax a bit once Amanda, at nineteen, had received and accepted a much-coveted offer of marriage from the Earl of Kingston. If not then, surely once the vows had been spoken in St. George's in front of hundreds. Or once the requisite heir and a spare had been born.

But if in fact Mama had ever allowed the phrase to fall into disuse, she soon took it up again when Amanda found herself a young, and most eligible, widow.

Though she loved her mother, Amanda despised being told to mind her step. To be forever minding your step meant worrying more about others' thoughts than your own. Making yourself small, fearful of taking up space. Always looking down instead of looking up.

But when the glorious June sun shone from a sky of cerulean blue, dotted with puffs of white clouds so fat and happy they appeared to have been added to the world's canvas by an enthusiastic five-year-old, then who, on such a day, would not rather look up?

Heedless of the potential for either gossip or freckles, Amanda tipped her face to the sunshine and reveled in its warmth, watching light and shadow dance across her eyelids in a rose-tinted quadrille. The sounds and smells of Bond Street washed over her like a raucous stream flowing around an unmoving stone. Clutching her parcel—a copy of Pascal's treatise on geometry in the original French—so that one sharp corner fitted against her ribs, she drew in a deep breath and—

A sharp blow to her left shoulder and elbow jerked her from her moment's reverie. Her chin snapped downward and her eyes popped open as the paper-wrapped book flew from her hands. Before she could bring him into focus, the man who had jostled her arm was already disappearing into the crowd.

The footman who had accompanied her on the outing—at Mama's insistence, for Amanda had been firmly of the opinion that a widow could surely go into a bookshop alone—had been trailing at a respectful distance. Now he surged forward and would have given chase had not Amanda instead directed him with trembling motions to rescue the package, which had skidded to a landing on the pavement several yards away. The book she'd bought for Jamie's birthday was in danger every moment of being kicked by careless feet into the gutter.

Just before it met an ignoble fate on the steaming pile left by a passing dray, the footman snatched up the package. In another moment, it was back in her kid-gloved hands, the paper wrapping scuffed and torn at one corner, the string holding the paper frayed but still knotted. No real harm done.

"Thank you, Lewis. Thank you." Once more, she clutched the book to her chest, heedless of the grime it had gathered.

"I'm only sorry I couldn't lay hands on the fellow who treated you with such disrespect, milady." A flush, part anger, part embarrassment, spread across his youthful cheeks and to the edges of his powdered wig, clashing miserably with the rusty orange of his livery. "Mrs. West will box my ears."

Her eyes traveled in the direction the stranger had been walking, but of course, he was long out of sight. She had caught no more than a glimpse of him, just the back of a drab greatcoat and tall beaver hat, an identical costume to the one sported by dozens of gentlemen strolling and striding along the busy street.

"I'm sure it was an accident, Lewis. I hadn't any business stopping in the midst of all this bustle." The crowd still surged around them, oblivious to the incident. "But I think it's best if my mother hears nothing of the matter. Now." She nodded in the opposition direction. "Let's make our way back to Bartlett House, shall we?"

Lewis sent a glance toward the package. If he had been carrying it, as was his duty, doubtless a passerby would have been unable to knock it from his hands as easily as it had been knocked from hers. But Amanda had refused when she first left the shop with it, and she made no reply to this silent repetition of his offer. He bowed. "As you wish, milady."

Away from Bond Street, the crowd thinned, and though the streets of Mayfair were not empty, they were quiet enough that one could pick out the notes of the birds perched high in the lush treetops. Now and again the air was split by the cheerful shrieks of children, barely contained within the nurseries whose windows had been flung open to the fresh morning air.

With a rueful roll of her aching shoulder, Amanda slowed her steps but did not stop again. She had lost a little of her taste for soaking up the sunshine. Perhaps later, in the seclusion of the garden at Bartlett House, while the boys made observations for their project about bees.

But first she intended to meet with the housekeeper about the week's menus, if Mama had not already done it. Then she had some invitations to which she wished to respond, if Mama had not already written on her behalf. And of course, George, Lord Dulsworthy, had promised to call on her today, and Mama was predictably delighted at the prospect....

A swallowed sigh pushed Amanda's shoulders a notch lower. How had things ended up thus?

When they reached Bartlett House, she paused to collect herself as Lewis preceded her up the stairs. While he held open the door, she ascended, watching the toes of her brown leather half-boots peep from beneath her skirts as they landed squarely on each step.

Inside, all was quiet—unsettlingly so, given that two young boys lived within.

Matthews the butler came forward with a reproving glance for Lewis and a hand outstretched for the package she carried. But before he reached her, the hand fell to his side and the movement folded into a bow. Lewis must have communicated, whether through mouthed words or gestures, that the assistance would be unwelcome.

"Mrs. West rang for her morning cocoa not a quarter of an hour ago, my lady," Matthews reported.

Mama was having a lie-in? *Good.* "And the boys?"

"In the drawing room with the fencing master, my lady."

"Oh? Is it...Tuesday?"

The butler very nearly smiled. "No, my lady. When Mr. Jacobs arrived, he indicated that Lord Dulsworthy had requested the change."

*Ah.* Not, of course, that she begrudged George having a say in her sons' upbringing. Her husband's will had named both of them guardians, after all. And in the first months of her widowhood, she had been grateful to have a friend in Lord Dulsworthy, to whom she could turn when the inevitable questions arose. Grateful too to her mother, who had swooped into Bartlett House and taken command so that Amanda could focus all of her attention on her grieving boys.

But months had turned to years. Nearly three of them. And though the Countess of Kingston was perfectly capable of handling matters herself, over time, people seemed to have forgotten it.

Including, occasionally, Amanda herself.

"Did Mr. Jacobs happen to say wh—?" She bit off the question, saving it for later. For Mr. Jacobs himself, perhaps, or for George when he called. "Thank you, Matthews. Please send Mrs. Hepplewythe to me in my sitting room."

If Mama had risen late, then the matter of the menus was yet to be decided, and Amanda could finally enjoy a week without—

"Certainly, my lady. I'll tell her as soon as she returns from Mrs. West's chambers."

Though tempted, Amanda did not suck in a sharp breath of disappointment or grimace or even shake her head. As her mother often reminded her, the servants saw everything and knew even more; therefore, she must mind her step around them most of all.

Occasionally she wondered if she might not be better off if she let a bit of her frustration show.

With a nod to Matthews, she climbed the stairs to her own suite of rooms at the back of the house, passing through the bedchamber, with its cheerful yellow curtains and floral paper; shedding her pelisse, bonnet, and gloves in the dressing room; and coming at last to her small sitting room, more than half filled by a velvet-covered divan, an overstuffed chair flanked by a marble-topped table, and her escritoire. At that elegant writing desk, positioned between two tall windows overlooking the garden, she sat down.

The small stack of invitations still lay on the center of the desktop. At least Mama had not taken the liberty of writing replies—yet. Nevertheless, she had made clear her opinion about the necessity of declining them.

But *why* must Amanda continue to limit her social engagements? She was no longer in mourning. Surely no one would think it improper for her to spend an evening at the theater with the Hursts?

This time, her sigh escaped, but the room's silence absorbed it.

More than twenty years her senior, James Bartlett, the late Earl of Kingston, had been a quiet gentleman of bookish tastes who had generally avoided frivolities. Though he had been gone for three years, Amanda had had no opportunity to discover anything of the supposed liberties a widow of her status might take.

Because now it was Mama who sorted through the post. And Mama had decided that the only invitation it was proper for her to accept was the one that lay uppermost: the invitation to Lord Dulsworthy's ball. Because George was an old friend and the boys' guardian. Because he always behaved with strict propriety. Because *everyone* knew that he intended someday to make Amanda his—

*Enough of that.*

She laid the package from the bookshop on top of the invitation, pressing down slightly as if to smother the folded note. She would rather think of the treasure she had found and imagine the light in Jamie's eyes when he saw it.

One look at the package brought back the memory of the jarring blow the stranger had struck against her arm. She could see the book fly from her fingers, arc into the air, and get lost on the ground among the feet of the crowd. Uneasily, she traced the torn wrapping, fingered the frayed string with which it was tied. Had the fall damaged the book's binding? Only one way to find out. She rummaged in the tray for the penknife, sawed through the twine, and peeled back the brown paper to reveal a little book bound in green leather.

In her mind's eye, she pictured the clerk's long, ink-stained fingers holding the slim volume out to her. But hadn't the cover of the book the clerk had put into her hands been *blue*...?

Reaching forward to lift the green cover, she caught herself holding her breath. Could she have been mistaken? For just a moment, as she flipped through the book, she was reassured by what she saw. French phrases. Numbers.

But as the pages sped past, fanned between her fingers and thumb, her eye caught more and more that did not belong in a treatise on mathematics. This was...why, this was a...a cookery book? Filled with recipes for elaborate pastries, it would appear, though her knowledge of baking came entirely from the eating side of things. The kitchen had been another of the places a lady of her station did not set foot, according to her mother: *The housekeeper is your intermediary with the lower servants, dear; make her come to you.*

"Oh, bother." Somehow the clerk had wrapped up the wrong book or given her someone else's package. Now she would have to make a second trip to the shop to set things right, and as soon as possible. What if they mistakenly sold the Pascal to someone else in the meantime? "Oh—" A stronger epithet rose to her tongue, but even in the privacy of her sitting room, she squelched it out of habit. "Bother," she finished again, though more emphatically this time.

"Mama, Mama! You must come and watch us. Mr. Jacobs says I'm a—a—" Philip was already halfway across the room, having burst in between the first and second *bother*, weaving between the chair and the little table and making its fragile top spin. She twisted toward him, welcoming both the distraction and the burst of energy he brought.

"Prodigy," his elder brother supplied, following a pace behind, tossing dark hair off his narrow brow with a jerk of his head. "But I shouldn't think so much of the compliment, if I were you, Pip. Uncle George pays him, you know."

Stockier and nearly as tall as Jamie, though the younger by almost two years, Philip looked surprisingly formidable as he squared his shoulders and crossed his arms over his chest. Perspiration shone on his round, red face and dampened his blond hair. "That's as may be," he retorted, glaring at his brother. "But I still knocked your foil from your hand, didn't I? Twice."

"Boys!" Amanda's mother was the next to sweep into the room, wearing a morning gown of pale blue and clutching a gauzy shawl around her shoulders. Thanks to her maid's artful arrangement, her hair still looked more blonde than gray. "What have I told you about barging in on your mama? You and your brother are young *gentlemen*, and a gentleman never interrupts a lady's much-needed repose."

"Oh, pshaw, Grandmama." Philip dismissed the notion out of hand, though Amanda rather suspected he hadn't the faintest notion of what *repose* might be. "Mama likes a bit of noise now and then, don't you?" he demanded, turning toward her.

*Yes*, she wanted to cry out. *Yes*. During the months of her late husband's illness, and for the period of mourning afterward, she had been cocooned within a muffled world of sickness and grief. Even now, her mother was still trying to wrap Amanda in cotton wool. She was almost as tired of the quiet inside Bartlett House as she was of watching her step whenever she dared to leave it.

But she was prevented from replying by the nearer approach of her elder son, Jamie, the eleven-year-old Earl of Kingston. A shadow of worry hung on his slight build and sallow complexion. "Is something troubling you,

Mama?" He spoke low, his voice almost inaudible beneath the clamor of Philip regaling his grandmama with his fencing triumphs.

Amanda could not keep herself from brushing the cowlick of dark hair away from his eyes, though he was growing old enough to be annoyed by the gesture. "Why do you ask, my dear?"

"You were saying 'oh, bother' when we came in. Has something happened?" Even before his father's illness, Jamie had been the sort of boy who always feared the worst.

"You're coming, ain't you, Mama?" Philip interjected. "I want you to watch me whoop him again."

"Don't say *ain't*, Philip," his grandmother corrected.

"Or *whoop*," added Amanda. "And don't worry, Jamie." She turned back toward her elder son even as she gathered the wrapping paper, the twine, and the book, along with the invitations on which it had been resting, and stuffed the lot into the escritoire's shallow center drawer. "I'm not troubled by anything. And neither should you be."

"I'd wait," Philip insisted, "until you've seen him fence. What's to become of him when he's old enough to be called out?"

"Gracious, Philip." Amanda avoided her mother's eye as she swallowed a laugh. "Why ever do you imagine anyone would challenge your brother to a duel?"

Philip considered for a moment before replying airily, "Oh, the usual things, I s'pose. Card sharping or trouble with a petticoat or—"

"That's quite enough from you, young man," their grandmama said, steering Philip from the room. With a shrug, Jamie followed. From the threshold, Amanda glanced back toward her desk. The matter of the book would have to wait until later.

Much later.

The next hour was given over to a display of fencing in the drawing room, with Philip crowing over every hit. Contrary to his brother's taunts, Jamie was not altogether hopeless, though Mr. Jacobs appeared more interested in striking poses than in teaching the boys much of anything. Amanda weighed whether to mention it to Lord Dulsworthy. Luncheon followed: "You never eat the creamed turnips, dear," Mama observed with exaggerated solicitousness. "I can't understand why, when I ask Mrs. Trout to prepare them especially for you." Afterward the boys declared it the ideal time to observe the bees at work in the spring flowers, though by three o'clock it would not have been an exaggeration to call the sunshine hot.

The slightest headache had begun to form behind her eyes even before they returned to the house to find George, Lord Dulsworthy, in the entry hall arguing with a stranger.

Well, no. *Arguing* implied a degree of passion that George would have found shockingly inappropriate under any circumstance. *Murmuring reprovingly*, then, his remarks directed mostly to Lewis rather than to the stranger, who stood apart from the fray.

After the brightness of the garden, the house was dim, and she had to blink away the spots before her eyes in order to bring the gentleman—tall, lean, brown-haired—into focus.

Or perhaps *not* a gentleman?

"—letting a tradesman in through the front door?" Lord Dulsworthy was scolding the footman.

If the cut and fashion of the stranger's clothes had been insufficient proof of his lowly status, he carried a small, paper-wrapped package.

And yet there was something in his bearing that made her wonder whether George had been quite accurate in his assessment of the man.

"Why, one might even wish to mention the matter to Matthews," George continued, and for the briefest of moments, Amanda wondered whether he would truly be so bold as to reprimand *her* servants. Doubtless if he did not, her mother would.

"My lord." With one hand, Amanda waved the boys into the library as she stepped closer, not quite into the circle of their conversation. George, Lewis, and the stranger all turned to look at her, and she sent a glance over her shoulder to see that Jamie and Philip had obeyed her silent command. The pair of them were just disappearing through the library door, though Philip moved jerkily, as if Jamie might be dragging him by the other arm.

Although she had addressed George, the stranger spoke first. "Lady Kingston?" He hadn't quite the deferential manners of a tradesman, either. When she nodded, he bowed, then held out the item he carried. "I believe this is the volume you purchased at Porter's bookshop this morning? As you may already have discovered, you were given an item intended for someone else."

"I had discovered it, yes." Readily, she took the book from him, though both George and Lewis had reached for it too. "Thank you."

The answering dip of his head was not the gesture of a shop clerk. Or an errand boy.

No, for a man of thirty-five or so, with broad shoulders and features that bore the stamp of experience with the world, the term *boy* was entirely inappropriate.

Nevertheless, Lord Dulsworthy seemed eager to dismiss him as such. "Well, well. You've got what you came for, what? On your way, then." With his still-raised hand, he motioned for Lewis to open the door.

The stranger made no move to leave. In fact, he gave no indication of having heard George at all. "If it's quite convenient," he said to her, "I'll take the other book now."

"Lewis can retrieve it," Lord Dulsworthy said, a command the footman thankfully did not immediately heed.

When she darted a glance up the staircase, she noted that the stranger's dark eyes followed the movement. She thought of the package tucked away in her escritoire, nowhere she wished a servant to pry. "I suppose I could go myse—"

Lord Dulsworthy broke in again. "Lady Kingston is too well-mannered to tell you that your request is quite *in*convenient at present. She has a prior engagement to go driving. With me. As you can see, she's just on the point of going out."

Now the stranger shifted his gaze, and his study of her, though brisk, was more than a little unsettling. She was still wearing a coarse holland apron over her morning gown. At her side, she dangled a straw hat by its ribbons—a concession to her mother's insistence that the sun would brown her dreadfully. Its broad brim was not always compatible with her close observation of the boys' lessons, however, and she had taken it off and on so many times over the course of the afternoon, her hair must be a tumbled mess. Indeed, she could feel a few straggling curls clinging to her damp neck.

No one, not even a tradesman, would mistake her for a lady ready to spend an hour or two on display among the fashionable set in Hyde Park. He must suspect that George was rudely hurrying him away.

Her cheeks, still flushed with warmth from the time spent in the garden, grew warmer still. But the stranger only gave a slight smile and a nod of acknowledgment. "Forgive me. Will you be so kind as to tell me when I may call for it?"

"She'll have her maid fetch it 'round to the shop," declared Lord Dulsworthy, now raising his hand as if to clap the stranger on the shoulder and direct him toward the door.

The man moved only slightly, not out of George's reach, but enough that George too could see his face, which had turned...Amanda could not decide how to describe his expression but settled at last on *stern*. George's hand fell.

"The book in Lady Kingston's possession is a rarity, sir," the man explained in a cool voice. "And much anticipated by another customer. I must insist on retrieving it myself." He returned his attention to her as he reached into his breast pocket, withdrew a card, and held it out to her. "A message here will always reach me, Lady Kingston."

The line of his jaw was firm and his dark eyes narrowed slightly. *Intense* was perhaps a better word than *stern* to capture his demeanor, but in any case, the look sent a prickle of uncertainty along her spine. All this, for a recipe book?

Awkwardly, she juggled the package into the crook of her arm to free one hand. Once more, out of the corner of her eye, she saw George's fingers twitch as if he were tempted to snatch the card from the stranger. He was always so protective of her, of the boys. But the card was safely within her grasp before he made any further movement.

Across the rectangle of stiff paper, the stranger's neatly manicured thumb nearly met her considerably grimier one. Like the broad-brimmed hat, gloves were sometimes an encumbrance during scientific pursuits. With a murmur of embarrassment, she took the card and tucked it beneath the string wrapped around the package. "Thank you. I'll be in touch soon."

"I await your message most eagerly, Lady Kingston." With another bow, he turned and was gone.

Almost before the door closed behind him, certainly before she could draw breath, the boys raced into the hall, their questions echoing off the high ceiling: "What book, Mama? Who was that man? Can I open the package?" As they fell to arguing between themselves over the honor, George resumed upbraiding Lewis, his voice only adding a deeper note to the cacophony. Amanda was surprised that neither Matthews nor her mother came running to shush them.

But no one came. No one even seemed to notice when she said, "I'll just take this upstairs, shall I? And freshen up? I'll only be a moment."

The stout door of her bedchamber ought to have restored everything to its usual quiet, but even in the silence, her head buzzed. The unaccustomed noise in the entry hall must have left her ears ringing. Or perhaps too much time in the sun had done it. Either way, her nerves jangled and hummed like a badly tuned pianoforte.

Out of habit, she reached for the bell to ring for her maid. With the other hand, she clutched both the book and her hat, now rather mangled, against her side. As her breast rose and fell with the slight exertion of climbing the stairs, the corner of the book pressed into her ribcage, its sharpness a reminder of that morning's scuffle. She glanced down at the package—the paper wrappings, the string, the calling card with no writing visible. She thought of the striking-looking stranger. She let the silk-tasseled bell rope slip through her fingers without pulling it.

Instead, she tossed her hat onto her dressing table with a flick of her wrist and stepped toward the bed. Against the ivory silk coverlet, figured with delicate embroidery of yellow and pink roses and green vines, the coarse brown paper and twine looked out of place. She slid the card free and put it aside without looking at it. There was nothing mysterious, certainly nothing interesting or exciting, about having received the wrong book this morning. Nothing intriguing about the man who had delivered the correct one.

Nevertheless, she caught herself holding her breath as she slipped the knot and peeled back the paper to reveal exactly what she'd expected to find the first time: a copy of Pascal's *De l'Esprit géométrique*, bound in tooled blue leather.

If she felt something like disappointment, she hid it, swiftly enfolding the book in the paper again. Jamie would be delighted. In the morning, she would send 'round a note to—to—

It required more resolve than it ought to pluck up his card from where it lay on the coverlet. *For pity's sake.* Why was her fancy determined to make something out of nothing? Mistakes were made every day. A shop certainly might employ a gentlemanlike sort of fellow to smooth them over. He'd said the recipe book was valuable. All the more reason to entrust the task of retrieving it to someone other than an ordinary clerk. Just because the events of today stood out in her mind, a splash of color on the canvas of her dull, ordinary life, it did not therefore follow that either the mix-up or the man was actually *interesting....*

When she swept the card toward her with two fingers, its sharp corner snagged one of the embroidered roses and unraveled a quarter-inch or so of pale pink silk thread. Absently, she smoothed the injury with her fingertip before turning over the calling card, wondering what the man's name might be.

But the card bore no name, and her pulse kicked up a notch in spite of her determination to be calm.

Half of the creamy-white rectangle was taken up with a black and white picture of a bird. Long-tailed and sharp-beaked. And beside it, a direction that did not belong to Porter's bookshop.

*Mind your step, Amanda. Mind your step.*

What exactly had she stumbled into this time?

"Nothing. Absolutely nothing," she scolded herself aloud and tried to shake off her foolishness. So she'd been given the wrong book. So the man who'd been tasked with exchanging it for the right one carried an unusual card. Her imagination was running away with her.

The sooner the mistake with the packages was resolved, the better. Lord Dulsworthy was waiting below to take her driving, and he would be wondering what had become of her.

She picked up the book and tucked it behind one of the mountains of pillows on the bed. Jamie wouldn't pry, but Philip might, and she did so want it to be a surprise. Then she turned toward the door to her sitting room, intending to lay the card on her escritoire, where she would sit down in the morning and write the note that would put an end to the matter.

Only the thought of her mother's curiosity, sharp as the edges of the stranger's mysterious calling card, gave her pause. After a quick glance around, she tucked it into her shift. It lay against her skin, cool and crisp.

As she crossed back to the bellpull to summon her maid, the corners of the card pricked her with every movement, yet she did not remove it from her bodice. Would Martha spy it there when she helped her change into a fresh gown?

If she did, then the snagged coverlet would be something to distract her with. The girl had an eye for detail and a knack with needle and thread.

This afternoon, she must keep her promise to go driving with dear, old George. But tomorrow evening, once the cookbook had been returned and quiet once more hung over the house like a pall, then Amanda would be at leisure to lie in her bed beneath the freshly mended coverlet, to trace the embossing on the stranger's card, and to embroider the memory of this little interlude to her heart's content.

# Chapter 2

With the stairs of Bartlett House pitching downward before him, Major Langley Stanhope paused to pinch the bridge of his nose between his thumb and first finger. He did not swear, though a few colorful phrases sprang to mind, remnants of a youth spent in quite another part of London than the wide, tree-lined streets of Mayfair.

Not that he'd failed in his mission. Not yet.

But he had expected to count it an easy victory.

Certainly it ought to have been. He'd wondered, at first, why General Scott had sent *him*. Anyone in Scott's service of highly trained intelligence officers could have been called upon to retrieve the package Lieutenant Hopkins had been forced to abandon in a moment of desperation. Nothing about the assignment suggested, even now, the need to involve the man once accounted Scott's best agent.

Then again, Scott's best agent was leaving without getting what he'd come for.

Langley fished in his breast pocket for his spectacles and carefully threaded them over his ears. The green smudges of trees sharpened into individual leaves fluttering and rustling in the afternoon breeze. He could even spot the cracks and joints in the elegant stone facades surrounding him, if he chose to look.

He would have liked to have seen Lady Kingston as clearly, to have had more than an impression of dark eyes surrounded by a frowsy halo of golden-brown hair. To have been able to judge her reaction to his request by the expression on her face.

But the spectacles were noteworthy. An identifying feature. So he often went without them in public, went without his uniform, too, without anything that might easily distinguish him from a hundred other gentlemen, tallish but not too tall, with brown hair and eyes, who dressed respectably enough but far from the first stare of fashion.

In the flurry following the news of Hopkins's predicament, there had been no time to plan a cover story more thorough than "shop clerk." No time to compile a dossier about the woman who, through sheer happenstance, now possessed some of the most valuable information in England. Langley hadn't expected to need either one.

Therefore, he also hadn't expected the widowed Countess of Kingston to be so young. Hadn't expected the pair of curious boys she'd hustled out of sight.

Armed with a duplicate copy of the volume she had purchased that morning at Porter's, he had intended to make a simple exchange of books. Certainly he hadn't expected to need to leave his calling card.

Would the simple etching of a magpie pique her curiosity about him?

If so, then he'd have to find a way to assuage it.

More likely, though, she wouldn't spare him another thought. Would she even remember to return the book, as she'd promised? Worse, would she take up the suggestion of the pompous ass who'd met him at the door and send it back to the bookshop in the careless hands of a servant? He'd need to set a watch on Porter's if that might be the case.

"Damn it," he muttered—or perhaps he *hadn't* muttered, given the shocked expression on the face of the elderly woman who drew abreast of him on Curzon Street at precisely that moment.

He lifted a finger to the brim of his hat. "Apologies, ma'am."

*Count yourself lucky it wasn't worse.*

Past St. James's, on a street lined with establishments that catered to gentlemen—clubs, discreet pleasure houses, even a gaming hell or two—Langley wheeled into a glass-fronted shop. The bell jingled merrily, unperturbed by the force with which he'd opened the door. The high walls were lined with drawers and shelves of jars, all filled with varieties of snuff and tobacco, their perfume spicing the air.

"Right with you, sir," called the proprietor, Mr. Millrose, a portly Black man with close-cropped silvery hair. He was perched on a ladder, leaning precariously toward a jar that was still almost out of his reach. The customer at the counter did not turn his head.

With one deft flick of his hand, Millrose swept the jar from the shelf into his arm and clattered back down the ladder, chatting amiably as he measured out and wrapped the other man's purchase.

When the door had closed behind the customer, but before the bell dangling above it had ceased its dance, Millrose shifted his attention to Langley. "Well, sir?"

Langley spread his hands on the counter. "I'll need a paper of the Kingston blend."

Millrose's gaze flickered from Langley's empty hands to his face, betraying no hint of recognition or surprise. "Right away, sir."

As Millrose turned toward the shelves behind him, Langley took a quick glance around the shop before ducking under an opening in the counter, sliding behind the ladder, and slipping through the door at the back of the shop.

A dozen years ago or more, when the war with France had been in its infancy, General Scott had ordered the purchase of the tobacconist's shop, to be used as a front for the intelligence officers whose work would be endangered if they were regularly seen coming and going from Whitehall. Hidden away on a side street, tucked between some of the wealthiest and seediest parts of London, the shop still sold tobacco, just as the shingle outside proclaimed. The number of men who passed through its door was therefore perfectly unremarkable.

But below, in place of what must once have been the kitchen and servants' quarters, now lay a warren of offices and spartan bedchambers, connected through a series of low-ceilinged passageways to what had been the kitchens and cellars of other establishments up and down the street. No one on the block seemed to know that beneath their floors, a hand-picked collection of secret agents and codebreakers worked day and night on behalf of the Crown.

No one, that was, but Mr. Millrose—Colonel Millrose, more correctly—who served as both General Scott's aide and a purveyor of fine tobacco products. Langley had heard the man complain more than once, and only half-jokingly, that learning to recognize the different varieties of tobacco by sight and smell in order to appease the suspicions of the most particular customer had been far more difficult than learning how to break a Vigenère cipher.

Despite his impassive expression, Millrose must have been disappointed to see Langley return empty-handed. In the wrong hands—and more especially in the right ones—a codebook was a far more deadly weapon than any cannon. Hopkins had risked his life to steal this particular one.

Langley, tasked only with the simple act of retrieving it from some confused widow who'd been handed the thing while out for a shopping spree, had let everyone down. Again.

At the bottom of a narrow flight of stairs, a series of doors branched off a dimly lit corridor. Langley opened the second door on the right. He should have gone straight into the workroom and confessed his failings to the codebreakers hunched over the tables there, waiting both for his arrival and word of Hopkins's fate.

Instead he threw himself onto a narrow rope cot, which all but filled the room that passed for his private quarters. He had inherited a house near Richmond, but he never visited it. Occasionally he reflected on the fact that he might have been sleeping on a feather mattress in a stately bedchamber overlooking a more scenic portion of the Thames.

Right now, however, comfort was the last thing he wanted.

An hour or so later—the passage of time was always something of an illusion, but never more so than in a windowless room—he heard a knock at the door.

"Major Stanhope?" A soft, feminine voice.

He made no answer.

*Tap-tap.* "Sir Langley?"

*Damn* that knighthood. Why had General Scott insisted he accept the honor?

"Come," he nearly shouted, jerking himself into a sitting position, and then to standing when the door opened and Mrs. Drummond stepped into the room.

Frances Drummond was the widow of a fellow officer killed in the line of duty. Having determined that she knew more than was wise, General Scott had quickly devised a plan to keep her as safe as possible. Officially, she managed the domestic affairs of what was known among the men as the Underground. Despite her somber black dress, however, she looked like no housekeeper Langley had ever seen. Even in the dim light spilling in from the corridor, her pale hair and blue eyes gleamed coldly.

Once, he had found her beautiful.

"Ah, here you are." Her mouth curved in a mocking smile. "When Colonel Millrose said you'd returned without the book, I though perhaps you'd gone into hiding."

"You know better than that, Fanny."

"Do I, Major Stanhope?"

They'd been friendly, once. Even, perhaps, friends. But she hadn't called him *Magpie* since…since Langley's error in judgment had led to Captain Drummond's untimely death.

"Any word about Hopkins?" He forced the question from between his teeth, even as he tried to push down the memory of Hopkins's last note, penciled on a scrap of the same brown wrapping paper that had covered the book he'd just handed over to Lady Kingston, his fearful scrawl its only encryption:

> *They're onto me. Managed to switch packages with a passerby, but don't know how long this geometry primer will fool them. Ask at Porter's—*

Who had discovered the truth of Hopkins's mission? And once they realized he no longer had the codebook, what might they do to uncover its whereabouts? Were they holding him captive? Or worse?

The crossing-sweep who had brought the note could—or would—reveal little of use. Nothing more had followed.

When word had arrived from General Scott, Langley had expected to be sent in search of Hopkins. Instead, he'd been told that the codebook was now in the hands of the Countess of Kingston, and he was to retrieve it from her. Despite his initial disappointment in the assignment, he understood. If he could not count be counted on to save his fellow soldier, he had only himself to blame. Scott was giving him a second chance, an opportunity to work his way back into his fellow intelligence officers' confidence.

Some job he'd made of it.

At his gruff question, Mrs. Drummond slid the folded note between her fingernail and thumb, creasing it. She did not answer. How he wished she would just scream at him, rail at him, have it out. The cool distrust, the distant resentment, was far, far worse.

Fanny passed a critical eye over him, her plump lips pursed. "I wish you'd stop sleeping in your clothes, Major."

He thrust out a hand for the paper she held. He needed to know what was in that note before her nervous movements rendered it illegible. "I wasn't sleeping."

The codebook was his priority now, the only way back into anyone's good graces. Even his own.

She slapped the paper onto his outstretched palm. "*Brooding*, then. The wrinkles are equally difficult to remove."

Before he could retort, she turned and left, closing the door behind her and leaving him in darkness. He fumbled to light a lamp, then sat down once more on the sagging cot to read by its flickering light.

> *Subject: A. B., Countess of K— (widow), aged 32 years*
> *Children: Earl of K— James, aged 11 years, and Philip,*

*aged 10*
   *Guardian: George, Lord Dulsworthy (Brook Street)*
   *Since death of late earl in '04, subject has lived exclusively*
*at Grosvr. Sq. residence with her mother, Mrs. D. West (widow,*
*aged ??)*

The document went on to name most of the household's principle servants: butler, housekeeper, ladies' maids. He noted the inclusion of a fencing master, but the omission of the boys' governess or tutor—inessential information, almost certainly, but unlike Millrose to leave off any detail.

The information regarding the countess's habits was similarly sparse. Either her ladyship went almost nowhere, or she was unusually clever about hiding her footsteps. Most people were not clever, whatever they might like to imagine. But what could Lady Kingston possibly have to hide?

The next words he read only confirmed his suspicions about her.

*Lovers: none (rumored understanding w. Duls.).*

He smirked at the abbreviation of the man's title. So, she was going to marry her sons' guardian, the dullard who'd tried to have him thrown out on his ear? How thoroughly conventional.

Nevertheless, a waste, in his not-so-humble estimation. Even blurry, the countess had struck him as attractive enough to do better. Then he shrugged off the thought.

Her love life—or lack thereof—wasn't his concern.

After reading through the note twice more, memorizing its details, he dipped a corner of the paper into the chimney of the lamp. When the flame caught, he watched it devour Millrose's precise penmanship, let it run up almost to his fingertips before dropping the blazing sheet of parchment. The charred remnants landed on a plate that still bore crumbs from the sandwich he'd scarfed down sometime late last night. Or early this morning.

*This morning...*

Given the time Hopkins's message had arrived, Lady Kingston must have been already leaving the bookshop while other ladies of her ilk were still studying their invitations and refusing their breakfast. An early riser, then. Or motivated.

*Motivated by a French geometry book?* He tipped his head to one side. Possibly it had meant something special to her, or to someone else. A gift, then...but for whom? Not Dulsworthy, surely. Perhaps one of her sons?

A curl of smoke rose from the ashes of the dossier, forming itself into a plan.

Though he was more night owl than early bird, he'd call again first thing tomorrow, before anyone went in or out of Bartlett House. His future in Scott's service rested on his safe recovery of the priceless intelligence in Lady Kingston's possession. Nothing else mattered.

But he could not shake his awareness that, as long as the codebook remained in her hands, she and her family could be in danger.

\* \* \* \*

Lord Dulsworthy had timed the conclusion of their ride through Hyde Park so that it would be difficult for her to avoid inviting him to tea. Amanda knew it, though she could not prove it. And of course, if she did not issue an invitation, her mother more than likely would.

So, while he stepped down from the carriage and gave the reins to a groomsman, she forced herself to brighten the rather strained smile she had been sporting since setting out. And when he reached up to hand her down, she managed to ask him in with enthusiasm that was not obviously feigned. George, pretending to be surprised, attempted to look flustered for a moment before accepting the invitation for which he had angled. Amanda tried hard not to laugh.

It was not that she disliked Lord Dulsworthy. He was the epitome of a decent fellow. Not handsome, to be sure, but not displeasing in looks, either. And always careful to treat her with the utmost propriety and respect. She would not, for example, have imagined it possible for anyone to drive a high-perch phaeton so sedately.

A woman could do worse, yes. But why, oh why, did so few ever consider whether a woman in her position might not want to do *better?* Might not want to remarry at all?

Still, whenever she grew annoyed by his attentions, she generally found it prudent to remind herself that George cared for her boys and wanted only what he believed was best for them. That her husband had trusted the man. That no matter how many times her mother might caution Amanda to mind her step, she no longer had the power to direct her daughter's steps down the aisle.

"Mrs. West is expecting you in the drawing room," Lewis told her as he accepted her bonnet and spencer and Lord Dulsworthy's greatcoat and hat.

Upstairs, her mother crossed to them as soon as the footman had opened the door. "There you are, my dear."

Lord Dulsworthy evidently heard a reproving note in her voice. When he spoke, he sounded sheepish. "I will gladly accept responsibility for the delay, ma'am."

"I do believe the weather bears no small share of the blame, Lord Dulsworthy," Amanda insisted, accepting her mother's kiss of greeting before choosing the green and gold striped chair her mother had vacated, rather than the settee closest to the tea table. "Was there a soul in London within doors this afternoon?"

"Quite a number of them, I should think," was George's too-serious reply. "Clerks and servants, unless their masters are shockingly lenient. The infirm. People who—"

"Shall I ring for tea, Amanda?" asked her mother, stepping to the bell as if determined to head off Lord Dulsworthy's prosy instincts. "I've already sent for the boys. They would be sorry to miss a visit from their uncle."

"An excellent notion, Mrs. West. I have already spoken with Jacobs about this morning's fencing lesson," he explained, turning toward Amanda as he arranged himself on one side of the settee, brushing a hand over the empty space beside him as a silent indictment of her choice to sit elsewhere, "but I should like to hear young Kingston's and Master Philip's assessment of their progress."

"Speaking of," Amanda ventured, "I did wonder why—"

"They'll make great strides, with a master coming twice weekly now."

"*Twice* weekly? Oh, I see."

She knew of no harm in increasing the frequency of the boys' fencing lessons. Still, Amanda narrowly kept herself from bristling at the intrusion on both her privacy and her parental prerogative. George might at least have consulted her on the matter.

He nodded sagely, oblivious to her displeasure. "Kingston will thank me, come September."

Despite the overwarm afternoon, and the prickle of sweat beneath her arms and along her spine, Amanda shivered.

Ordinarily, the mere mention of a month in the latter half of the year would not turn her blood cold. But the particular mention of *September* renewed an ongoing debate over Jamie's education, George's determination that he attend Harrow as his father had done, and Amanda's decided preference for keeping him at home.

George had wanted to send him away last autumn, just past his eleventh birthday. Then she had pleaded Jamie's slight stature, his natural reserve, his grief. Now, with her elder son's twelfth birthday rapidly approaching, she knew those arguments—never strong ones in George's eyes—had weakened considerably, though Jamie was much the same as he had ever been.

In Lord Dulsworthy's view, twelve was past the point at which boys like Jamie—lordlings and future leaders—should be at school, forming bonds with other young men, not tied to the apron strings of a nervous mother.

The terms of the guardianship left the final decision in George's hands, though it was clear her late husband had expected George to consider Amanda's wishes. But the education of boys was a matter for men—at least, according to the rules by which their society operated.

Amanda's last, best hope was to persuade George to wait one more year, until Philip—stronger, tougher, and more outgoing—would be old enough to accompany his brother. "I think, my lord, that we ought to consider whether—"

Before she could complete the sentence, Jamie and Philip burst into the room—well, Philip *burst* and Jamie walked, carrying an open book, with eyes only for its pages. He was very like his father, even in looks.

"Have you heard, Uncle George?" Philip threw himself onto the vacant place beside Lord Dulsworthy. "Mr. Jacobs says I'm a prodigy. Where's the tea things, Mama? I'm famished."

Jamie came to lean against the tall back of her chair, closing his book around a finger to mark his place. "You're a prodigious bore, Pip, that's for certain."

George, who would never be mistaken for a wit, blinked blankly at Jamie before turning to Philip. "Indeed, I had a ripping report from Jacobs. You must have worked up quite an appetite, young man."

On that cue, Betsy arrived with the tea tray and placed it on the table between George and an empty chair, which Amanda's mother came to occupy. "Allow me to do the honors, Lord Dulsworthy," she said, in the saccharine voice she seemed to reserve only for him.

"But there's no cake!" Philip's scandalized cry drew every eye to the tray, which bore the teapot and cups, a plate of bread and butter for the boys and cucumber sandwiches for the others, but no cakes—indeed, no dainties of any kind.

"Is something amiss in the kitchen, Betsy? It is a baking day, is it not?"

Betsy colored. "Yes, ma'am. It's only…well…You see, Cook did try—"

Displeased with the maid's stammering reply, Amanda's mother broke in. "Send Mrs. Hepplewythe to us," she said dismissively and fluttered her beringed fingers toward the door.

"Bread and butter's better for you anyway, Philip," said George, accepting his cup from Mrs. West. "Make you strong."

"Then Jamie had best eat *two* pieces," he declared, which earned him a sneer from his brother and a frown from his mother.

As if she had anticipated the summons, the housekeeper soon made her appearance, clasping her hands nervously before her even as she dropped into a deep curtsy. "My apologies about the state of the tea tray, Lady Kingston. Mrs. Trout tried three different recipes from that book Mrs. West gave her and nothing came of them that either of us thought worthy of gracing a table in this house. But that left no time to prepare aught else. She's most vexed, ma'am. Said it must be some mistake in the book's printing."

"Sadly, it sounds to me as if your cook's skills are in decline," Lord Dulsworthy said, polishing off his third sandwich.

Amanda's mother blushed. Mrs. Hepplewythe bristled. Amanda said only, "Which book?" though she knew already what the answer must be.

"The one Mrs. West gave to me just after luncheon, ma'am. French pastries, 'twas said to be, though I don't know..." Amanda tried to keep her expression impassive, but the housekeeper's voice trailed off all the same.

Her mother took up the explanation. "The recipe book in the drawer of your writing desk, my dear. I went into your sitting room to, er, borrow a piece of paper and found it there." Amanda said nothing, certain her mother had been in search of the invitations, to decline them. Then, to her surprise, her mother explained, "I urged Mrs. Hepplewythe to have the cook try something new. I thought it might tempt your appetite, dear."

George took a great slurp of tea. "You are unfailingly thoughtful of others, Mrs. West."

"Yes, indeed, Mama," agreed Amanda. Her headache had returned in force, perhaps had never entirely left, and masking her frustration required a more than usually heroic effort. "Sometimes, though, I wonder whether you oughtn't to give yourself so much trouble."

"Oh, well, I—"

Amanda turned to the housekeeper. "Mrs. Hepplewythe, would you please retrieve the book from Mrs. Trout and bring it to me?"

"Very good, ma'am." The woman curtsied once more and was gone.

In the interval of her absence, Philip regaled Lord Dulsworthy with a familiar tale of his triumph in the fencing match that morning. Jamie, a slice of bread and butter in one hand, perched on the arm of Amanda's chair and returned to his book.

"I hope you are not unhappy with me, my dear?" her mother said, low.

"Of course not, Mama." Amanda knew it would be too impolite to admonish her, and hints of displeasure were of no use whatsoever. "You meant well."

Before many minutes had passed, Mrs. Hepplewythe returned, clutching the small green volume with both hands. "Here 'tis, ma'am. Mrs. Trout is most aggrieved and hopes you won't take things amiss."

"Certainly not," Amanda reassured her. She could guess how the larder had been decimated by the failed attempts. "Tell her to send Lewis to the market if she is in need of anything."

Mrs. Hepplewythe's posture visibly eased. "Thank you, ma'am. I will." She curtsied again before reaching out to hand the book to Amanda.

Lord Dulsworthy leaned forward to intercept it. "I say, Lady Kingston. This wouldn't be the book that chap was here about earlier?" Depositing his teacup on the table with a clatter, he began to thumb idly through it.

*"That chap"?* Oh, how she longed to correct him! *My dear Lord Dulsworthy, you couldn't possibly be referring to the gentleman who left the intriguing calling card that's currently tucked in my shift?*

Instead, she swallowed that spiteful retort and dipped her head in acknowledgment. "It is. I shall write to him directly and have the matter done with."

"No need for you to trouble yourself," he insisted, snapping the volume shut and waving off her suggestion with a flick of the hand that held it. "I'll take it to the bookshop myself."

"I don't—" She thought of the stranger explaining the book's rarity and value, his insistence on retrieving it. She tried not to think of her own silly disappointment at having no excuse to see the man again. "There really is no need, Lord Dulsworthy."

"Nonsense. I'll see to it on my way home."

Fearing that a weak smile of thanks would betray her displeasure, Amanda only nodded again and lifted her teacup to her lips to hide behind it.

For the next half hour, she chatted amiably, scolded fondly, listened attentively—yet always some corner of her mind, and occasionally even her eye, was drawn to the book, resting on George's knee, tucked into his greatcoat pocket, and finally carried out the front door of Bartlett House.

She could feel the mask of her good spirits slipping as the door closed behind him. Over a book? *What utter foolishness!*

Her mother ascribed her suddenly somber mood to a far different cause.

"Do not fret, my dear," she said, picking up Amanda's hand and patting the back of it consolingly. "The day will come soon enough when you need never be parted from Lord Dulsworthy again."

Amanda's mouth dropped open, and a gurgle escaped from her throat—whether a failed laugh or a strangled scream, even she could not be certain.

*Mind your step.*

She covered her lips with the fingertips of her other hand and coughed discreetly. "Pardon me, Mama. I'll just go check on the boys."

She slipped away before her mother could say anything more. But she did not go in search of her sons. She went to her sitting room, perched on the chair in front of the writing desk and, after sucking in a deep breath, fished in her bodice for the stranger's calling card.

The rectangle of paper was no longer cool and stiff, but warm and slightly softened, the cream-colored paper now bent in a shape that echoed the gentle curve of her not especially ample breast.

She smoothed the card on the blotter.

*A message here will always reach me, Lady Kingston.*

Where was "here"? The direction on the card might as well have been in quite some other part of the globe. She certainly did not recognize it.

Nonetheless, she drew a sheet of paper toward her, uncorked her ink bottle, and dipped her pen.

*Dear*

Pausing, she brushed the tip of the feather across her lips, studying the stark engraving of the bird. Quite well versed in apiology, thanks to the boys' bee project, but no expert in ornithology, she tipped her head to the side and squinted at the image on the card. It could be some sort of crow. Or maybe a raven? Better to be general, if she was not certain. But no one wanted to get a note addressed to *Dear Mr. Middling-Sized Sort of Carrion Bird…*

*Dear Sir,*
*I regret*

Her regrets were numerous, and at the moment, most of them revolved around allowing Lord Dulsworthy to continue imagining he could have any place in her affections. But a stranger would not care about that.

She twirled the quill between her thumb and fingers. Dusk was starting to settle over the garden. *A message here will* always *reach me*, he had said. But she hated to send Lewis out at this hour, hated to think of disturbing the gentleman when the bookshop would soon be closed.

*I regret not retrieving the book for you earlier today,* she thought of writing.

But it would not be the truth. She had wanted some excuse to prolong the little adventure of the book—and what a very *little* adventure it was! The gentleman would laugh to know the leaps of her wild imagination, and all over a cookery book that, according to Mrs. Hepplewythe, wasn't even any good.

Absently, she laid the pen in the tray and picked up the card, running the pad of her thumb over the printing and around the edges of the engraved bird, flicking meditatively at one corner of the stiff paper with her fingernail. Hard to believe the stranger had given it to her just that afternoon.

But as only a few hours had passed since his visit...surely the note could wait until morning?

She sent a furtive glance around the room, as if she expected to find someone spying from the folds of the drapery or the embossed scrolls on the wallpaper, laughing at her reluctance to be done with the matter of the mysterious book.

Then, with a private smile, she slipped the stranger's card back into her bodice.

# Chapter 3

Colonel Millrose had sent other agents to keep watch at the bookshop, in case the volume was returned. Hopkins's whereabouts were still unknown. Langley was supposed to be catching a decent night's sleep, for once.

But even in the darkness, he could not shut out the memory of the despair, the anger, the distrust on the faces of his fellow officers when he had finally forced himself to go into the workroom and confess that he had failed to retrieve the codebook.

At last he dragged himself from the bed, still fully clothed in his shopkeeper's garb, splashed cold water on his face, and donned his spectacles. In the corridor, a pale yellow seam of light gleamed beneath the workroom door. He knew it must be very late, but work went on in the Underground at all hours.

Fortunately, at least Fanny had retired for the night, and he could slip away without being chided for the rumpled state of his coat or his unshaven jaw.

For the first quarter of an hour, he walked aimlessly, through streets he knew well from many a previous midnight ramble. The few souls he met paid him no notice, and he returned their indifference. Though he ought to have been focused on devising a plan for retrieving the codebook and saving Lieutenant Hopkins, his thoughts were as fuzzy around the edges as his vision would've been without his spectacles. What would become of him—who would he be—if he failed in this mission? If General Scott, who once had bravely and generously taken him in, finally decided to turn him away?

No matter how long he walked, the cool night air never lessened his searing guilt. Eventually, however, it succeeded in sweeping the cobwebs from his mind, or at least in making him regret having stepped out without greatcoat or hat. When at last he paused and took note of his surroundings, he discovered that his feet had brought him to Mayfair and Grosvenor Square. To Bartlett House.

Every window in the impressive, impassive facade was dark. No sign of wakefulness, nothing to indicate which rooms might belong to the countess. Yes, he'd intended to call on her first thing, but even dawn was still hours away. At this hour, a knock at the door would only earn him the scorn of whatever servant he managed to rouse.

As he leaned against the railing and let his eyes drift over the house, he mentally ticked off the information contained in the dossier. The two boys, the young earl and his brother, likely had a room on the uppermost floor. Ten and eleven—too old for a nursemaid. But where was their governess? And what about the countess? Quarters to the front of the house, or the rear? Did her maid—Martha, wasn't it?—sleep lightly nearby, ever attentive to her mistress's call? Or was the whole house virtually unguarded at night, left to the lookout of some drowsy footman? The residents of Mayfair were ignorant enough to imagine themselves safe, after all.

But really, what did Lady Kingston have to fear? His wild imaginings were fueled by his own desperation to recover the codebook. Outside of General Scott and a few others, all trained and trusted intelligence officers, no one even knew she had it.

Unless, of course, Hopkins had been forced to reveal what he'd done with it…

In the distance, steady footsteps echoed off the buildings. Langley pushed himself away from the chilled metal bars. He had no desire to attract unwelcome notice from a passing watchman. He should take himself off—back to bed, if he were wise.

Instead, he walked along the south side of the square and around to the mews, softening his stride so that his boot heels did not strike the ground firmly enough to ring out. Here, no street lamps burned, and the shadows were more inviting, if the stench of slops and stables was not.

Not entirely sure what he sought, he counted off as he went, making note of the faint signs that divided the houses from one another, a change in the brickwork or the paling, the plain wooden doors that led down to kitchens or into coal cellars. Then, from the back of what must be Bartlett House…a light.

Just out of the reach of its illumination, he paused. Unlike most, Bartlett House had a small garden at the rear. He supposed that explained Lady Kingston's apron and the state of her fingernails that afternoon.

A few rogue branches of a tall hedge poked between the slats of a taller wrought-iron fence. Between them, he glimpsed two neat flower beds, each bordered by a low stone wall and divided from one another by a narrow flagstone path that led up to a morning room, where a lamp gleamed. He saw no sign of the person who had lit it.

Cautiously, he crept to the gate in the outer fence, and when the latch lifted easily, he did not know whether to praise his good luck or curse some careless servant. If he could make his way into Bartlett House, so could others. How long before someone else discovered that the codebook lay within?

Perhaps it was that same careless servant who had failed to oil the hinge. Or perhaps the squawk of protest had been deliberately courted as a sort of alarm. In any case, he sucked in a sharp breath through his nostrils as its rusty shriek split the night, and was rewarded with the sweet, rich perfume of roses just before a thump on the back of his head sent him to his knees.

Langley Stanhope was far too hard-headed to lose consciousness. But his spectacles flew off and landed somewhere farther off, along the stone path, based on the clatter. When he tried to shake off the blow, he only succeeded in hurrying the onset of a headache. Dazed, but not so impaired that he could not move quickly, he hoisted himself into a crouch and spun, raising one arm to ward off any successive strikes as he turned to face his attacker.

The first thing he saw was the raveled end of a silk tie, the sort generally used to close a gentleman's dressing gown. As his gaze rose, he discovered that the gentleman's dressing gown in question had presumably once belonged to the Earl of Kingston. At present, it was wrapped around the tall, willowy form of that late gentleman's wife.

She too had one arm raised, clutching the remaining fragment of the clay flowerpot with which she'd clubbed him. And on her face, an expression that somehow mingled both shock and horror, along with more than a dash of pride.

He wasn't entirely sure which emotion had won out when she dropped the shard of pottery and began to babble as he got fully to his feet. "Oh. Oh, my. I *am* sorry! I couldn't sleep, so I came out here. The weather was so fine today, wasn't it?...though I suppose that wasn't wise, so late at night. Still, I should never have done such a thing if I'd realized *who*... but in the shadows, it's quite impossible to tell—"

He raised his hand again, partly to stop the flow of words, and partly to try to ease the pain shooting through the back of his skull. "Don't apologize, Lady Kingston. It's your garden, and I was trespassing. You have every right to protect yourself."

Obligingly, she stopped speaking for a moment. But her nervous energy next found its outlet in reaching forward to brush the dirt and pottery fragments from his shoulders and even his hair. Her fingertips moved over him lightly, gently, the sort of touch a man could come to crave.

"And no idea who I really am," he rasped, pushing her away with words when he could not seem to command his body. He knew better than to make himself vulnerable.

Her hand fell away and something like fear fluttered into her eyes. She was studying him as she had earlier that day—or yesterday—when they had stood facing one another in the entry hall.

Langley was unaccustomed to being the object of scrutiny.

And having lost his spectacles in the fracas, he could not return the favor as fully as he would've liked. Though they stood closer together now than they had then, she was still a bit blurry around the edges. The combination of lamplight and moonlight was insufficient to put a firm name to the color of her eyes or her hair—*brown* wouldn't do, in either case—and the dressing gown hid everything else of interest from view. Still, he knew beyond a doubt that she was pretty.

"But of course I do. You're—" she began and broke off again, backing a step away in her uncertainty. "Are you hurt, sir?" she asked abruptly. It could not have been clearer to him that the question she really wished to ask was, *Do you mean to hurt me?*

To both questions, spoken and unspoken, he swiftly answered, "No."

Nevertheless, she withdrew another step, and another, out of the reach of his vision, out of his reach, until—

*Crunch.*

"Oh dear. What have I—?"

"I believe, Lady Kingston," he said calmly, "you'll find those are my spectacles under your foot."

"Your spectacles? But you don't—that is to say, earlier you weren't wearing—" As she spoke, she crouched, her eyes never leaving his face as her fingers brushed across the flagstone path near her feet until she found what he'd known she would. Her voice dropped as she finished her sentence: "—spectacles."

When she rose, their twisted remains lay on her palm, but she did not stretch out her hand to given them to him. Neither did he step forward to take them from her, having no desire to find out what might happen if he took her by surprise her a second time.

"I'll pay for their repair," she offered.

"That won't be necessary. If you'll just—"

At last he thrust out his hand, but she shook her head and her other hand joined the first in wringing what life was left from his mangled spectacles. The moonlight made a sort of halo of her loosely arranged hair. "I can guess why you're here. But I—I haven't got it."

For a moment, he wondered whether the blow to the back of the head had indeed knocked him senseless. He hadn't the faintest notion what she meant, and it was only after the passage of an awkward silence that he recalled why he'd come to Bartlett House to begin with. His heart began to pound with such fury he felt certain she must be able to hear it hammering against his ribs.

"The book, do you mean? You haven't got the book?"

Her teeth, small and pearly white, came out to gnaw at her lower lip, and she first nodded, then shook her head. "You see, I sat down earlier this evening to send you a note about it, but I really couldn't figure out from your card, Mr.—Rook, is it? Or—or perhaps Crow? I'm really not very good with birds… If it had been a bee, then maybe—the boys are doing a project on bees, you know. Well, no, of course you *don't* know. Anyway, it seemed awfully rude to address you by the wrong name, so I—"

"It's none of those, your ladyship," he spoke across her. "The bird on my card, that is." Unbelievably, he found himself fighting down a laugh. Had he gone stark raving mad? Or had she? "It's a magpie. A sort of… *nickname*, if you will."

Her answering giggle did nothing to reassure him about the state of his mind—or hers. "A magpie, you say?" She seemed to have decided to carry on as if this were an ordinary conversation. "I suppose I should have guessed it eventually. Although…those are the birds attracted to anything shiny, aren't they? Whereas you seem rather…"

Rather *what?*

She reminded him of a bird herself, chattering nervously, pecking aimlessly at the twigs of words and phrases but never quite weaving them in a whole thought. Rocking forward with an uneasy step, she held out his spectacles, and he took them, curling his fingers around the ruined frames. The metal was still warm from her hand, and he would have been tempted to tighten his grip to capture that sensation if not for the prickle of broken glass. "Well, as you yourself said, I really *don't* know who you are." She rocked back, knotting the fingers of her empty hands. A pause, heavier and more serious than any that had preceded it. "Who are you?"

He narrowed his gaze, just enough to bring her features into sharper focus. "If I answer that question, Lady Kingston, how can you be sure I'm telling the truth?"

As she swallowed, a bit of white fabric at the base of her throat—her nightdress, he supposed, otherwise hidden beneath the heavy brocade dressing gown—slipped in and out of view. He wondered what had kept her from sleep. The book? Or something else? "Well, I—I suppose I can't." Once more, she looked him up and down. "But I suspect you aren't a shop clerk."

That earned her a slight, and slightly wry, smile. "Well spotted, Lady Kingston. I am not a shop clerk. But you are better off without that book here, anywhere near you or your sons."

Her brow furrowed. "My...sons? But it's just a—a—I think I should warn you that Mrs. Trout, our cook, tried to make a few of the recipes from it, and she said the proportions were all wrong. You said it was priceless, but I don't understand how a cookbook with bad recipes can be—oh." In the pause, a slight breeze stirred the scents of the flowers, and her frown deepened. "It's not a cookbook, is it?"

For years he had trained, practicing the best ways to interact with innocent civilians and learning how to withstand expert interrogation. Nothing had prepared him for this conversation. Lady Kingston was the most unexpected combination of scatter-brained and sharp-witted he'd ever met. He'd already given her his codename. Now he hardly knew whether it was right or wrong to tell her, "No."

"I...see. Well, Lord Dulsworthy took it," she explained after a moment. "He said he would return it to Porter's on his way home."

Langley knew if it had arrived at the bookshop this evening, he would have heard the news already. Lady Kingston too seemed to understand that his presence in her garden in the wee hours of the night meant that good old *Duls.* hadn't kept his promise.

"No doubt he'll see it delivered there in the morning," Langley tried to reassure her, feeling anything but reassured himself. Had Dulsworthy entrusted the return of the book to someone else? Or had he kept it for some reason? If he had, what next?

Lady Kingston seemed to read his thoughts. "And if he doesn't?"

Despite the limits of his vision, Langley glanced around the little garden, at the green-black swathes of leaves dotted with splotches and streaks of color, flowers that had burst into glory in the heat of the afternoon and some that had hidden themselves away again at nightfall.

Nothing was clear, anymore.

"Then I'll be in touch." After tucking his broken spectacles into his breast pocket, he gave another crisp bow. "It's late. You should retire, your ladyship. Does this gate lock?"

"Yes."

"Then see that you lock it after I leave." Before she could say anything more, he slipped back through the gate and into the shadows, pausing only to listen for the grating sound of a key in a lock.

From Grosvenor Square he made his way to Brook Street, where he knew Lord Dulsworthy resided, though the dossier hadn't included the number. He strode up and down the street twice, spotting just one window in which a light burned. It might be anything, of course: a sick room, a servant lost in the forbidden pages of a novel. Only a fool would imagine the lone candle belonged to Dulsworthy, up half the night, poring over the codebook he now had in his possession.

Surely the best explanation for the man's behavior was the simplest one. He had taken the purported French cookbook from Bartlett House purely for the comfort and convenience of the woman he was to wed. He meant to save her the trouble of having to return it to the bookshop. Something innocuous had delayed him. In the morning, when Dulsworthy did return it, Langley would recover it and be one step closer to recovering his good name in the process.

So why was he standing on an empty street in the dark, weighed down in equal parts by unease and something like regret?

He ought to be glad the damned thing was out of Lady Kingston's hands. Ought to feel relieved to be free of her headache-inducing chatter—to say nothing of her headache-inducing flowerpots. Why, she probably wasn't even as appealing as his shortsightedness gave her credit for being. She probably *wanted* to marry Dulsworthy and settle into the safe, predictable sort of life a man like him offered. And if that was the case, then Langley would do well to keep his distance.

The last thing the Magpie had to offer any woman was safety.

The bells of St. Martin-in-the-Fields were chiming three when he returned to the Underground and left word with the watchman on duty to wake him if nothing had been heard from Porter's by ten o'clock. Then he closed himself in his dark cell, shucked off his boots, and collapsed face down on the bed, for once falling instantly asleep.

Sometime later—minutes, hours—something roused him, calling him back from sleep, from the edges of a familiar dream—or nightmare. As always, no faces he recognized, no voices he understood, only shapeless anxiety, like hands dragging him down into the abyss. He had to shake free of them, had to get away, or else...or else...

Then the dream shifted. The aroma of flowers—roses—hung heavy on the night air, and the touch transformed, drawing him closer, coaxing him, and he wanted—needed—to chase that sensation, to reach out, to touch in turn....

*I'll be in touch....*

"Wake up, Major Stanhope."

That chilly voice chased away the last fragments of the dream, replacing its vaguely pleasant promise with a dull, throbbing pain at the base of his skull. The scent of roses still filled his nostrils. *Perfume.* Of course. He turned his head toward the woman who wore it but did not open his eyes.

"What is it, Fanny? It can't be ten already."

"Just past six, actually."

He cracked an eyelid, grateful not to be able to see clearly the expression on her face, the one that no doubt matched her voice.

A flash of red greeted his half-opened eye. The scarlet coat of his uniform, which she dangled from one fingertip. He scrambled upright. "What's happened?"

"General Scott's had a message from Lieutenant Hopkins's captors," she said, tossing the coat toward him, having apparently forgotten her earlier disdain for wrinkles. "He wants to see you right away."

# Chapter 4

Shortly after dawn began to streak the sky, Amanda was summoned to her mother's chamber. Despite her fatigue Amanda hurried to her bedside, uncertain what could have roused Mama at such an hour.

Mama was sitting up in bed, her breakfast tray across her lap. "Did you sleep well, my dear?"

Amanda had retired last night, just as the stranger—Magpie—had ordered. But sleep had eluded her. Instead she'd replayed their second encounter, weighed it against the first, and tried to come up with some explanation for both his midnight return and his concern over a cookbook that wasn't *really* a cookbook.

Every explanation that presented itself made her fear she might be going a bit mad.

"Well enough, Mama," she lied. "And you?"

Mama sighed, managing to sound fatigued, though she looked as fresh as she always did. "I confess, I shall rest easier when you are married again, though of course a mother never really stops worrying about her children." She paused to stir her cocoa, then gestured with the spoon for Amanda to sit down at the foot of the bed. "I only want you to be safe. And sometimes...sometimes you do not seem to realize the dangers that surround you."

It was an old argument, one Amanda knew she could never win. "Are there dangers lurking in my writing desk, Mama?" she dared to ask as she perched on the edge of the mattress.

Her mother bristled. "Did you think I was snooping?"

Amanda said nothing. Her silence was answer enough.

"Even after all this time, you seem to have very little sense of what might happen to a woman, even one of your position, if society disapproves of her conduct." Mama shook her head, fixing her with a pleading gaze. "I only want you to be safe," she said again.

*Must safety always take priority over happiness?* Amanda wanted to reply. But she feared her mother's answer might be yes.

To avoid an argument—some lessons, Amanda had learned well—she rose, kissed her mother's papery cheek, and excused herself to the schoolroom. Noon found her once more in the garden, drowsing on an uncomfortable iron bench while the boys observed the bees at work in the flowers. Mama was preparing to make morning calls. Perhaps now Amanda might sneak back into her chamber for a nap.

Or would her curiosity flare again as soon as her head hit the pillow?

A woman of good sense would have raised an alarm at the discovery of a man slipping into the garden after dark. A woman of good sense would not have been in the garden after dark to begin with.

A woman of good sense definitely would not thrill a tiny bit at the thought she might have stumbled into an intrigue with a spy.

A spy? Every time the thought occurred to her, common sense tried to dash it away. *He's a clerk in a bookshop. A nosy one who suffers from sleeplessness—just like you.*

But did bookshop clerks, even insomniac ones, generally have...a codename?

*Magpie...* What did it signify? Surely there was a copy of Bewick's *History of British Birds* in the library. Maybe she would just go inside and look for it.…

"Mama, come look at this fat little fellow," called Philip. "He's gathered up more pollen than he can carry."

"He'll manage it," insisted Jamie, lifting a glass to his eye to study the bee. "Size isn't the same as strength, you know."

She rose, trying to shake off her drowsiness—and her foolishness—as she shook the wrinkles from her skirt. Before she had taken a step in the boys' direction, however, a pebble skidded in front of her.

The very idea that a single pebble skipping across a flagstone garden path would be noteworthy seemed at first to be confirmation of her sensitized, sleep-deprived state. Evidently her mind was capable of making something from absolutely nothing.

Except that something—someone—had put the pebble into motion. Not the boys, who were closer to the house. Not she; her feet hadn't moved and her hems did not brush the ground. It had come from behind her, from

somewhere near the fence and the narrow alleyway that divided the houses
of Grosvenor Square from their mews.

*I'll be in touch.*

She darted a quick glance toward the tall hedge, trying to decide if she
could make out a masculine figure hidden by its branches.

"Come, boys," she said, steeling herself against her sons' inevitable
protests. "No, now, it's nearly time for luncheon. Go in and wash up. You
can resume your observations this afternoon."

Philip glanced skyward. "It's going to rain."

"Not for some time yet, I'm sure." Earlier, she had noticed the thickening
clouds, but now she did not look their way. "But if it does, think of it as a
chance to see where the bees go. Inside, inside." She spread her arms to
usher them toward the house, then paused. "Oh, dear. I must've dropped
one of my gloves beneath the bench. I'll just—no, Jamie," she warded him
off, "I'll get it. Go inside."

She walked toward where she had been sitting, taking care not to hurry.
Jamie and Philip, quickly reabsorbed by their earlier squabble, paid no
attention. Hardly had she reached the back of the garden when a low voice
coming from beyond the fence said, "Sit down. Don't turn. Pretend to
look for your glove."

Obligingly, she sank onto the bench and leaned forward, as if searching
the ground beneath it.

"Lord Dulsworthy never returned the book."

"Oh?" She wondered if her reply, sent from somewhere near her knees,
could be clearly heard. "That's not like him. He's always so…responsible."

"Can you think of any reason why he might keep it?"

Amanda started to shake her head, then a laugh squeezed itself from
her lungs. "Maybe he's trying to get you in trouble at the bookshop. He
didn't seem to like you very much."

An answering chuckle, more than a trifle wry, came from behind the
bushes. "I have that effect on some people."

"What happens next? Did you—did you want me to go to his house
and look for it?"

A pause. "Are you on such familiar terms with the gentleman?"

She sat up, clutching both kid gloves in her lap. "Before I answer that,
I wish you to tell me who you are and what this is really about." A daring
glance over her shoulder was rewarded with a glimpse of his profile, the
rest of him hidden by overgrown shrubbery. She ought to have turned
and faced the house again immediately, but instead she rose slowly and
stepped closer to him. To her surprise, he moved further into the clear.

Yesterday, in the comparative dimness of the entry hall, her own eyes still recovering from the bright outdoors, she had taken an impression of him. Last night, the near darkness had added few details to the picture. But now, she saw him in the clear light of day—albeit shadowed by greenery.

His brown hair was a few shades darker than her own, a rich walnut sort of color under the midday sun. But his eyes were lighter than hers, more hazel than brown. No spectacles, of course. And his features were lean, sharp, as she'd noted before. Sharply handsome. Definitely not the face of a boy. Five and thirty, at least, and she found herself intrigued by the sort of living he'd done in those years. He was…well, *dashing* was the first adjective that came to mind.

Most intriguing of all, though, was the flash of red that caught her eye, the color of his coat beneath his greatcoat. She stepped closer still, looking him up and down all the while. "You're a soldier?"

Too late, he thrust his hands into the pockets of his greatcoat and crossed them, trying to hide the uniform beneath. Why didn't he want her to know?

A moment passed, a few seconds, perhaps, though it felt longer. At last, he ground out, "Major Langley Stanhope, your ladyship."

Silently she mouthed the name, committing it to her memory. "A pleasure, sir. So I take it that the cookbook is—"

"Isn't a cookbook, just as you said last night. It may be the most priceless piece of military intelligence we have. The agent who collected it discovered he was being followed and needed a way to hide it. I gather you happened to be coming out of Porter's bookshop with a similar package."

"He—he bumped into me on purpose?" Absently, she rubbed her arm and elbow, though they no longer ached. "Yes, of course he did. Causing me to drop my book on the pavement. And when I—or rather, my footman—picked it up…"

"The switch had already been made. That agent managed to send a message, alerting us to what had happened. I had only to discover who had purchased a copy of Pascal's treatise on geometry and switch the books back. Or so I thought."

A nervous laugh bubbled in her chest. "It's—it's a birthday present for Jamie. My older son. I don't suppose he would have been too pleased to unwrap a French cookbook."

He held up a finger. "I'd appreciate it if you said nothing more of the book. Now, regarding Dulsworthy's house," he prompted.

"Oh, yes. Right. I do occasionally call on him at his home, on matters of business. We share the guardianship of my sons, you see."

"During such a call, would you be a liberty to explore—?"

She cut him off with a shake of her head. "He would consider that highly improper."

Understandably, Major Stanhope's—*Magpie's*—concern for the fate of the book was no ordinary concern. But how could she possibly poke around in George's house?

Realizing she had balled her gloves in her hands, she smoothed them over one palm, soothing herself by stroking the pliant leather. The answer to her quandary lay upstairs in the drawer of her writing desk—unless Mama had got to it already.

"Tomorrow night he is giving a ball." *In my honor, if the gossips are to be believed.* "He's been quite beside himself with preparations. Doubtless that's the reason he forgot to return the—ah, the item. I'll be going, of course," she added after a brief pause, although she'd been trying for days to concoct an excuse to avoid it. "I can try to slip away and look then."

"A ball," Major Stanhope repeated, and his eyes narrowed, as if he were performing some complicated calculation—or trying to see something beyond the range of his vision. "Interesting. I'll try to find a way to get inside, take advantage of the bustle to look around."

An unexpected wave of disappointment crashed in her chest. Was this to be the end of her adventure? "I can do the looking," she offered.

"No. I don't want you to take an unnecessary risk."

"Any right-thinking Englishwoman in times like these would surely be prepared to take risks, Major Stanhope. Or—or should I call you Magpie? It's kind of exciting, isn't it?"

His features settled into something closer to a scowl of disgust. "Lady Kingston, you don't know what you're saying. You haven't the first idea of the danger involved—"

"No," she agreed. "I suppose I don't. What happened to the man who made me drop the—the item?"

"I can't tell you that."

His expression was inscrutable. "Can't, or won't?"

"I don't know what became of him," he said after a moment and with obvious reluctance. "He hasn't been heard from since."

A hard lump rose in her throat, which she at first struggled to speak past. "I—I'm sorry to hear that." Then she thrust her chin forward. "But now you can't say I don't know the risks. And I still want to help, Major Stanhope. I want to do *something.*" His expression didn't budget. "Please. You haven't the first idea how dull my life is."

It was an incredibly foolish, childish thing to say, the sort of excuse Philip would give for rule-breaking, for scrambling up one of the tall trees in the square when his grandmother wasn't looking.

*Mind your step.*

Nevertheless, it drew a sort of half smile from Major Stanhope, along with a shake of his head. "And it's my job to see it stays that way. I won't involve a civilian. Particularly not a lady."

"I know my way around the house," she reminded him. "You don't."

He appeared to weigh those words for a moment before shaking his head again. His gaze traveled to the door through which the boys had disappeared. "You'd best go inside before your family misses you."

For once in her life, she did not swallow her sigh of resignation as she turned toward the house. She had gone only a few steps when he spoke low.

"'Til tomorrow night, Lady Kingston. Don't look for me. I'll find you."

Excitement surged through her, like flames roaring up a chimney. "Really?" She spun back to face him.

But he had already disappeared.

As soon as she entered the house, she accosted the first servant to cross her path. "My mother—where is she?"

The young woman, a kitchen maid holding a pair of heavy shears, evidently sent up from below to fetch some herbs from the garden, goggled for a moment at being addressed thus, and then shook her head.

Abashed at having frightened the girl, Amanda gave her an apologetic smile before hurrying on her way. Finding the library door open, she poked her head inside and found Mr. Matthews, the butler, directing Lewis, who was perched on a ladder, removing books from a high shelf so that the parlor maid could dust them. Motes twinkled in the sunshine streaming through the tall, street-facing windows.

"Have you seen my mother, Mr. Matthews?" Amanda asked, more mindful of her tone this time and reining in her expression to something like mild curiosity.

"Mrs. West?" He glanced at Lewis for confirmation before shaking his head. "No, your ladyship. We did hear Lord Kingston and Master Philip on the stairs not a quarter of an hour ago."

Another smile rose to her lips, this one amused. She rather liked to imagine a ruckus when two healthy, energetic boys thundered upstairs to wash before luncheon, no matter how often they had been scolded to silence. "Thank you. I suppose she's gone out, but if you see her, please let her know I'd like to speak with her."

"Yes, your ladyship. Of course."

Upstairs, she found no one in the dining room or the drawing room. Mama had already left, then, and no telling whom she planned to visit this morning, or what she would tell them. Belatedly, Amanda realized that she ought to have asked Mr. Matthews whether her mother had put any letters to post. What if she'd already written to decline George's invitation?

Amanda's lips curved again, this time abashed and embarrassed. How disrespectful of her to feel interest in attending Lord Dulsworthy's ball only now, because she looked forward to meeting another gentleman there.

But he *was* a gentleman. Not a shop clerk. *Major Stanhope.* That was a title of responsibility, respectability. *Oh, bother.* She sounded like her mother now. And truth be told, Amanda really didn't care a whit for the man's rank in society. No, her interest was even shallower than that: he was intriguing, exciting, and quite the handsomest man she'd ever seen.

Everything, in other words, that George was not.

"What are you smiling about, dear?"

Despite the object of her quest, the sound of her mother's voice nearly caused Amanda to stumble, she'd been so lost in her thoughts. "Oh, nothing, Mama. I was only thinking—*looking*, that is. I was looking. For you."

Her eyebrows lifted in surprise. "Yes?"

"You're going out, I see. I won't keep you. I only wanted to speak to you about—about the invitations I'd left in my desk…"

"I thought I was relieving you of a burden by managing the household correspondence," she began, her cheeks pink. "Truly, I never intended to pry, Amanda."

"Of course not, Mama. But if you did happen to answer any of them…"

Mama pressed her lips together and let a frown dart across her brow. Amanda knew it must be serious business, for her mother ordinarily took such care to avoid any expression or strain that might wrinkle her skin. Finally, Mama nodded. "I told the Hursts you would be delighted to join them at the theater. You should remember to mark it on your calendar, dear. Tuesday evening."

"Oh! I—" Caught entirely off guard, Amanda could hardly form a reply. Her mother had insisted for so long that all such invitations must be refused, for the sake of propriety.

"Did you not wish to go?" Now Mama looked vaguely hurt, or perhaps worried.

"Indeed, I am most eager to see the play, Mama," Amanda insisted, taking her mother's hands between hers. *Whatever it is.* "It will be splendid, I'm sure. Thank you. But I—" She gnawed at her lower lip with her teeth, a gesture that never failed to earn a reproving glance. "But just now, I happened to be thinking of the invitation to Lord Dulsworthy's ball."

She knew how her mother would interpret such breathless curiosity, such urgency. She watched the familiar sparkle of excitement light her mother's eyes. Amanda felt vaguely ashamed of herself. She would be getting *everyone's* hopes up.

If she weren't careful, she would find herself walking down the aisle with Lord Dulsworthy yet.

But at this very moment, the intrigue over the book and the promise of seeing Major Stanhope again had left her too giddy to worry about such eventualities. At this very moment, she believed she might even be able to contemplate a future with George with resigned aplomb if she could cling to the memory of one little adventure.

"I haven't answered that invitation, no," Mama said, speaking each word carefully, as if she did not wish to do anything to upset the delicate balance of this moment. "I wasn't sure whether—"

"Of course I wish to go, Mama," Amanda insisted, though half an hour earlier the answer would have been a lie. "It would be astonishingly bad manners to refuse him, and you raised me never to—"

"Certainly not. I never thought you would—that is, I never thought you wouldn't—oh, never mind. You'll send your answer this very minute," her mother said, freeing her hands from Amanda's only to take her by the elbow and guide her toward her own chambers, evidently having discarded her previous intention of going out. "And then we must figure out what you're going to wear. Blue, you know, is Lord Dulsworthy's favorite color. I think you must have my Sarah do your hair. I don't trust that girl of yours...."

Amanda heard none of it, though her thoughts were running along parallel lines. A ball, after all these years. The music, the dancing.

George...

Why hadn't he returned the book to Porter's, when he'd promised to? Where in his house might he have laid it?

And if she found it, would that be enough to earn a look of approval from the Magpie's bright, warm eyes?

* * * *

Standing for inspection had never been Langley's favorite part of army life. When the inspectors in question were Mrs. Drummond and Colonel Millrose, so much the worse.

At long last, Fanny gave a nod of reluctant satisfaction. Millrose had called her in to have a lady's eye, and though Langley knew she preferred to keep her distance from him, she certainly seemed to be enjoying the opportunity to find fault. "It's fortunate that Lord Dulsworthy had to hire extra servants for his ball."

"Yes, yes," Langley agreed, forcing himself not to fidget beneath the weight of their combined stares. Perhaps no uniform was ever comfortable, but he was rapidly discovering a footman's livery was worse than most. The powdered wig, especially. It itched.

"And fortunate that you're tall enough to carry it off. A little long in the tooth, though," she added with one of her usual wry smiles as she patted his cheek—a little too firmly for comfort. Earlier, she had smeared his face with some stinging concoction that was supposed to...well, he couldn't quite remember *what* the stuff was meant to do. She'd used words like *smooth* and *soften*, and he half wondered whether it was something for improving the look of one's skin or one's old shoes.

"Especially fortunate that one of the newly hired men was taken ill," Millrose said, stepping forward. At that, Fanny—thank God—moved back. "No one will pay you the least mind, Stanhope. Unless, of course, you drop a tray full of dishes in some grande dame's lap."

Langley forced a smile. "If you two are quite through?"

"I wish we'd been able to supply you with a floorplan of the house."

"I'll manage." He'd told Millrose nothing of his previous afternoon's exchange with Lady Kingston.

"Of course you will, Magpie. It's only..."

At his speaking glance, Fanny gave a shallow curtsy. "I must see to matters in the kitchen. Best of luck, Major Stanhope."

Even after the door closed behind her, leaving them alone in Millrose's private office, neither one spoke. Weak afternoon light filtered through the single small, high window, whose mottled glass offered the only view of the outside in all of the Underground, a view now further distorted by streaks of rain.

Millrose retreated behind his desk. There, the light was strong enough to highlight both the silver in his hair and the worry in his expression. "Be careful, Langley. General Scott doesn't want to lose you too."

"Did he tell you that?"

For answer, the other man glanced down at the papers scattered across the desktop and idly shifted two or three with his fingertips.

In spite of himself, Langley laughed. "I didn't think so."

His meeting with the general yesterday morning had been brief and brusque, a quick reporting of Langley's attempt to secure the codebook and nothing more. No one who had observed the exchange would have imagined the thirty years of history between the two men. Scott had revealed nothing of what he knew of Hopkins's fate, nothing to the agent he'd once proclaimed his best. The closest the general had come to showing any emotion at all had been a strange sort of smile when Langley had admitted he would have to return to Bartlett House to meet with Lady Kingston a second time—when, in other words, Langley had admitted his failure.

"I'm sure he—"

"Save your breath, Billy." He started to raise a hand, but paused when the coat tautened uncomfortably across his shoulders. How did footmen manage to get any work done, when they were apparently dressed for show? "You'll both have a full report when I return," Langley assured him instead. He knew what he had to do win Scott's approval. "With the book."

He arrived at Dulsworthy's Brook Street house in the pouring rain. "You're late," snarled a man Langley assumed to be the butler, Mr. Evans, who was at present organizing an entire regiment of servants to go into battle.

Only after Mr. Evans had shouted at a florist's boy, wobbling beneath an arrangement twice his height and probably half his weight, and then reduced a housemaid to tears by calling her a slattern, did he turn his full attention to Langley. Unsurprisingly, his eye was far more critical than either Fanny's or Millrose's had been. He tugged at Langley's lapel, straightened his wig. "I don't remember asking the employment agency to send me an old man."

Langley did his best not to bristle at the comment, though at thirty-seven he was considerably younger than Evans. "There's a war on, sir," he answered, knocking some of the usual refinement from his speech, but not so much that anyone might guess where he'd really been born.

"I am aware." The butler thrust a closed umbrella into Langley's chest. "Out front with you. No one will notice your crow's feet in the rain."

Langley nodded and turned away to take up his post. The assignment had one advantage: he'd see every person who entered the house. But he would have to find an excuse to get inside later to look for the book.

"If even one lady enters this house with a damp hem," Evans called after him, "you'll be lucky to find yourself mucking stables at your next job."

"Yes, sir."

He lost the next hour to skulking under a temporary awning with another footman, who was considerably younger but evidently no more satisfactory to Evans's critical eye, with his freckled face and unfashionably slight frame, which did not fill out the uniform. "We're to wait until we hear the clock on St. George's chime eight before we roll out the carpet," he repeated, every so often. "Mr. Evans don't want it sopping wet."

The lad didn't offer his name, nor any further comment. The monotony of waiting in the chilly rain was broken only by an occasional word from a deliveryman or a coachman. Mostly, Langley was at liberty to imagine the house's interior—warm, dry, half its rooms alight with the blaze of wax candles, the rest dark, closed off to guests.

Where had Dulsworthy stashed the book?

And when would Lady Kingston arrive to search for it?

Her early morning visit to the bookshop suggested the sort of person who would land on the doorstep precisely at the hour specified on the invitation. Her midnight traipse through the garden, however, had revealed a woman somewhat at odds with the dossier's rather staid description of her. Something about her demeanor yesterday afternoon had also hinted at a certain reluctance regarding Dulsworthy's ball. Now, Langley hardly knew which to hope for, promptness or fashionable lateness.

Most disconcerting was the discovery that he was hoping anything at all. He'd been wrong to accept her offer of assistance. He was putting her in unnecessary danger.

He hadn't any business looking forward to seeing her tonight.

At long last, the sound of eight bells rippled along Brook Street and there was a bustle to unroll the carpet and light the last lanterns before the first carriage rattled to a stop. She was not the first to arrive, nor the second. In fact, he'd lost track of how many crested coaches had deposited lords and ladies dripping with silk and jewels—a dozen, at least—when he saw her.

Langley nearly had to shoulder the freckle-faced lad out of the way to ensure it was he who helped her from her coach and walked slightly behind her from the street to the house.

As she descended, her face nearly disappeared into a calash of dark green, paired with a satin cloak entirely inadequate to the weather, tied loosely around her neck and open enough to offer a glimpse of the rest of her: an enticing display of bosom in a low cut gown made of some flimsy reddish stuff over a pale underdress. The effect was to make it seem as if one could see right through to her bare skin.

No, Lady Kingston was not at all what he'd expected when he'd been told she was a widow.

She briefly touched his palm as she stepped to the ground, and with the other hand, he clutched the handle of the umbrella in a death's grip, afraid he might give in to the temptation either to reach across and wrap the cloak more securely around her—or worse, to unwrap her entirely.

They were halfway up the walk before he remembered to speak. "My lady." He kept his voice low, hardly parted his lips. "Once you are inside, you must—"

"Oh, it *is* you," she began and turned toward him slightly before seeming to think better of it and walking on. "I wasn't certain—you make a masterful footman, by the way. Even better than your bookshop clerk. I think I understand now why they call you Magpie. I read up on the species in Bewick's Birds this morning, you see. 'Crafty and familiar,' he says. They're great mimics apparently. Do you know, they can be made to repeat whole sentences? I suppose that's why some people try to domesticate them."

"My lady—"

But that was that. They were at the door, where conversation between them could too easily be either seen or overheard, and would in any case be regarded with suspicion, given the part he was playing. He was obliged to bow and back away, handing her over to the care of another liveried footman just inside, who had the honor of helping her to remove her cloak. Rubies glittered at her ears and throat. He might have lingered for another look if not for the sound of an approaching carriage.

He had had no chance to convey his plan. No notion of how or when he'd reconnect with her tonight. If Dulsworthy caught her snooping, it could mean trouble—for both of them.

Yet his thoughts, such as they were, had once again wandered far away from codebooks and Lieutenant Hopkins. Far even from this Brook Street mansion. Some walrus-faced nob had to speak sharply to him before he realized he was letting the rain drip off the edge of his umbrella and down a lady's back. Evans would have his head, and might even fire him before he had a chance to sneak into the house.

Still, he was lost in the winding stream of Lady Kingston's silly chatter.

*Crafty and familiar.*

*A mimic.*

Was that how she saw him?

If she only knew...

# Chapter 5

Amanda drew back her shoulders, lifted her chin, and walked toward the ballroom, fighting with every step the impulse to make sure her bosom was still contained within the shallow bodice of her gown.

Guilt, not gravity, lay behind the impulse, as she well knew. She'd had to engage in subterfuge to escape the house in this dress, rather than the one her mother had chosen, which had been blue, of course, and perfectly demure. A dress not for dancing and flirting and adventure, but for sitting in a straight-backed chair on the fringes of the ballroom with the other matrons.

So Amanda had arranged for Martha to come, just as soon as Mama had seen her in the blue gown, and say that Philip was complaining of the stomachache. Everyone had played their part with perfection, even the unknowing actors: Martha had worn a wide-eyed expression of concern, Amanda had bustled and fussed and been on the point of declaring she couldn't go to the ball, and Mama had protested and insisted all would be fine and declared that she would personally go upstairs to look after the boys.

Before ten minutes more had passed, Martha had helped Amanda out of the blue gown, into the rose one, and out the door.

The guilt that prickled at her now wasn't entirely because she had deceived her mother, though. Certainly at two and thirty, she hardly required a chaperone. No, it was in larger measure the knowledge that she had insisted on the low-cut rose gown not to please George, who would almost certainly *not* be pleased by it, but to attract the notice of someone else entirely.

But would Major Stanhope even see it?

Not that she expected compliments from him if he did. Even knowing him so little, she felt certain it was not in his nature. She would have been contented with a few other words from him: some explanation of how he imagined the evening would proceed, at what hour she was to go looking for the book, and how she was to return it to him if she found it. But the walk into the house had been so brief—it had taken her more than half the time to decide whether it was really he beside her—and now, here she was, alone, moving through the receiving line and refusing to look down at her bodice.

Oh, who was she kidding? Her bosom was neither the size nor the shape to be prone to bursting out of its confinement.

On the threshold of the ballroom, she curtsied to Lord Wrexham, George's brother-in-law, whose town house was by design too small to host the grand entertainments his wife adored. From here, Amanda could see guests milling about in what yesterday had been the receiving room, now cleared of most of its furnishings and transformed into a ballroom. Not a crush, but respectable nonetheless.

"I've so been looking forward to this evening, Lady Wrexham," she said, squeezing her hostess's fingers.

"As have we all," Lady Wrexham replied with a sly glance toward her brother, who was studiously refusing to allow his gaze to travel any lower than Amanda's chin.

"May I have the honor of the first pair of dances, Lady Kingston?" Lord Wrexham asked, and she knew then that the gossip-mongers had not been wrong. She and Lord Wrexham were to open the ball, with George and his sister following. Every eye would be upon her, every tongue would wag about her inclusion in the family circle. George almost certainly intended this evening to be the prelude to something momentous. A question. An announcement.

If she gave him the chance.

"Of course," she murmured with another curtsy, before turning a dazzling smile on George, who gaped and stammered and could not quite muster the words to ask her for the second set before she glided past him into the ballroom.

The scent of flowers, the glow of a hundred candles, the sound of the musicians tuning their instruments—all of it made her heart beat faster, just as it had when she was little more than a girl, nervously stepping out on a very different sort of adventure. Then, she'd been thinking of marriage, of doing what she must to attract the proper notice of a proper gentleman. Of minding her step.

Quite the opposite of what she was thinking about tonight...

As she moved about the room, she nodded and spoke to the acquaintances of what seemed a lifetime ago. She kept her chin up and did not mind that her long-delayed return to society was likely the subject of at least some of the whispering that was presently going on behind gloved hands and fans. The Countess of Kingston had no reason to hide.

When the music began, Lord Wrexham approached and they took their places at the top of the dance. He was a pleasant-enough partner, though she knew his heart and mind were upstairs in the card room. She could hardly fault him for that: her own thoughts were almost entirely filled by a small green book and poor Major Stanhope in footman's livery, standing in the rain.

*Don't look for me,* he'd instructed, but it was difficult not to wonder when and where she would see him again.

Even as her feet went through the motions of dancing with Lord Wrexham, in her mind's eye, she traveled over the unlighted parts of the house, anywhere Lord Dulsworthy was likely to have laid down a book and forgotten about it.

Though the figures of the dance brought her in frequent contact with George—the touch of hands, a little walk, ample opportunity for conversation—she managed to evade any and every question he might be primed to pose, by keeping up a steady stream of chatter herself.

Despite George's clear intent, Mr. Hurst secured the next dance. Mrs. Hurst had been a school friend of Amanda's, and that gentleman was eager to report his and his wife's delight at Amanda's unexpected acceptance of their invitation to the theater. *Cymbeline* was to be the play, and they spent a pleasant half hour moving through the steps while discussing both Mr. Shakespeare's genius and Mr. Kemble's.

By a stroke of something that at the time seemed far from luck, her third partner was Lord Penhurst, whom everyone present knew to be penniless— and in search of a wife who was not. Given that oleaginous gentleman's predicament, he naturally made every effort to be charming. He was not, however, an accomplished dancer. Still, partnering him allowed her to avert a tête-à-tête with George for yet another set.

But she knew she could not avoid her fate forever. Foregoing the duties of a host, George had carefully watched the progress of her dance with Penhurst, ensuring he was at her side as soon as the sweaty-palmed younger man released her hand.

After a quick glance around the assembled company, and a silent prayer that she might discover Major Stanhope searching for her in one guise or another, she faced George and favored him with a smile. "Yes, of course, Lord Dulsworthy. I shall be honored to partner you. I only wonder it has taken you this long to ask."

Amanda had little hope that George would prove a superior dancer to Lord Penhurst, but she dutifully took her place in the line, performed the requisite curtsy with her eyes lowered, and discovered she owed the younger man a debt of gratitude after all.

She had been painfully aware that Lord Penhurst had trod more than once on her foot. But she had not noticed until just that moment that he had also stepped on the hem of her gown.

The overskirt of delicate organza was gathered in scallops along the bottom, each one suspended by a small rose fashioned from the same amaranth-red silk. In one spot, the thread holding the rose in place had broken and a swath of fabric now trailed on the marble floor. Another careless move, her partner's or her own, and the dress could be torn beyond repair, even beyond the abilities of Martha's needle. For once, she really did need to mind her step.

Thank goodness for Lord Penhurst's clumsiness!

"Oh, dear," exclaimed Amanda, gesturing at the damage. George did not look, still steadfastly refusing to take in the splendor of the low-cut gown, with its daring suggestion of translucence, lest he glimpse something improper. "Please forgive me, but I must pay a visit to the ladies' retiring room."

"Ah, hmm," was Lord Dulsworthy's only reply, and she was soon halfway across the dance floor, slipping past the other couples and into the freedom of the hall.

The retiring room was empty of guests, and the maid stationed there for just such a purpose would have made quick work of pinning the rosette back into place and averting further disaster. With very little effort, Amanda could have returned to George's side before the Boulangère began.

Instead, she gathered her skirts in her hands and hurried upstairs.

In the drawing room, the card players were too much occupied to notice her passing the double doorway. In the dining room beyond, servants bustled to prepare for the late supper that was to be served. She overheard George's butler, Mr. Evans, speaking sharply to someone about the parmesan ice cream. Glancing quickly around to ensure she wasn't spotted, Amanda slipped into the shadowy corridor past the dining room, where the sconces had not been lit, signaling that the rooms there were not open to guests.

A dozen silent steps took her to the door of George's study.

She surprised herself with the firmness of the hand she stretched out to open it, though what lay beyond that door was a familiar battleground, the site of innumerable discussions about the boys and their future. No trembling—except, perhaps, with excitement. If the book was inside, she would retrieve it and smuggle it to Magpie below… *Oh.*

How *did* she intend to sneak out of the house in the middle of the ball carrying a French cookbook?

The less-revealing blue gown might have been better suited to the evening's activities after all.

*No matter.* She could…why, she could stash the book somewhere else in the house and return for it at the end of the evening.

And with that plan, she opened the door and plunged herself into the study's total darkness.

\* \* \* \*

By ten o'clock, the street was quiet, and the footman inside the front door had departed for other duties, ordering Langley and the freckle-faced lad to give admittance to any late-arriving guests. Langley knew better than to be surprised that Dulsworthy's guests were not the sort to start their evening closer to midnight. In fact, he supposed it would not be long before the stodgiest ballgoers would be calling for their carriages to take them home. If he was to get inside and have a look about, he needed to act now.

"Damn this rain," said his partner, shifting uncomfortably. "Makes a chap need to take a piss, eh?"

"There's bushes t' the side," Langley offered with a jerk of his chin. "Nobody'll notice if you give 'em a little extra water."

The lad needed no further encouragement. With a nod of thanks, he hurried down the steps and disappeared around the corner of the house and into the shrubbery.

Likely before the other man had unbuttoned his fall, Langley had shed his wig and livery coat, stuffed them behind a stone urn, and entered the house wearing the tight-fitting attire of a gentleman, running a hand through his hair to give it a rakish air, transformed from a lowly footman into a late-arriving guest.

With no one the wiser, he stepped easily into a stream of dancers leaving the ballroom for the supper room. In the crowd and without the aid of his spectacles, he held out little hope of finding Lady Kingston—although the color of the dress she wore might prove helpful in that regard.

When he saw no telltale flash of red, he once more wondered whether to curse his luck, or praise it. Had she already managed to slip away from Dulsworthy to go in search of the book?

He ascended the stairs, mingling so thoroughly with those around him that no one seemed to notice he had not been there before. A lady who clearly had had too many glasses of something stronger than lemonade reminded him that he still owed her a set. "After supper," he promised in a drawling voice that was no more his than the one he'd used with Evans and his fellow footman, then fobbed her off on some hapless chap just leaving the card room.

He couldn't be certain he was heading in the right direction, but he'd seen no library on the ground floor, and Dulsworthy might just as well have laid the book aside in his dressing room as anywhere else. An unlit corridor and the suggestion of private rooms beckoned ahead, and while a dozen people bustled past him, calling out to an acquaintance or debating whether they smelled goose or duck, he disappeared into its shadows.

The first door he opened led into a room so dark he had to pause just past the threshold to gather his bearings. The mingled scents of leather, paper, and beeswax hinted at a study, a library, an office. The row of large rectangles scarcely visible along the far wall must be windows, though they shed no light, only suggested something less than utter blackness. He waited for his eyes to adjust, though without a candle it would be impossible to search for anything here.

Beneath the rumbling noises on the staircase, the clatter and conversation from the nearby diners, all in this room lay utterly still. Yet awareness prickled along his spine and sent him onto the balls of his feet.

He was not alone.

After a moment, he began to make out the shapes of furniture, and recognized the reflection of the windows in a mirror above the mantle. He would likely find a tinderbox there, but the pathway to that promise of light was still too indistinct, doubtless cluttered with chairs and small tables his eyes had yet to identify. He waited in silence.

*"Caw-caw-caw."*

The sound was low, uncertain. He tried to tell himself it had come from outside the room.

But after a moment, he heard it again. Closer. Louder.

*"Caw-caw-caw."*

The call was vaguely reminiscent of a crow's. Or rather, someone trying to imitate a crow. But why—? And who—?

*Ah. Of course.*

"Lady Kingston?" he whispered into the dark.

"Oh, thank goodness." The reply came on a rush of relief as a figure hurried toward him from somewhere near the fireplace. "I thought it might be you, but at first I couldn't work out a way to be sure without revealing myself. And you just stood there for so long. I realize it's terribly dark in here—the natural effect of a rainy night, I suppose, and we're quite at the back of the house—but I began to fear—"

He reached out his hands and caught her shadowy form by the upper arms before she ran into him, prompting another gasp. "Was that—was that meant to be a…bird call?" he asked.

"A magpie, yes." She tipped her chin up and the bit of light that had managed to make its way into the room from the windows glittered in her eyes. "But I confess, I don't really know what they sound like. I read up, as I told you before, so I know they often mimic other noises—other birds, I suppose. But what their natural call might be, I couldn't—"

"Harsher. More grating." His own voice was low and rough, but he held out little hope she'd take any hint from it. "Thoroughly unpleasant to the ear."

This time he felt her breath catch, rather than heard it, and her whole body went still. "Oh."

"Have you had a chance to look for the book?"

She shook her head. "I've only just managed to get away from the dancing."

He wasn't surprised the countess was a desirable partner. She certainly could be charming enough. And with her in that red dress, even a gentleman would look for any opportunity to draw her lithe figure close.…

"No matter," he said, abruptly releasing her and setting her a little apart. "I think it's best if I look and you return to the party. I don't want to make Dulsworthy suspicious of your behavior."

Her lips parted on a tiny huff of sound that might have been intended for a laugh. "No, that wouldn't do, would it?"

"Is this room the most likely place for him to have laid it? Has he a sitting room off his bedchamber, for instance?"

Though he was no longer touching her, he felt her bristle. "I wouldn't know, Major Stanhope. Lord Dulsworthy and I are not on such intimate terms as that."

"I didn't mean to suggest—" he began.

But in truth, he *had*. For reasons that he was beginning to fear lay far beyond the scope of his usual investigations, he wanted—needed—to know whether she and Dulsworthy really did intend to marry. Whether they were, in fact, already lovers.

Never before had a vague, incomplete dossier troubled him quite like Lady Kingston's did.

"Where else might he have stashed it?" he asked, trying to shift the subject.

"I—I suppose it's possible he tossed it in his phaeton on his way home— we'd been out driving that day. Or palmed it off on a servant when he returned to the house."

*Damn.* Perhaps he'd shed his borrowed livery too soon.

"It's—it's so unlike him to be careless," she murmured.

Less and less did Langley think the man's behavior was a sign of carelessness, but he still did not know the meaning of it. "Then it seems most likely to be in this room. You go enjoy the supper, make up some excuse for your absence. I'll light a candle and have a look arou—"

The door rattled in its frame, as if something had fallen against it. Then someone whispered—or thought he whispered—drunkenly, "How 'bout here?"

A feminine giggle, followed by somewhat quieter words in a voice he could have sworn belonged to the woman he'd passed on the stairs. "Ohhhh. You're an eager one! But upstairs…" she pleaded.

Langley pictured her pulling the man along the corridor with her, in search of some hidden place for a tryst, a theory confirmed when the door rattled again as if the man's weight had been lifted from it. Langley dared to let himself breathe.

Then the latch clicked and the man said, "I'm not waiting for a proper bed."

Lady Kingston flailed in the darkness and, finding his arm, gripped it and whispered frantically, "What are we going to do?"

They could hide, of course. The drunken couple would be too busy to bother noticing they weren't alone in the room. Of course, that would mean crouching with Lady Kingston in the darkness, just feet away from whatever went on between the other two. Waiting. Overhearing…everything.

The list of things a man and woman might do, even without a proper bed, was long.

"Kiss me," Langley said, throwing his arms around her again.

When the door flew open, the faint light of the corridor would illuminate just enough of the two of them, locked in an apparent embrace, to persuade the couple they needed to look elsewhere for a trysting spot. Not enough that he and Lady Kingston could be identified. He hoped.

"I beg your pardon?" Within the circle of his arms, she grew rigid but did not struggle. "Did you say—?"

"Kiss. Me." He almost growled the command the second time, no opportunity to explain his plan as the door swung inward.

For once, she didn't babble or ask questions. She did as she was told.

Pressing her body against his, she rose up onto her toes and brought her lips to—well, to the edge of his jaw. Her aim must have been thrown off by the darkness. Then she dragged her petal soft lips along the determined stubble that had reappeared over the course of the evening, at last reaching the corner of his mouth. Was that—*Christ have mercy*, was that the tip of her tongue?

He dropped one hand to her hip to turn her slightly out of the path of the light, out of the view of the intruders. He had no fear of being recognized, but he had to take care she wouldn't be either. At this angle, nothing of her would be visible but perhaps the edge of her skirts, and in the semi-darkness, their color could not be easily identified.

God, but her dress was just as wicked to the touch as it was to the eye, the way that filmy red layer—the one that promised to reveal everything to a man's eager gaze—slipped and skated over the silky stuff beneath, revealing her curves to the palm of his hand. His fingers curled almost convulsively in the fabric, against the flesh beneath. He needed—

He needed to take control of this kiss. The cold sharpness of the jewels at her throat pressed into his palm when he lifted his other hand to the back of her neck, squaring their mouths, keeping his determinedly closed.

It didn't help.

Her own lips were still slightly parted, still soft and inviting, and for all that his brain knew this kiss was a ruse, his body seemed to have other ideas. On a groan, he drew her closer, tipped his head, and claimed her mouth with his.

His own eagerness did not entirely surprise him. It had been an age since he'd been with a woman, and longer still since he'd kissed one, since he'd tasted such sweetness or drunk his fill of those little feminine sighs. He moved his lips hungrily over hers, wanting to imprint every clinging curve of her mouth on his mind.

Her eagerness, though, was a revelation. The way she claimed him in turn, no battling for dominance, no awkward bumping of noses or clashing of teeth. As if she'd already made a mental map of his mouth and was traveling familiar roads. Yet along the way she seemed to discover new pleasures, the sort that made her wander back to a spot she'd just passed for a more thorough exploration. No rush to hurry on to other points on the journey. Just here and now, this kiss, for as long they liked.

*She's only playing her part, doing what you asked*, warned his brain, at present entirely disengaged from his actions. *She's clever—she understands what's at stake.*

But did he?

Dimly, he heard another giggle from somewhere near the door. A masculine voice. "Looks like this spot is already taken. Come, my love." Another click of the door latch. Total darkness again.

For a moment more, he went on kissing her, telling himself it was necessary to maintain the pretense, in case the other couple returned. At last, however, he dragged his mouth away from hers, set her on her feet, and dropped his arms to his sides. Tried to bring his ragged breathing under control—all the while reveling in the sound of hers.

"That was—" He drew another steadying breath, licked his lips. Tasted her there. "That was well done, your ladyship. I don't believe they suspected a thing."

"They were coming in here to—to—" He could almost hear her blush.

"Yes. Such things do happen at society balls."

"Do they?"

The question sounded earnest. Was it possible for a widow—especially one who kissed like Lady Kingston—to be so innocent?

"So I've heard," he said. "Something about the environment encourages people to...to give in to what would no doubt be, in the clear light of day, an ill-advised, even forbidden attraction."

"Oh." A rustling sound in the darkness revealed she was straightening and smoothing her dress. When she spoke again, he heard something strange in her voice. "George wouldn't approve."

Of that, Langley was certain. And if he weren't more careful than he'd been tonight, Dulsworthy would catch on and call him out. Worse, General Scott would have his hide.

He was here for the codebook. Nothing more.

"You should return to the party, ma'am. I'll search for the book on my own." When she neither moved nor spoke, he added, "On behalf of the Crown, I thank you for your assistance." The words sounded absurdly formal, even to his ears. "We shan't require anything further from you."

She must have nodded. Her ruby earbobs winked in the faint suggestion of light coming through the window. He strained to catch the whisper of her slippers across the carpet, but the next thing he heard was the click of the door latch.

He was alone.

# Chapter 6

Amanda snuggled more firmly into her pillow, determined to ignore the tentative *tap-tap-tap* on her chamber door, which sounded to her aching head more like a volley of gunshots.

Never having consumed three and a half glasses of wine at one sitting before—the remainder of the fourth had spilled when Amanda had strangely misjudged the distance to the table—she had no prior experience with how she would feel the morning after such folly.

Another *tap-tap-tap* at the door, this one accompanied by a soft *"Mama?"* Jamie's voice.

She managed to lift her head, despite its inordinate weight. "Yes, dear? Come in."

Martha had not yet opened the draperies, so the room was full of shadows. In the ochre-tinged light that passed through the panels of yellow silk, her elder son looked as sallow as ever. He paused a few feet from her bedside and tossed his dark hair from his eyes.

"Are you feeling all right, Mama? It's nearly nine."

Amanda pushed upright and swiped at her mouth with the back of one hand. Ordinarily at this hour, she would be in the schoolroom, breakfasting with her sons. "Yes, dear. Yes, of course." She felt as though she were speaking around a wad of cotton. "Only it was quite late when I got home last night, so I—"

"Uncle George seems chipper enough." She heard a note of judgment in Jamie's voice, and he looked at her with a critical eye as he spoke. He knew, of course, that she'd been out late at Lord Dulsworthy's ball. She wouldn't put it past him to have waited up. "He's downstairs," he explained then, a little twist of annoyance curling his lips. "And he's brought you flowers."

Those words set her thoughts spinning, which did nothing for the state of either her head or her stomach. She'd managed to avoid a proposal last night. But if George was determined, she wouldn't be able to avoid him forever. "How…kind of him."

"He's asking to take Philip and me for a drive. I suspect Pip's already got the reins in his hands. But I thought we'd just better ask permission, and Grandmama…well, you know…"

"Doesn't like to be wakened early. Yes, I do know." Amanda glanced toward the window, at the light seeping around the edges of the drapery and the hint of blue sky beyond. "It looks like a fine morning after yesterday's rain. Do you *want* to go for a drive with Lord Dulsworthy?"

Jamie lifted one shoulder in a shrug, but she saw in his bright eyes the telltale signs that at least some portion of his reluctance was feigned. Though he was quieter and more bookish than his brother, he was not indifferent to a high-perch phaeton and prime horseflesh, even when they belonged to George. Perhaps with the boys, George allowed the horses have their heads.

"Go on with you then. And tell Pip I said he's not to whoop and holler until you're well out of Mayfair," she called after him, before collapsing on the pillow once more.

Flowers, an early call…at least George hadn't insisted on speaking to her. *Yet.*

Martha entered a moment later, bearing a tray of coffee and toast. "When you didn't join Lord Kingston and Master Philip upstairs like usual, I thought you might rather take something in your room, milady." She placed the tray over Amanda's lap with exaggerated care, so nothing rattled—nothing but Martha herself. Mama was appalled by the maid's tendency to chatter familiarly, and just now, Amanda was inclined to agree with her mother. "I've only just managed to fix that frightful rent in your gown, ma'am. Must've been quite a night." Martha's expression was nothing short of sly.

But Amanda could hardly fault the girl for thinking that her mistress had stayed out too late and had too much to drink. It was true, after all.

What would she say if she knew it had all been at the service of a spy? A spy had needed her, Amanda Barlett's, help.

And now, he…didn't.

Amanda had heard rumors that forgetfulness, even oblivion, might be found at the bottom of a glass. Last night at supper, she'd held out hope that at the very least, she might blur the edges of her memory.

Now, however, all she had to show for her intemperance was a dry mouth and a headache. Everything about the evening remained crystal clear.

George's expression as he demanded to know where she'd got off to, his brow creased by a deep frown of disapproval he'd tried to pass off as worry.

Lord Penhurst's curse when what remained of her fourth glass of wine had landed in his lap.

The spice of Magpie's kiss. The bitter tang of his parting words.

So much for her little adventure.

* * * *

At some hour well past midnight, following a swift but thorough search of Dulsworthy's study, Langley returned to the Underground empty handed.

All was quiet. The faint light beneath the workroom door suggested no more than a single candle still burned within. Against his better judgment, he opened the door but found the room unoccupied.

Anything truly valuable to the war effort had been locked away by the last person to leave. The signs that remained of the work that went on in that space—crumpled bits of paper, the trimmings from pens, open books left lying face down—put him in mind of an untidy schoolroom.

With the swipe of an arm, he cleared a space, sat down in a sturdy chair, and laid his forehead on the scarred wooden tabletop, resisting—but only just—the temptation to strike his head against the cool, unforgiving surface until sense returned, or was driven from his brain forever.

A few moments later, the door opened behind him. Not bothering to sit up, he twisted his neck to identify the arrival.

"No luck, eh?" Colonel Millrose said, studying him from the threshold. Langley knew that dawn must be approaching, for Millrose was dressed in his shop clothes. He opened the tobacconist's early, for the business that came when the hells and clubs closed their doors and unwitting men, half-drunk with fatigue or entirely drunk on illicit French brandy, wandered in with occasionally interesting stories to tell.

Langley's only reply was to turn back to his prior position, hiding his face from the other man.

"I'm sorry to hear it." Millrose strode toward the table, scraped a chair across the floor, and sat down. "But I'm glad to have a chance to speak with you in person. General Scott sent a message just after you left."

"Finally realized he chose the wrong man for the job, eh?"

Langley wasn't entirely sure who the right man would have been. But he was positive the task should belong to someone who wouldn't have connived for a kiss with the countess at the first opportunity, who had the self-control not to grope her arse. It was more than likely Scott had assigned him to this mission to humble him, to teach him a lesson. But impossible that Scott had foreseen his supposed best agent lusting after A man—*Lady Kingston.*

Millrose ignored his words. "He's heard—don't ask me how; it's as if the man has some vast secret network, spying on his spies—that Hopkins's captors have managed to figure out who has the codebook."

They would have had to torture the information from Hopkins. But that was not the first concern that rose to Langley's mind. He dragged himself upright and eyed Billy, who sat a few feet away, his arms folded over the back of the chair he was straddling. "I pray you mean Dulsworthy."

"I'm afraid not."

"Christ." He was on his feet before he knew he'd moved, the heavy table skidding forward with the thrust of his arms and his chair toppling onto the floor behind him. "Then she needs—she and her family need protection."

Unperturbed, Billy waved the fingers of one hand, gesturing for calm, for Langley to sit down again. But he couldn't. Not if—not when—

"I've got men guarding the house, front and back. So long as she stays inside, she'll be perfectly safe."

"But?" Langley spoke the word the other man had left unspoken.

"It seems she has plans for the theater tonight. Covent Garden. A box with her friends Mr. and Mrs. Hurst."

Langley raked a hand through his hair. "A ball last night, the theater tonight. Didn't the dossier—didn't *you* imply the woman never left the house?"

Hell, *she* had implied it. *You haven't the first idea how dull my life is,* she'd told him, pleading up at him with those rich brown eyes as she'd insisted on a chance to play a part in the search.

Billy shrugged as he rose from his chair and swung his leg over the seat to stand beside it. "It would seem the Countess of Kingston is finally out of mourning." He reached a hand into his breast pocket, withdrew a folded paper, and laid it on the table. "Your ticket to *Cymbeline.* Eight o'clock. I've heard Kemble is extraordinary as the hero."

Langley swore and kicked the fallen chair for good measure. "Which exactly is it I'm being ordered to do? Search for the codebook? Or tail her ladyship about the town?"

A knowing smile split the man's face. "Yes."

* * * *

Well before the longcase clock in the entry hall chimed seven, Amanda had been ready and eager to escape Bartlett House. She felt rather as she imagined a fox must feel during the hunt, hurried and harried from its den, and from every subsequent hiding place it found, until it simply gave itself up to the hounds.

With no other plans for the day, Mama had been at liberty to follow her from room to room, enquiring about the ball in that saccharine voice that set Amanda's teeth on edge. And with every remove, Mama had ordered poor Lewis to fetch the vase containing George's flowers, ostensibly to discover the ideal place to showcase their beauty.

They *were* lovely, a hothouse arrangement studded with red roses that echoed the gown she had worn to the ball. Amanda wondered whether they had been chosen for that purpose, and if so by whom, for George was unlikely to make the connection. Their heavy perfume had done nothing to alleviate her headache.

Lord Dulsworthy's call late in the afternoon had been mercifully brief, to enquire after her health and to return her hot, tired sons to her care. But his parting request for a private audience with her in the morning—"to discuss young Kingston's future"—had left her palms as damp and her mouth as dry as they had been when she'd first waked. As they would have been if he'd got down on one knee right then.

Worst of all, though, were the memories that nipped at her heels, undiscouraged by an occasional kick.

Once, in her first season, she'd allowed a notorious rake to maneuver her onto a secluded terrace and pretended to believe his whispered promises, hoping he would teach her what the matrons whispered about and the wallflowers would never know. Mama had discovered her missing before any damage had been done—and before any real knowledge could be imparted. In all the years of Amanda's marriage, in Kingston's kind but dispassionate embrace, she had refused to let herself remember the possibility that there might be something more. Until last night...

*Kiss me*, Major Stanhope had commanded, and it had taken but half a moment for her to understand why: such a pose would both excuse their presence in the darkened room and persuade the other couple to leave them in peace.

And as a result, Amanda did not think she would ever know peace again.

Because she had kissed him with the hunger she had pushed down, deep inside herself, so deep she had almost forgotten its existence.

But oh, she remembered it now.

It still quivered in parts of her body she generally tried to ignore.

"Amanda, dear, are you feeling all right?" Rebecca Hurst leaned toward her in the carriage, concern etched onto her delicate features. "You're quite flushed. Open a window, Charles," she urged her husband. "She needs fresh air."

"I'm quite well, thank you," Amanda insisted, though not quickly enough to forestall Mr. Hurst's efforts. The pane of glass slid down into the door, and a warm breeze gusted into the carriage, scented strongly of horse.

"Now, where did I lay my fan?" Rebecca patted the seat around her until Amanda reached out a staying hand.

"Truly, I'm fine. I seem to be compelled to keep remembering last night's embarrassment, that's all."

"The spilled wine, you mean?"

Amanda mustered a tinkling laugh at her own expense. "What else? Now, Mr. Hurst, tell me about the play, if you would." She needed to turn the conversation and give everyone in the carriage something else to think about.

As Mr. Hurst began to sketch out the story—involving a wicked queen, a duped king, a daughter denied the right to marry her true love, and two sons, kidnapped in their infancy and restored to their places in the succession to the throne at last—Amanda fought to keep her attention from wandering back over the various plot twists in her own life. Despite her careful upbringing, the girl of nineteen who had once so enjoyed an outing such as this had been ill-prepared for the life—and death—that had followed. But what she'd lacked in wisdom she had gained in strength, the strength required to be a countess, to bury her husband, to shield her boys. If she hadn't the savvy to spy on behalf of the Crown, she at least had what little wit it took to outmaneuver Lord Dulsworthy.

"I am so glad you've joined us at last, Amanda," Rebecca said as the carriage rolled to a stop near Covent Garden. Her voice dropped a note lower. "I'd begun to think you'd decided to mourn Lord Kingston forever."

She had the grace not to sound skeptical, though she certainly had reason to be. Though over the years she had developed an affection for the man she had married, Amanda had never pretended to be making a love match. No one would have expected it of her—least of all her husband.

"Mama has been very protective of me," Amanda answered after a moment.

Her friend nodded, a knowing expression in her eyes. "Mrs. West always was, as I recall."

Amanda only smiled. Mama still wanted to shelter her, to give her the best, by which she meant the safest—and the dullest—life possible. If she knew about Amanda's involvement with a codebook, a secret mission, a handsome spy…well, she would probably have heart palpitations.

Fortunately, all that was over. Mama's heart was perfectly safe.

Amanda gave herself a little shake and looked about at the bustle, the great variety of people, the gowns and the jewels and the headpieces. A night at the theater offered ample distraction, and she would not ruin its pleasures, or the enjoyment of her friends' company, by sulking.

The Hursts had excellent seats, a box near enough the stage that Amanda could immerse herself entirely in the performance, but not so near that she was distracted by the thick paint the actors' wore or the spittle that flew from their lips. Mr. Kemble was, as promised, extraordinary as Posthumus, the princess's would-be lover.

So lost was Amanda in the story unfolding before her, Rebecca had to tap her twice on the knee with her folded fan to pull her attention from the stage. "My dear, do you recognize that gentleman over there?" She tipped her head slightly toward a box on the other side of the theater, where a dark-haired man sat alone. "He has been staring at you all evening."

Not wishing to return the favor, Amanda sent a quick glance in his direction, too quick to be sure of much of anything.

"Oh, of course he would return his attention to the stage now." A huff of somewhat amused annoyance underscored Rebecca's whisper. "He must know I've caught him at his rudeness."

Amanda looked again. Looked, but would not stare. Each time she let her eyes drift across the theater, another piece of him came more clearly into view. Rather outrageously dressed, the sort of person who wished to draw attention to his clothes. A pink silk coat, an embroidered floral waistcoat, and a collar so high and so stiff he must have difficulty turning his head. And twirling a quizzing glass in the fingers of one hand.

With each glimpse, her chest tightened, until she was nearly breathless. Brown hair, darker than she had first imagined. A chiseled profile.

She was imagining things. It couldn't possibly be…

He turned toward her then, lifted the glass to his eye so imperiously, he might have been a duke. He gave no nod, made no acknowledgment that he had been seen.

*"Magpie."*

Her lips shaped the name, but made almost no sound.

"I beg your pardon?" Rebecca said, leaning toward her in a way that momentarily blocked him from Amanda's view.

"Whoever he is, he's a preening sort, I'll say that much." With an exaggerated movement, Amanda squared herself in her seat and would look nowhere but at the stage.

But beneath that performance of indifference, her heart clattered in her chest and heat threatened to rise to her cheeks.

*We shan't require anything further from you.*

So what was he doing here tonight?

She held herself stiff for the remainder of the performance, willing herself not even to glance in his direction again. So stiff that Mr. Hurst was obliged to help her to her feet when the play was over.

"Did you enjoy it?" he asked.

"Marvelous," was her reply, though she no longer had any sense of what she'd witnessed.

Thankfully, that was a sufficient reply to encourage Mr. Hurst to launch into his own analysis, comparing this performance to ones he had seen in the past, decrying the modern practice of changing the endings to certain plays. Most of all, he mourned the inestimable losses when Shakespeare's genius was cast before indolent, indifferent audiences, like pearls before swine—"too rich and too comfortable," he complained as they fought their way to their carriage. People nearby cast him looks ranging from tolerant amusement to anger. "Not as it once was, when everyday sorts of people jostled for position in the pit and the actors had to keep them hanging on every word if they wanted to be heard above the crowd."

*The crowd.* Amanda would *not* look for Major Stanhope, would not try to pick him out among the milling throng of theater-goers, turned loose into the warm night. He had as much right to an evening's entertainment as the next fellow, and doubtless Rebecca had exaggerated his notice of her.

"Still, it was a fine cap on the season," Mr. Hurst was saying as he helped first his wife and then Amanda into the carriage.

"Indeed," Amanda murmured her agreement, only half hearing him.

"Yes, town will be deserted soon enough." The streetlight streaked Rebecca's face, making her expression impossible to read. "Will you be leaving for the country soon?"

Since James's death, she had kept to the confines of Bartlett House, unable—or perhaps *too* able—to imagine herself restlessly wandering the endless corridors of Foxhaven.

But as her mother occasionally reminded her, Philip needed a wider scope for his energy, space to run and climb and ride, and the fresh, clean air would do Jamie good. Besides, he ought to be familiar with the ancestral home of the earls of Kingston. Foxhaven was his, after all.

And after last night, a change of scene would have the added recommendation of distracting her from the intrigue over that silly book and Langley Stanhope.

Most of all, she did not believe George would follow them into the country unless invited. And she had no intention of inviting him.

But wouldn't such a trip also hint at a sort of a last hurrah? Possibly their final weeks fully as a family, before first Jamie and then Philip went away to school at their guardian's insistence and she... She *what?* Finally gave up and gave in to her mother and to George? Reluctantly became Lady Dulsworthy?

Oh, of course it was not as if she would never see her sons again. There would be school holidays—though even now she could picture in her mind's eye Philip's ill-spelled (because quickly dashed off) missive begging her to let him spend those few precious weeks at the home of a friend. She could see Jamie, older, thinner, paler, retreating further into himself, refusing to speak much of how he fared at school because he did not wish to worry her.

And over it all loomed George, their—*their stepfather? oh, God*—answering Philip's note in the affirmative without telling her, or slapping Jamie on the shoulder, urging him to take his nose out of his books. Then, later, laying that same beefy hand on her shoulder, and...

The shudder that passed through her made her teeth rattle.

"Lady Kingston?"

Mr. Hurst's voice, concerned, bewildered, brought her back to the present: the darkened interior of the Hurst's carriage, the quiet streets of Mayfair, the wide-eyed expressions on her friends' faces.

"The night air has grown cool, don't you agree?" she asked, rubbing her hand over her upper arm. Her cloak had slipped over her shoulder, exposing the narrow strip between the bottom of her sleeve and top of her glove, where her skin was pebbled with gooseflesh, though in fact the evening was still warm. Oppressively so. "No, I have no plans to go into the country this summer. The boys and I are quite content at Bartlett House."

It rolled into view just as the words left her lips, the gray stone face familiar, impassive, a little like a prison.

"Then you all must come and stay with us in Richmond," offered Mr. Hurst.

"Yes," Rebecca agreed. "We shall have picnics on the river." As the carriage swayed to a stop, she reached for Amanda's hand. "It would do you good to get away from town for a few days."

"I daresay you're right. Given the pleasant spring weather we've enjoyed, July is sure to be beastly. Oh, thank you," she said, squeezing her friend's fingers. "Thank you for tonight, and for—" *For not giving up,* she wanted to say. But instead she said, "for everything," her voice so earnest that the worry in Rebecca's eyes only deepened.

Fortunately, in another moment, the footman had opened the door and lowered the step, and she could clamber down to the pavement without waiting for Mr. Hurst's assistance.

"I trust you had a pleasant evening, milady," Matthews said, bowing her into the house.

"You needn't have been the one to wait up." Though the few candles that remained burning could hardly be said to illuminate the entry hall, she could see the dark smudges beneath the butler's eyes, the lines on his weary face.

"You are too kind, ma'am," he said with another bow. "Mrs. West insisted."

She drew in a sharp breath in an effort to contain the words that rose to her lips. But a few of them escaped nonetheless, very similar to the ones with which she'd answered Rebecca Hurst. "My mother can be overprotective, Mr. Matthews."

To that, of course, the poor butler could offer no reply. He simply held out a hand as if to assist her with her wraps.

Amanda willingly slipped the cloak from her shoulders, but she did not then make the expected move toward the stairs. "Please tell Martha she may retire, Mr. Matthews. And you must follow suit. I'm going to sit for a while in the garden. The night is too fine to waste."

Something flickered into the butler's eyes. Surprise, perhaps. But not disapproval. "Very good, milady," he said, before folding the cloak over his arm and preceding her to the back of the house, he making his way to the servants' stairs, and she to the narrow freedoms offered by Bartlett House's garden.

From the windows of the morning room, she studied the hedges and vines and espaliered fruit trees that had been carefully planted to disguise the garden's high walls and tall gate. She could still see through them, to the unyielding stone and cold metal. How had she ever persuaded herself that going into the garden was an escape?

But it was all the escape she had. She stretched forth both arms, swung open the French doors, and stepped out, letting the train of her skirts trail carelessly over the three wide steps that led down to the flagstone path, curving gently between flower beds on either side. As she walked, she fluttered her fingers through the sleeping flowers and stirred their scent. Roses, their perfume quite unlike the hothouse blooms George had sent, though it was enough to make her think of him, and of last night's disastrous ball, and of—

Was that a noise? The house behind her and the walls to either side muffled the sounds of the great city. Surely, everyone closer at hand was asleep. The boys in their beds, the bees in their hive, the birds in their ne—

Her chin jerked up and her pulse began to knock as she peered into the shadows beyond the gate.

She wasn't alone.

# Chapter 7

What had Amanda been thinking of as she stood inside, looking out over the little garden?

Whatever it was, Langley had fully expected her to turn around and disappear into the depths of the house again. The night air was damp, all lay in darkness, and the hour was late. She certainly ought to be safely in bed.

When instead she pushed open the doors, making a surprisingly dramatic exit—or entrance?—he did not know what to feel.

On the one hand, this sudden enthusiasm for going out would cause no end of trouble. She would be more difficult to guard, to protect. If the men who had got hold of Hopkins managed to get hold of Lady Kingston, they would not hesitate to do whatever was necessary to pry information from her. They would not be put off by her protests that she knew nothing at all about the contents of the codebook or its present whereabouts. Though she was a countess, they would not be chivalrous.

On the other hand, he had spent the whole evening watching her from afar, straining to bring her into sharper focus.

He could see her now.

Not with perfect clarity, no. But well enough.

She had shed her cloak, and in the deep darkness of the garden, the silvery stuff of her gown shone like moonlight, paler even than the skin of her throat and her arms. She moved with an easy, graceful stride among the flowerbeds. Above her brown hair—no hint of its golden warmth visible now, as it had been earlier beneath the lights of the theater—swayed a pair of creamy plumes, held in place by a circlet of diamonds that gleamed in what faint light they could find.

He slipped a hand inside his coat, reaching for the stubby jeweled handle of the damned quizzing glass he'd been toying with all evening. Billy had suggested the disguise, a dandy whose clothes and manner would draw all the notice, leaving *him* quite overlooked.

At first, Langley had protested the costume, until Fanny had said, with icy humor, "I thought magpies *liked* all the shiny bits and bobs," and the need to clamp his jaw against a string of epithets had left him unable to tell Billy no.

But as it had turned out, the glass had been good for more than deflecting any theater-goer's untoward curiosity about his identity. Still missing his spectacles, he'd found this little substitute unexpectedly useful for keeping an eye on…things.

He slid the quizzing glass from his waistcoat, the garment so fashionably tight-fighting that he swore he heard a little *pop* when he tugged the round glass free of the slit pocket. Slowly, he raised it to his eye to bring Lady Kingston into sharper focus, then stopped.

What the hell was he doing?

Standing guard, yes, of course—he'd relieved another soldier of his duty for the privilege of lurking all night in this stinking alleyway, wearing a kit even less comfortable than the footman's had been, to make sure Lady Kingston and her family did not come to harm.

But what exactly was it he wanted to see?

The glass tumbled from his suddenly nerveless fingers, falling, falling, until it reached the end of the silk ribbon by which it was tethered to a button of his waistcoat, jerked in surprise at its arrested momentum, sprang back, and clanged against a wrought-iron fence post.

Amanda froze mid-stride and searched the darkness beyond the gate.

*She's not foolish enough to investigate a noise in the alley after midnight.*

She took a step closer. Two steps.

*She'll never know it's you if you don't move.*

"Magpie?"

Stiffly, he moved into the gap between the hedges, where the narrow gate stood.

"Lady Kingston."

Her face, which had been creased with worry, eased into a smile. "I hoped it was you."

*She had?*

"Better a spy than a thief, I should think," she explained through upturned lips.

He ought to waste no time in correcting her assumptions about spies. About himself in particular. Ought to tell her right now of the dangers she faced, the knowledge of which would surely wipe away her pleased expression. He even opened his mouth to form the words.

But of course, she spoke first.

"Did you find the b—?" She bit her lip to stop herself from saying more, and for a moment, he could not think why. Then he remembered having asked her not to mention the book. "Did you find what you were looking for last evening?"

*Had he?*

He looked her up and down. At this distance, hampered only by the wrought-iron fence and the prickly offshoots of an overgrown hedge, he could see her quite clearly without any mechanical aid. The way the silvery silk of her gown highlighted her tall, slender form, though not quite as the red one had last night. More like a marble statue, inviting a connoisseur's appreciation.

Surely a man could admire a woman's appearance dispassionately, could he not?

The persistent memory of the way she'd felt in his arms—not at all like cold, unyielding marble—was another matter entirely.

"No," he answered gruffly. "I did not. I made as thorough a search as I could of that room, without drawing attention to myself or the light. By then supper was ending and having shed my footman's livery, I did not dare venture further into the house."

"Oh, I'm sorry. It must have been very frustrating."

Briefly, he closed his eyes against her present beauty, against the recollection of last night. "Yes. It was."

"If I'd known, I should have sent you a note this morning to tell you he was out all day. He took my boys for a drive into the country. But I didn't—that is, he didn't ask my permission—not that he has to, of course, as he is their guardian—I only meant to say I didn't know beforehand about the outing, or I could have told you the house would be empty."

He'd taken her boys without asking? Langley liked Dulsworthy less and less with each passing conversation about the man.

"Anyway, I have been wondering whether you were successful. It's kind of you to take the trouble to let me know the outcome of last night's… mission." Before speaking the last word, she glanced around them and dropped her voice to something even less than a whisper, for she had already been speaking quietly, though there was no one to overhear them.

He did not correct her assumption about why he was there.

"I'd invite you in," she said next, still softly, "but the lock..." She pinched her lips into a sort of amused frown and stepped closer, curling her fingers around one of the wrought-iron cross bars. Almost, but not quite, touching him. "I don't think anyone had turned that key in all the years since the garden was first planted. It was nothing but rust, and the next morning, after you were—and we—well, anyway, one of the maids came out to, to, ah—" Her other hand circled in the air, as if to conjure the rest of the explanation from thin air.

He could guess, based on the smell of the alleyway, that the maid had been emptying the slops. He could also guess the unfortunate servant would not have been pleased to find the gate unexpectedly locked and barring her from completing her task.

"She found half of the key lying on the ground, and the rest—well, it was apparently still in the lock. It just...disintegrated. Mr. Matthews has sent for a smith to have it repaired, but the fellow won't be here until Tuesday next."

"It's just as well."

He meant it, too. Not only because he had no business poking around in Lady Kingston's garden, but because no one else could get in this way either.

But the tone of his voice—fatigue had made it gravelly and he deliberately avoided any temptation to soften it for her—evidently took her aback. Quite literally. She straightened her shoulders, released her grip on the cold metal, and stepped away from the gate. When she spoke again, even her voice was more remote. The sort of tone one employed when speaking to a stranger.

Which she was.

"Did you enjoy the play tonight?" Despite her sudden reserve, the question was still polite. It seemed there were some habits she could not break.

"Not particularly." Enjoyment had not been his purpose for attending. "*Cymbeline* cannot make up its mind to be either a tragedy or a comedy."

She appeared to consider his assessment for a moment. "I suppose it makes a certain sense that you prefer predictable outcomes in your entertainments—they must be rare enough in your line of work."

He almost laughed at such a ridiculously simple explanation.

And might have done, if not for the damned ring of truth.

"I confess," she said then, "I like a happy ending too."

But of course she did. He shook his head at himself, at the notion they had anything in common. Other than the obvious, the physical, there ought to be nothing about her that attracted him. She was talkative, cheerful, sweet—everything he wasn't. She had no connection to him or his world.

Or hadn't, until Hopkins had been forced to hand off the codebook to an unsuspecting passerby, and Langley had got himself mixed up in the matter.

Until he had kissed her.

"But it must be difficult to enjoy any play without your spectacles. I *am* sorry—"

He raised a hand to forestall another apology. "I often manage without them."

"Oh?" She tilted her head to the side, studying him. "I suppose they don't fit in with certain...disguises." She spoke that word with the same inflection she'd earlier given to the word *mission*.

He answered her with a brusque nod. He had not intended to invite her scrutiny, and he would not let himself enjoy her gaze sweeping over his features like a delicate, searching touch.

"Forgive me for disturbing you, Lady Kingston. I should withdraw and leave you to the pleasures of your garden."

She tossed a glance over her shoulder, leaving him momentarily bereft of her warm, dark gaze. "No, I should retire. I only come out here sometimes to—to clear my head, I suppose. Though I don't know as it does any good," she added with a self-deprecating laugh, turning back toward him without meeting his eye. "I am tired. I'm not used to keeping such late hours. It's been many years since I had two evenings out in a row, you see. So many years taken up with my husband's illness, and my mourning, and my children..."

"A quiet life is not always to be regretted," he said, deliberately avoiding the word she had used the other night. *Dull* was not the same as *quiet*, was it?

As if he had any experience with either one.

"Besides," he added, "I'm sure that for one tasked with raising two boys, a quiet life is rarely on offer."

A little huff of laughter—wry, skeptical—lifted her chest. "You might be surprised." Then her breath caught, as if a sudden pain had stabbed through her. "And it will soon be quieter still..." Those words were spoken almost entirely to herself.

At last she lifted her eyes to her face and with an obvious effort, mustered a smile tinged with sorrow. "I have just remembered that Lord Dulsworthy will be out of his house again tomorrow morning. He is to call here at ten o'clock, to discuss his intention to send Jamie—Lord Kingston—away to school."

"*His* intention?" Langley echoed without meaning to.

"A young nobleman's education is not a matter to be left in the hands of a woman, Major Stanhope," she said, and he knew from her stiff way of speaking that the words did not belong to her. Who had told her such a thing? Her late husband? Dulsworthy?

The affair was nothing with which he need concern himself. He ought to be considering how best to use the information that Dulsworthy would be from home. He ought to be thinking of his mission.

And he was. Just not in the way anyone, including General Scott, would have anticipated when the assignment was given.

Then again, he did have *two* missions. And he had not earned the title of Scott's best agent by doing only what was expected.

"I thank you, ma'am. I will do my best to make something of the opportunity." He gave a rather pointed bow, as if taking his leave, though of course as he had already relieved the other guard from duty, he would be going nowhere tonight.

As he had hoped, she mirrored the gesture with the dip of a curtsy. Then, as he had *not* dared to hope, she laid a hand on the iron railing again. As if reaching for his hand. As if reaching for him.

He held himself rigidly still, never more a soldier than in the endless moment until her hand fell away once more.

"Good night, Major Stanhope."

Was it his imagination, or was the fatigue in her voice now tinged with disappointment?

"Good night, Lady Kingston."

He slipped back into the shadow of the hedge and from there, watched her make her way into the dark house.

\* \* \* \*

Amanda woke at the usual hour the next morning and did not wince at Martha's ringing voice or the light stabbing through the curtains, though her sleep had been checkered with shadowy dreams.

Dreams rarely bore scrutiny in the morning, she had found. They slipped through one's fingers like water. And since a good many of her dreams last night—or had it all been one long, repetitious nightmare?—had ended with George arriving to announce she was not fit to have charge of Jamie and Philip, she had no particular desire to try to shape those hazy fragments into something like a memory.

Instead she rose, dressed, and went upstairs to the schoolroom for her usual breakfast with her sons.

The room at the top of the house was not overlarge, but light-filled with its rows of high windows around three sides. The furnishings she had kept deliberately simple: bookshelves, wooden chairs, a table almost too big for the space. Already the chairs' lower rungs bore the scuff marks of restless, swinging feet, and the table, the scars of pen knives and spilled ink. Those signs of schoolboy use brought a soft smile to her lips.

On either side of the stairwell, on the wall without windows, sat two doors. She tapped softly on the one to her right.

"Jamie? Philip? Ready to begin the day?"

Time was, the boys would have been up before her, the table covered with toy soldiers or spillikins—some charged battle between them—while they impatiently waited for breakfast and for her. But they were growing older, less eager for their mother's companionship. Jamie in particular would as soon not rise at first light, and both of them had declared that she must not open the door before they were dressed.

So she sat down at the table, traced with one fingertip the start of an angular P that had been carved into its top, and took her turn at waiting in the schoolroom quiet.

Too quiet.

She was on her feet again a moment later, straightening some books on one shelf before crossing to the second door, which opened onto a room almost too narrow for the bed and washstand it contained. A nurse had occupied it when the boys were small, and under more ordinary circumstances, it would then have been turned over to a governess. Amanda used it for storage.

When she emerged a moment later, bearing two rolled-up maps and a box of geometric shapes, Lewis was just stepping into the schoolroom with the breakfast tray.

"Good morning, milady. I didn't see you there." He placed the tray on the table, executed a swift bow, and then hurried forward to relieve her of her burden.

"Good morning, Lewis," she said, blowing from her eyes a lock of hair that had worked its way loose during her search and then brushing the dust from her hands.

"Just say the word, milady, and I'll see that storeroom made spick and span."

"Oh, it's hardly worth the effort," she answered, seating herself as he poured her coffee. "If it were all clean and organized, I might never find anything again."

Lewis dared a smile. "Yes, milady. Will there be anything else?"

"Thank you, no."

He bowed in acknowledgment but nevertheless paused before descending to give a considerably firmer rap than she had on the boys' door. "Breakfast, Lord Kingston, Master Philip. Your mother's waiting."

She still had time to butter and eat her toast, sample the eggs, and start on her second cup of coffee before two sleepy faces joined her at the table, Philip first, declaring he was famished, as always, and Jamie a moment later, yawning as he pushed his hair out of his face.

"Good morning," she said, her cheerfulness not forced—she was happy to see her sons, though dread of the coming conversation with George hung over her like a cloud. "We are in danger of becoming dilettantish with our lessons, boys. Noses to the grindstone today, I'm afraid." She paused for a sip of coffee, fortifying herself not against the chorus of their grumbles but against the words she was determined to say next. "But first, I have a question."

Jamie and Philip turned toward her, Jamie's eyes dark like her own, Philip's blue like his father's, both pairs bright with curiosity despite the general air of sleepiness. They were good boys, growing into good young men. She could not expect to keep them by her side forever. They might even *want* to go away to school. Either way, they deserved to have some say in their future, in the plans Lord Dulsworthy had for them.

"Later this morning," she began, "your Uncle George will be calling to discuss something of importance with me."

He called frequently enough that the visit could not be a matter of particular interest to either of them. Philip, though generally optimistic, turned back to his breakfast while waiting to hear the rest, evidently having decided that another outing in the phaeton was unlikely to be on offer. Jamie, however, narrowed his gaze—only slightly, but enough to make her think that he suspected something.

That look was enough to weaken her resolve. "And so I wondered whether you would rather begin this morning with drawing," she gestured toward the box of shapes, "or defer that lesson until after the interruption and start with geography instead?" She laid her hand on the rolled-up maps, hoping to disguise its tremble.

"Geography," declared Philip around a mouthful of porridge. He generally lacked the patience for drawing.

"Whatever you think is best, Mama," said Jamie, his trusting, steady gaze freighting the words with additional meaning.

Or so she chose to believe.

"Very well, then. Geography it is," she said, rising to set aside the box and clear room to unroll one of the maps. "Finish your breakfast and we'll begin."

Not quite two hours later, she left the boys with a project to sketch the major rivers of Europe and Asia and went downstairs to freshen up before her meeting. She wished to appear cool and collected, not harried and a little dusty. And she did not want to be late, either.

She had already arranged to have Lord Dulsworthy shown into the library, not the drawing room. She would greet him from the chair behind her late husband's desk, to remind him of the authority she still held as the boys' mother and the Countess of Kingston.

She opened the library door and found…her mother.

Most mornings at this hour, she would still be in bed, drinking her chocolate, reading through her post and the newspaper, meticulously arranging her daughter's life.

Now she stood in the library, running a finger over a row of book spines, apparently searching out a tome on agriculture and estate management— unless Matthews's cleaning project of a few days ago had resulted in a total reorganization of the shelves.

"Mama, this is a surprise."

She turned sharply, eyes wide. The hand that had been trailing over the bookshelf fluttered down to her chest. "Goodness, Amanda, what a fright you gave me. I never heard you come in."

If she didn't know it would violate her mother's strict sense of propriety, Amanda might have suspected Mama of having once considered a career on the stage. Though not the *London* stage. Perhaps a troupe that traveled to villages and country towns where the audience's expectations of the actors' skill were considerably more modest.

"I suppose you must've already heard. Lord Dulsworthy is to arrive momentarily and I've arranged to have him shown in here."

"Really?" Mama pretended to choose a book and crossed the room with it. For just a moment, Amanda allowed herself to hope that she intended to show herself out. "I suppose this is a comfortable enough room for entertaining," she said, sitting down on the sofa near the front of the room, part of a grouping of softer, more comfortable furniture placed to balance the enormous mahogany desk at the other end.

"I'm not entertaining, Mama. He's coming to discuss the boys."

"Oh." Disappointment flickered into her mother's eyes. "Nothing…*else* to talk over? Since the ball, I mean."

"No."

She rose again. "When your Papa died, I had no thought of marrying again. But after a time, there were offers." Amanda could not help but start at that revelation. She had often wondered but never known. "I didn't wish to appear unseemly in my haste, however. So I waited…too long, as it turns out. I only wish that you…" She paused and shook her head. "I will not always be here to protect you, my dear."

"Protect me from what, Mama?"

"The world, I suppose," she replied with a self-deprecating little laugh. "Just as you wish to protect your sons." Amanda stiffened at the comparison. "As a child, even as a young woman, you were like Philip—impulsive, a bit of a thrill-seeker," she continued fondly. "But of course a lady mustn't—"

Amanda was quite familiar with the list of things a lady mustn't do. Fortunately, Mama was interrupted by the sound of voices in the hall. George had arrived.

"I should go," Mama insisted. "I would not wish to intrude."

"Don't forget your book." Amanda gestured toward a curved-leg table, its marquetry top almost entirely covered by the volume her mother had laid upon it.

"I'll—I'll come back later for it."

Then Lewis was opening the door and George was coming in, greeting her mother as she slipped past, out of the library. Amanda hadn't a moment to dart across the room and station herself behind the desk, as she'd planned. She had no choice but to smile and invite him to sit down on the sofa her mother had just vacated, while she perched herself on the edge of a nearby chair.

"I suppose," George began, settling himself and looking about the room, "this is a fitting spot to discuss schooling." With a lazy, almost possessive hand, he picked up the book her mother had abandoned, raised an eyebrow at the title—*Proper Drainage and Cultivation of Fens and Marshland* or some such thing, she felt sure, given the shelf from which it had been ignorantly plucked—and tossed it back where he'd found it, making the delicate table shudder beneath its weight.

"Er…yes," she agreed, instantly regretting she had not made him climb four flights to the schoolroom and sit on an unforgiving wooden stool instead.

"Though there's a good deal more to a boy's education than books, ma'am." He brought his gaze to her as he spoke, and her own fell to her hands, folded in her lap. "But I wouldn't expect a lady to understand that."

The demure interlacing of her fingers tautened into a painful knot. "I assure you, my lord, I am quite capable of understanding a great many things, especially where my sons are concerned."

"Then you must know young Kingston will be well-served at Harrow, as his father and I were. It will be the making of him—as a man, I mean. He needs toughening up."

She started to protest that she did not want Jamie to be *tough*. *Tough* was for old shoe leather and the woody ends of asparagus. But George thought in absolutes, in stark alternatives, and she would not sit here and listen to him deride her son for being *soft*.

"I have a proposal," she said instead. "An alternative to sending Jamie off alone this September."

George slid across the silk damask cushions of the sofa, until he was at the end closest to where she sat. "I too have a proposal, Lady Kingston—Amanda, if I may." He reached out for her hand, but she could not seem to make her fingers disentangle themselves from one another. "Say yes, and in future, I'll gladly defer to your wishes about your sons."

At first she thought the ruckus she heard was the rattle of her pulse, the steady beat of *botherbotherbother* through her skull. George's clumsy offer of marriage did not surprise her. But his offer regarding Jamie and Philip…? Oh, she couldn't think clearly, didn't know what she ought to answer him. Why should keeping her children with her require her to give up both body and soul?

"I do beg your pardon, Lady Kingston." Lewis was at the door, bowing more than usually low, and when he straightened, his cheeks were pink with embarrassment. "But this gentleman insisted you would want to see him right away. I did tell him you were occupied with Lord Dulsworthy, but he—"

"Do your job, boy," growled George, his evident frustration jerking him from his seat. Amanda rose too.

Then another voice slipped into the room above the others. "Forgive me, my lady."

Amanda searched past Lewis's shoulder for the source of that voice.

At first she had thought the entire interruption might be a figment of her imagination, part of her brain's feeble attempt to keep her from having to answer George. She *was* feeling distinctly lightheaded.

But in another moment a man had stepped past Lewis and into the room, sketching a bow that was gentlemanly but not obsequious. His clothing too bespoke the gentleman, though neither a wealthy nor a fashionable one. Blue coat, buff breeches, crisp linen, well-polished boots. Neither a shop clerk nor a dandy out for a night on the town.

*Magpie.*

She mouthed the name but did not speak it, finding her lips suddenly parched and her breath rather uneven.

"I thought, as the boys' new tutor, it would be best if I were a part of this conversation."

*T-t-t*— Amanda couldn't seem to wrap her mind around the word.

But George suffered from no such inability. "Tutor?" he exclaimed. He spun toward her. "What is the meaning of this?"

"This is Mister, er—"

She stumbled over what came next, in part because she was not sure what name to use. Did the Magpie generally employ a new alias with each new disguise?

But equally to blame was the fact that her thoughts no longer seemed to be hers to command.

He was wearing spectacles. In keeping with the part of a tutor, she supposed, though certainly no one would think to call him bookish. Steel-rimmed spectacles ought not to have made his face more handsome, and yet…

She licked her lips. "Mister, um—"

"Stanhope, my lord," he supplied swiftly, dipping his head in greeting at George before stepping closer with hand extended.

To her surprise, Lord Dulsworthy shook hands with him, if not pleased by the gesture then not displeased by the strength of the other man's grip. "Not a clergyman, I take it," George said with a satisfied nod, looking him up and down, oblivious to the fact that he had dismissed the same man as the bookshop's errand boy less than a week ago. "Thank God."

Major Stanhope mustered a smile at what he evidently mistook for an attempt at humor on George's part. "My father did have me in mind for the church, my lord," he conceded, rocking back on his heels and folding his hands behind his back. "I was educated for it, kept the necessary terms at Oxford. But it's an uncertain future without a preferment, as you must know. And I have found I enjoy the privilege of shaping young minds."

She caught herself nodding along with the story, as if it confirmed what she already knew. Except it was also a reminder of everything she did *not* know:

Who he was.

Where he came from.

Why he was in her house.

"So you hired him," George said, turning toward her, his voice now laced with disapproval.

"You've made your opinion on the matter of the boys' education amply clear, Lord Dulsworthy, but I worry they are not ready for one of our fine public schools."

"Their instruction *has* been rather irregular," he agreed, directing the comment at Major Stanhope with a sharp look for her.

"Which is why I hired Mr. Stanhope. To remedy any defects he might find. To offer his professional judgment about their abilities and the best direction for their educational futures."

Major Stanhope dipped his head in agreement with her makeshift explanation for his presence. George's face grew redder with every word she spoke.

The two men were standing close enough together now that it was impossible not to compare them—though such a comparison was doubtless imprudent of her.

Lord Dulsworthy had always seemed to her a sort of cartoon sketch of the ideal Englishman, minus the tweed coat. He was not unhandsome and, though approaching fifty, had not lost his sandy hair. The breadth of his barrel chest was testament to the fact that in his youth, he had been a sportsman, shooting, riding to hounds, boxing, fencing. If some of that powerful chest had begun to slip a tad lower over the years, his tailor was careful not to let it strain the buttons of his waistcoat.

Major Stanhope, in contrast, was lithe, hard. If she dared to lay a hand on his shoulder, she knew she would not find his coat padded. He was not quite forty, she thought, though nearer it than she. His face would one day—and sooner, rather than later—bear the lines of a man who had done a great deal of living. He wore his dark brown hair slightly longer than was the fashion—the better to style it according to his various disguises, she supposed.

Then there were the spectacles. They…well, they suited him. She knew no better way to describe it. She understood now why he did not always choose to wear them, though, for they brought distinction to an already distinguished face. She felt as if she were seeing him, the real him, for the first time.

And she knew when he leveled his gaze on her, he was seeing her clearly too.

She swallowed hard.

"And how long will this professional assessment take?" George asked.

Major Stanhope once more dipped his head, this time in her direction. "As the matter concerns Lady Kingston's sons, as it was she who hired me to the post, and as this is her house—until young Lord Kingston comes of age, of course—I must defer my answer. I am entirely at her ladyship's disposal."

That little speech was all very proper and very polite, and yet she did not wonder that George shifted his weight between his feet before taking an almost imperceptible step back from Major Stanhope. "You mean to live in, then?" Some of the bite had gone out of his voice.

"Of course, my lord." Oh, but she hoped it was the correct answer to give. "I've already put the maids to work making ready the chamber off the schoolroom," she lied.

"I'm sure I shall be most comfortably accommodated there," Major Stanhope said.

George gave a skeptical "*Harrumph!*"

She very nearly echoed it. In her mind's eye she pictured the cramped, dusty chamber adjoining the schoolroom. The narrow bed. Mightn't even a soldier balk at such quarters?

But she had no business imagining alternative beds in which he might lie.

"Should you like to go up now and meet your charges, Mr. Stanhope?" she offered, turning toward the door.

Lord Dulsworthy had other ideas. "Our conversation here is not finished, Amanda."

*Oh, how* dare *he!* To address her so familiarly before another, to act as if she welcomed his address, to make it seem as if his claim had already been staked. For the first time in all the years of their acquaintance, her palm itched to slap him, and she might have done if she had not at just that moment glimpsed Major Stanhope's hand, hanging loosely at his side, curl into fist.

She shook her head, both amused and bemused by the two men's posturing. What on earth had got into Lord Dulsworthy? And why should Major Stanhope care? They were worse than Jamie and Philip, spoiling for a fight.

"The rest of what we have to discuss can surely be deferred until Mr. Stanhope has something to report," she said. "Good morning, my lord."

She did not wait to see how he accepted his dismissal, but marched through the doorway and toward the stairs, praying the Magpie followed.

# Chapter 8

Langley had been impressed—

*Reluctantly* impressed—

Well, by all rights his response *ought* to be reluctant where Lady Kingston was concerned—

He gave a vigorous shake of his head, then straightened his spectacles. *Good God.* His thoughts were in danger of becoming as fragmented and jumbled as hers.

Though he could not help but notice that she fumbled and rambled less when speaking to Dulsworthy. Oddly, he doubted it was a mark of her comfort in the other man's presence. She had conducted herself well in the library, to be sure, and had managed the fellow with aplomb. But whatever Dulsworthy inspired in her, it was not confidence.

And then Langley found himself wondering what it might mean that she was so willing to speak freely, to be herself, in front of *him*....

"You are to have use of any of the books in the library, of course, Mr. Stanhope," she was saying, her voice echoing slightly as she crossed the high-ceilinged, marble-tiled hall. "Now, if you'll follow me upstairs..."

He did as he was bid, hustling to catch up, as she seemed in a great hurry to be off. Dulsworthy grumbled as Langley nearly collided with him, the other man striding purposefully, even angrily, for the door. A footman, the same one who'd admitted Langley a few days past, bowed Dulsworthy out, and Langley could have sworn he glimpsed a twitch of a smile on the servant's face.

Now Langley had to trot up the steps, for Lady Kingston had already reached the turning and was saying something he couldn't quite catch about the dining room on the first floor. "The family apartments are on the second and third floors," she explained as they reached the landing but did not pause.

He was still a step or two behind her, enough to give himself a chance to look at her without being observed. Without his spectacles, he had been confident in his assessment of her beauty, but equally certain that she benefitted from the softening effect of his short-sightedness, as most everything and everyone did.

Now, however, he could see that she required no such help. Her skin was as flawless, her features as delicate, as they had first appeared to be. This morning, she wore her golden brown hair in a style somewhere between the easy looseness of their first meeting and the elegant arrangement of last night. The weight of its honeyed coils gave a saucy tilt to her chin. He liked it.

The skirts of her blue and cream striped gown swayed, summoning him like a bell. Trotting up the steps, he closed the remaining gap between them, expecting a chiding, questioning look from her dark eyes, or a series of fumbling questions from her lips.

He got nothing, not even a glance, as she droned on in a voice that hardly seemed her own, the sort of rehearsed speech about architecture and paintings he might have expected from the housekeeper of a grand country house frequently tasked with showing the place to visitors and hoping for a perquisite at the end of the tour.

When they reached the stairway to the fourth floor, some of the house's grandeur fell away. The steps were narrower, uncarpeted, steep. And they opened not onto a landing but right into the schoolroom itself, a sparsely furnished but pleasantly light-filled space.

At a large worktable sat the two boys he'd caught only a glimpse of on his first visit to Bartlett House. One dark head, one fair, both bent over some joint project spread out in front of them.

"Blue paint, please," the darker-haired one said.

"I'm using it," was the reply. "Have the brown."

"We're meant to be drawing *rivers*. They can't all look like great sludge-filled worms."

"The Thames does—ow! Why'd you hit me?"

Less a hit than nudge, really, the dark-haired one having realized the two of them were being observed and pushing quickly to his feet. The elder, Langley guessed, though he was slighter of build. The young earl.

"Mama?" the lad asked uncertainly, his dark-eyed gaze reserved entirely for Langley.

"Oh, Mama," the other said, eagerly scraping back his chair, "you're back. Would you kindly tell Jamie he needn't—ow!"

An elbow this time, and considerably sharper. "Hush, Pip," the elder pushed past barely parted lips. "Turn around."

Pip—Master Philip Bartlett—did as he'd been bid, though not without a scowl for his brother, the force of which caught Langley too as it passed. "Who're you?"

"Boys," Lady Kingston tightly reprimanded her sons. "This is Mr. Stanhope. He's…" A frown darted across her forehead and she glanced questioningly toward him. "He's…"

She was uncertain how far he meant to carry his performance, he realized. Not wanting to say too much.

For just a moment, he hesitated too. His first priority was finding the codebook, but he wanted to protect Lady Kingston and her family in the process. In order to do so, he'd presented himself in disguise. Could he be who he'd said he was below and still fulfill the rest of his mission?

"I'm your new tutor," he supplied, inclining his head at the boys.

"Tutor?" Philip looked and sounded scandalized. "Why on earth should we need a—"

"Yes, Mama," young Kingston spoke over his brother, his demeanor more polite, perhaps, but his demand no less urgent. "Why?"

"Change is sometimes desirable," she reassured them, though Langley did not think any of them—Lady Kingston included—believed it.

She stepped closer to the table and laid an arm around either set of shoulders, turning the boys back toward their work and shaking her head. "I can see, however, that your drawing lesson is still urgently needed. Philip, if you'll carry the box," she said, nodding her head toward a small crate of wooden shapes, the sort used to teach angles and shading, light and shadow, "and Jamie, if you'll fetch paper and pencils, we'll repair to the library and work there. Mr. Stanhope will need time to settle in."

"And after luncheon?" young Kingston queried.

"The bees, of course," she said, which drew smiles from both boys. "We mustn't abandon the project now. Tomorrow, I think, will be soon enough for Mr. Stanhope to begin his educational duties."

She looked toward him but did not quite meet his gaze, and her grip on the boys' shoulders tightened almost imperceptibly. Clearly, she was not ready to relinquish them, not ready to entrust them to him.

"I am entirely at your disposal, Lady Kingston," he said, deliberately echoing what he'd told Dulsworthy in the library. It wasn't quite true, of course. He rather suspected General Scott would have something to say about the matter when Millrose told him what he'd done. But in the meantime, he meant to do what he could to keep her safe. "When Lord Kingston and Master Philip are ready, I will be most eager to discover what they know."

"Yes, sir," said young Kingston with a crisp bow, and his brother echoed him, though with notably less enthusiasm at the prospect.

The boys gathered up the materials their mother had requested, and she ushered them toward the stairs, once more with her arms around them, a mother hen guarding her brood.

But it was not Langley's interference she needed to fear.

When the noise of their footsteps had faded, he examined the schoolroom more thoroughly. The small and rather haphazard collection of books on the shelves beneath one row of windows surprised him, though of course they had the massive library downstairs at their disposal as well. Scattered hints of history, science, mathematics. Clearly their mother was involved in their instruction, but was she entirely responsible for setting the boys' lessons? Men's and women's educations were different, making Dulsworthy's concern about their preparation for school suddenly easier to understand.

Opening the door to his left, he peered into the boys' shared bedchamber but did not go beyond the threshold. Needless prying was not the way to inspire trust. A bed sat on either side, one crisply made, the other rumpled— not difficult to guess which belonged to whom. Rather surprising that the sons of a nobleman were expected to make them up at all.

At last he went to the other door and found what he had anticipated finding, a room set aside for a nurse or a governess. Or a tutor. It reminded him of nothing so much as his quarters at the Underground, though at least here he had a window.

Unfortunately, he couldn't reach it at present. The narrow channel between the bed and the opposite wall was filled with crates, boxes, and an ancient brass-bound trunk; rolls of canvas—specimens of the boys' artwork, perhaps—lay stacked like logs atop the unmade mattress.

He recalled Lady Kingston saying something about ordering a space to be cleared for him, though of course, that could not have been true, as he had not been expected. No matter. He did some of his best thinking while his body was otherwise occupied. He shrugged out of his coat, hung it over the rail of one of the straight-backed schoolroom chairs, rolled up his sleeves, and got to work.

Sometime later, his progress was interrupted by the arrival of a housemaid, bearing an armload of linen and a basket of cleaning supplies, the handle of a broom threaded carefully through the lot, like a knitting needle through a ball of yarn.

"Let me help you with that," he offered, brushing the dust from his hands and his clothes.

The young woman, reddish haired and ruddy cheeked, appeared startled, as much by his dishabille as his offer. She blinked at him, her eyes moving up and down, then dropped her gaze. "Th-thank you, sir."

He juggled the cleaning supplies onto the table and laid the linens on the seat of one chair. "I've only just managed to clear a path through there," he said, gesturing toward the piles he'd tried to arrange neatly around the perimeter of the schoolroom, beneath the windows and on the shelves. The trunk had been filled with old clothes—costumes for home theatricals, by the look of things. Boxes of books, mostly primers and moralizing tracts for children that did not look to have seen much use. Maps. Toy soldiers, their painted uniforms worn away by more than one generation of hands. A globe that had been made when the American colonies were still, well, colonies. Displaying the collection of odds and ends gave the schoolroom a busy, well-used look. He suspected the boys wouldn't mind it, but he was not so sure about Lady Kingston.

"I managed to wrest open that window, too," he called after the maid, who had disappeared into the little bedchamber. "Someone had painted it shut."

He'd been determined to get the better of it, though, for nature dictated that heat rose, and here on the fourth floor of the house, the air at midday was stifling.

His shirt clung damply to him as he now set about opening more windows, inviting a warm, desultory breeze through the larger space of the schoolroom. Remembering the maid's scandalized expression, he unrolled his sleeves and picked up his wool coat, though he couldn't bear to don it just yet.

While she worked, whistling tunelessly, he made a more careful examination of the boys' map of rivers and whatever else of their work he could find. Compositions. Even a few poems. Most of it showed promise, though the poetry was plagued by rather clumsy rhymes.

He would have to play at being a real tutor, if he did not want his presence in Bartlett House to raise more suspicions than it doubtless already had. Would have to set them lessons and hear them recite.

He'd worn many disguises over the years. Rich men. Poor. Somehow, though, the particular irony of pretending to be a schoolmaster, a model of behavior and intellect, for two privileged and sheltered boys…

A bark of a laugh erupted from his chest.

"How's that?" the maid called out, popping her head past the door jamb. "Something you wanted, sir?"

He shook his head and ran thumb and forefinger beneath his spectacles, wiping away a sheen of sweat. "Nothing, thank you."

"Lady Kingston, Mrs. West, and the boys will shortly take luncheon, if you"—again her eyes flickered over him and her already red cheeks grew redder still—"wanted to make yourself presentable and join them."

"No," he replied, a shade too quickly, once more scandalizing the maid. Tutors and governesses did sometimes eat with the families who employed them, of course. But he hadn't been invited to join the family here and by the look on Lady Kingston's face when she'd left the schoolroom, he did not expect to be. "I never take luncheon," he made excuse.

Her head bobbed in an uncertain nod before she returned to her work. He resumed worrying at the problem of how best to proceed. The opportunity— the idea of inserting himself into the household—had presented itself only last night, and he'd had no chance to formulate a detailed plan. No sleep, either, but that was nothing new.

*Mrs. West*, the maid had said. He'd nearly forgot Lady Kingston's mother. What sort of woman was she? Protective? Interfering? The other watchmen had reported that she was considerably more social than her daughter, which meant she would be an easier target if Hopkins's captors sought a vulnerable point at which to launch their attack against Bartlett House. Langley glanced out the windows at the bright but sunless sky, the color of polished steel. Dare he hope Mrs. West was the sort to stay home when it rained?

And then, of course, there was Lady Kingston herself. *Lady Kingston.* He made himself repeat her title every time the name *Amanda* intruded into his thoughts. Dulsworthy had dared to address her as such, and he hoped the man knew how fortunate he was to have left the library unscathed. Not because Langley would have—could have—called him out on his rudeness. Dulsworthy needed to believe he was the tutor, and it was not a tutor's place even to notice such things. But if Langley were not very much mistaken, Amanda—*Lady Kingston*—had had to restrain herself from slapping her name from Dulsworthy's drawling lips. He had his doubts about the notion that the two planned to wed. Clearly, she did not like the man—and with good cause.

The memory of that flash of color in her cheeks, the swift curl and splay of her fingers, hidden behind her back but visible to him, brought a satisfied smile to his lips. Langley was just devilish enough to *enjoy* that hint of her fierceness, though he knew he had no business enjoying any such thing. Nevertheless, he understood its appeal in a way he might never understand the appeal of her sunshine and good cheer, though he could not deny that they attracted him too.

The ghost of that sly curve, a glimmering of his more disagreeable nature, must still have been lingering on his face when the maid emerged from the bedchamber with her apron streaked with dust and loose tendrils of hair clinging to her damp neck. "The room's all set," she began, and then froze when she saw him sitting there. Something sharper than surprise flared in her eyes. Something more like fear. She swallowed and bobbed a curtsy. "Sir."

Had he let his mask slip so entirely?

"Thank you." Jerking to his feet, he slid back into his current guise more swiftly than he slid his arms into his coat. The harmless tutor again, almost one of her own.

He'd let his voice trail upward, fishing for her name. She shook herself—casting off the foolish notion that he could be anything other than the gentleman Lady Kingston had hired to teach her sons—and supplied it. "Mary, sir."

"Thank you, Mary. I'm Stanhope."

"Shall I bring you some hot water, Mr. Stanhope?" Once more, the maid's gaze raked over him, this time openly appreciative. "You might like to freshen up."

"That would be most welcome, Mary. And I had a valise with me when I entered the house."

With a smile, she was gone, appearing perhaps half an hour later with the requisite items, having made shift in the meantime to freshen up herself, he noted. He refused her offer to unpack his scant few items of clothing and began to think he would be obliged to refuse an as-yet-unspoken offer to help him strip off his shirt and wash, when a woman's voice called up the open stairwell. "Lud, that's Mrs. Hepplewythe," Mary gasped. From the dossier, he recognized that name as belong to the housekeeper. The maid hurried off to her work.

The remaining hours of the afternoon passed with restless languor, as he paced the schoolroom, wondering what went on below and when he might have an opportunity to sort matters with Lady Kingston and begin his real work here. Dinner was brought on a tray by a footman he didn't recognize and who was not inclined to converse. An hour or so later, the boys trudged upstairs, their expressions still a mixture of curiosity and resentment. After dutifully mumbling their goodnights, they disappeared into their room to make themselves ready for bed.

He pretended to do the same, though the hour was ridiculously early for a grown man to retire for the night. Twilight had only just fallen. He was exhausted, though—could hardly recall a time when he had not been. Waiting, doing nothing, was frequently the most fatiguing mission of all. He plucked off his spectacles and laid them on the washstand. Perhaps he would just stretch out on the cool, crisp linens for a few moments...

All was dark when he awoke. Night had fallen while he slept, but the usual coolness had not accompanied it. The air of the little room was heavy. His shirt was once more damp with sweat.

He pushed to his feet, stretched away the familiar stiffness of sleeping on a sagging rope bed, splashed tepid water on his face, and scrubbed his palms over a day's growth of beard.

The window over the washstand still stood wide open, though it brought no relief. He peered out through the doubled layers of rippled glass, the lower sash pushed up over the upper. Rather like exploring the world through the wrong end of a spyglass. In the distance, lightning streaked the sky. But below, far below, wasn't that...?

He fumbled for his spectacles, tucked them over his ears, and looked again. *Yes.* His modest quarters overlooked the back of the house. And despite the rapidly approaching storm, Amanda—*Lady Kingston*—was in the garden, pacing along the flagstone path. Anxious? Sleepless again?

What he had to tell her would not help to set her mind at ease.

But he could not deny this was the opportunity for private conversation he'd been waiting for.

Hoping his movement did not alert the boys, that the hinges did not squeak nor the floor creak, he crept from his chamber, across the schoolroom, and down the stairs.

* * * *

Having reached the point in her well-worn path where the broken gate impeded further progress, Amanda paused, tempted to grab the bars and rattle them like a caged creature.

When the poor things in menageries behaved so, were they frightened? Or frustrated? Or angry?

A combination of all three, if her current mood was anything to go by.

After a deep, steadying breath, she turned back toward the house and discovered Major Stanhope standing in the morning room, watching her pace. The discovery did not improve her wild mood one jot.

She quickened her step back toward the house, just as he opened the door and trotted down the steps. A half-dozen long strides from each of them brought them toe to toe in the middle of the garden, where the perfume of roses was strongest.

"My lady," he began, all politeness and propriety, as if they were not meeting in the darkness for the third time—*or the fourth? Heavens, she'd lost track*—and he clad only in his shirtsleeves.

His cravat had worked loose, revealing the notch at the base of his throat and a hint of dark hair on his chest. The sight of it, much like the sight of his spectacles earlier, made something strange happen inside her. Sent a rush of sudden warmth to her belly, and lower. Shallowed her breathing and made her breasts chafe against her corset with their rapid rise and fall.

Or maybe those reactions were all simply caused by the exertion of her brisk walk and the dreadful, sticky heat of the night air.

She had made it a rule not to dwell on a man's looks. When she had been on the marriage mart, it would have been an exercise in futility to focus on gentlemen's faces and figures, when her parents' decision would be entirely guided by other qualities. And once their choice had been made, it had never occurred to her nineteen-year-old self to think of Lord Kingston as attractive. He'd been positively ancient when they'd wed—which was to say, approximately the age of the man standing before her now.

It seemed at thirty-two, she was more than capable of finding a man of thirty-seven or thirty-eight handsome indeed.

The way his shirt clung to him most provocatively, confirming the breadth of his shoulders and highlighting his taut abdomen.

The way his dark eyes pierced her through those steel-rimmed spectacles, making her want to gnaw her lip like a schoolgirl and express her willingness to learn whatever lesson he offered to teach.

"Are you even qualified to be a tutor?" she blurted out. "*Oxford*, you told Lord Dulsworthy. But I—I'm not even sure what's real anymore. Secret codes and spies and...*the Crown shan't require anything further from you*, you said," and she deepened her voice in mock imitation of his. "But now you're here, living in *my* house, and claiming to be—I don't know—no. I won't let him send Jamie away in the autumn. I can't, I just can't. But, oh God, you see, he...he *can!* Lord Dulsworthy, I mean. The will said—but Kingston can't have intended—and—and—oh, surely this can't all have happened because of a-a-a cookbook?"

She snapped her jaw shut on the word *cookbook*, having momentarily forgotten that Magpie had asked her not to speak of it. The click of her teeth was audible in the silent garden.

Even to her own ears, she sounded hysterical. Nonsensical. If George ever heard such a stream of chatter from her, he would declare her unfit to have care of her sons. And if the alarmed expression on Major Stanhope's face was any indication, he might concur with the assessment.

As usual, she'd been waving her hands about as she spoke. Their fluttering movements sometimes seemed to make the words come even faster. When she'd been a girl, Mama had urged her to sit on them whenever she talked to break the habit.

When, exactly, had Major Stanhope caught hold of them? His grip was firm, implacable. The resistance made the muscles of her arms ache.

But then his thumbs chafed over the thin skin on the backs of her hands, first one, then the other, and some of the tension eased from her. After a moment, her shoulders drooped in surrender.

He did not release her hands.

"Now, then." His voice was calm and calming. Quiet, but not a whisper. An accent slightly different from any she'd previously heard him use. Less refined? No. Not *less* anything, she decided. More…authentic. More *him*.

*Probably just another disguise,* a familiar inner voice warned her. *Mind your step.*

"I did go to Oxford, if it's any reassurance to you. Though with no intention of becoming either a clergyman or a tutor, I confess. And Rugby before that, from the time I was about the age of your sons." A wry smile lifted one side of his mouth. "Go ahead. You may well look surprised. I was."

It was a curious thing to say. Young gentleman of the sort who went to Rugby and Harrow were not generally surprised by the privilege. They considered it their due.

Had he perhaps been a scholarship boy?

*Clever. An exceptional mimic.*

*Magpie.*

She wanted to unravel the mystery of him, and that, she feared, was even more foolish than her wanton desire to drag her fingers—no, her mouth—along the bristled edge of his jaw.

"You have been giving them their lessons, I take it?"

She nodded. "I began when their father took ill. Before that, he had managed it himself. He was a man very interested in books and learning—as I suppose one might gather from the library here." When it had become necessary to stay in London to be closer to his physicians, Kingston had ordered crates and crates of books brought from the still larger library at Foxhaven. "In any case, my teaching them was only ever meant to be a temporary measure. My husband, you see, was to have got well."

He squeezed her fingers and, mercifully, said nothing.

"And afterward…well, at first Lord Dulsworthy told me that if I wanted to play at nursery-governess, he would not stop me. Now…" She shrugged her shoulders but found herself hoping Langley would not mistake it as a bid for freedom and release her. If she were to continue this explanation, she needed to be able to draw strength from his touch. "In a matter of days, Jamie will be twelve. The book from Porter's was to be a present for him, you see. He's very bright. But I…I do not think he is ready for Harrow." She paused, tried once more to gather her wits. "And when you arrived this morning, Lord Dulsworthy was on the point of declaring that if only I would…then he wouldn't…"

While speaking, she had deliberately focused her gaze elsewhere. The loose knot in his cravat. A spot somewhere over his shoulder. Now she lifted her eyes to his face, searching for the words to explain.

Jamie's fragile spirit.

Dulsworthy's abhorrent proposal.

Her selfishness.

Her guilt.

"If you would…*what*?" he prompted gently.

"If I marry him," she whispered, "he won't send my sons away."

A pause. "And you don't wish to marry him."

Not a question, but she shook her head. "I've been married, Major Stanhope. I see little benefit to repeating the experience."

Lightning flashed, near enough that she shivered against the electric charge in the air. The storm was getting close.

By that sudden glare, Langley searched her face, his expression unreadable. "You are never…lonely, then?"

Heat prickled through her, a mixture of awareness and embarrassment. She knew the sort of loneliness to which he referred. "If I am, must I marry to find a cure?"

When he spoke again, it was not an answer to her question. Or not exactly, at any rate.

"I am more than prepared to set your sons' lessons in algebra and Latin. More than willing to tell Dulsworthy whatever you wish about their prospects. But," his grip on her fingers grew tighter still, past the point of reassurance, almost past the point of endurance, "I think you know that's not why I've come to Bartlett House."

At just that moment, the sky split open, pelting them with cold rain. He glanced upward as if in disbelief. Then he turned, releasing one of her hands, clearly intending to tug her along after him, into the shelter of the morning room.

She set her feet.

Her resistance slowed him, though she hadn't the strength to stop him entirely if he were determined. He looked back at her, baffled, water streaking over his brow, spattering his spectacles, plastering his hair to his head, dripping off his chin.

"It's too late," she said, raising her voice to be heard over the clatter of the rain. "We're already soaked. Just tell me—tell me why you're here."

He closed the arm's length between them, bringing them once more toe-to-toe. Nearly chest-to-chest. The fine cambric of his shirt was almost sheer now, and she tried not to imagine the similar state of her muslin gown. With his free hand, he pulled off his spectacles, blinking against the raindrops that struck his lashes.

"You're in danger, your ladyship."

She was tall for a woman, but he was taller. She had to tip her face into the rain to meet his eye. "From you?"

Something sparked between them, like lightning traveling between ground and sky and back again. Almost involuntarily, she lifted onto the balls of her feet, bringing her body closer still to his. She could feel his breath, almost taste the rain on his lips.

"I'm here on assignment, Amanda," he growled, his voice rumbling through her, stronger than a peal of thunder. Until that moment, she had not known that the sound of man speaking her name had the power to turn her inside out—and that she would crave the sensation. "Another kiss between us would be a grave mistake."

She shook the rain from her eyes. "But two nights past...?"

His gaze cut away. "That was...unavoidable. Regrettable."

In those callous, indifferent words, she recognized an attempt to persuade himself he believed what he was saying—and perhaps to persuade her as well.

But for all his talk of mistakes and regret, he still had not let go of her hand.

"I've been ordered here to protect you," he went on. "The men who took my fellow agent captive have figured out the identity of the person to whom he passed the codebook."

Cold knifed through her, born of the shards of icy rain driving into her skin, his refusal to stoke the heat between them, shock. "But I—I don't have it."

Surely he knew that? Surely he believed her?

Not that it mattered—or ought not, at least. The villains after the codebook were the ones she needed to convince.

Still, relief surged through her when he gave a curt nod of understanding. "But it won't be a simple matter to persuade them. In order to divert their attention away from you—and to rescue Hopkins—we need to find the thing. Until we do, you—and your family—will not be safe."

*We.*

Under such circumstances—under *any* circumstances—the word should not have sent a thrill through her. For so long, she'd craved adventure, excitement. Longed to be a part of something important, even with all the risks he'd tried to warn her of.

Well, no. Not *all* of them. Standing here in his arms, she was beginning to suspect there were other risks to be weighed.

Despite the dangers he represented, was she truly reckless enough— *ill-advised*, to use his words from the night of the ball—to want to get closer to him?

"Then we must find it," she said simply, choosing action over fear. "Where do we look next?"

"No." The protest rumbled from his chest, past his clenched jaw. "I didn't mean—" He looked resolutely past her, even as his grip tightened. "Not *we.*"

"You told me as much once before, as I recall. And yet, here we are."

His lips parted, prepared to make some retort. Then he looked down at her, his eyes sweeping over her body. Her rain-soaked gown hid little from his view, she well knew. At last his narrow-eyed gaze flickered up to her wet lips, and she watched his resolve begin to unravel. In another moment, his mouth would be on hers.

"Good night, Magpie," she whispered as she slipped from his stunned grasp, contenting herself for now with that small victory over his self-control.

As she turned and made her way toward the house, satisfaction surged through her—and with it, a tremor of desire, a reminder that she had never been truly satisfied.

# Chapter 9

Langley awoke with a shiver so violent it nearly rattled his spectacles off the washstand. He'd lain for hours atop the bed in his wet clothes, refusing to warm himself with the memory of Amanda pressed against him, her rain-soaked muslin no barrier at all.

*You're in danger, your ladyship.*

No. Not from him.

He would not let his desires distract him from a mission—again.

Just in case, he had deliberately made himself uncomfortable, never imagining he could fall asleep under such conditions. Now, at God knew what hour, sunlight streamed in through the open window and with it, the considerably cooler air that had followed the storm. He fought back another shiver, forcing his stiff muscles to move at his command.

The rain-swollen sash was no more eager to slide down this morning than it had been to slide up yesterday afternoon, but at least this time he could welcome the warmth of the exertion. Afterward, he stripped off his still-damp clothes and rubbed himself vigorously with the towel before donning yet another clean shirt, a pair of brown woolen breeches, and the same blue coat. If he'd had his greatcoat handy, he might have put that on too. A shave would have to wait for warmer water.

The schoolroom was comparatively cozy and smelled marvelously of hot coffee. He followed his nose to the worktable and found a breakfast tray, laden with food. In a matter of moments, the same good scents lured the boys from their chamber, Kingston looking and sounding much as he had the night before, Philip sleepy and tousle-haired, but dressed and at least willing to grunt "G'morning, sir," in reply to Langley's greeting.

After a fortifying plateful of coddled eggs and kippers, Philip found the strength to say, "My mother usually breakfasts with us...sir." Resentment still rolled off the lad in waves. "Where is she?"

Langley returned his cup to its saucer. "I daresay she's enjoying her first breakfast in some time that didn't involve staring down a half-washed face and an uncombed head."

The young earl disguised his smirk of satisfaction at that setdown of his brother by taking a bite of toast. Philip spluttered a moment before tossing back, "Yes, well, at least she was always clean-shaven."

"Pip, you dolt," Kingston said, favoring his brother with a withering glance. "If you're going to talk back to our new tutor, then at least fashion a retort that doesn't insult Mama."

"Why, I didn't—I would never—oh. Well," here Philip shot Langley a narrow-eyed glance, "he knew what I meant."

"I did indeed," Langley said, standing abruptly. It wouldn't do to wink at their antics, despite the rusty laugh building in his chest. "You meant to try to put me in my place, young man. But my place, whether or not you approve, is here." He tapped the scarred wooden table with a fingertip, firmly enough that Philip flinched. "Now, finish your breakfast, wash up, and be ready for lessons to begin in a quarter of an hour."

With a stern look for each of them, Langley turned and strode back to his little chamber to do battle with his beard over the icy water in the washbasin.

*What—in—the—hell—are—you—doing?*

The question pounded through his head with the rhythmic *fwip-fwop* of the stropping of his razor.

He'd played a hundred different parts in his time as an intelligence officer. Why should the role of tutor to two spoiled, smart-mouthed boys be particularly difficult? Time to conjure the memory of every sharp-eyed, sour-faced teacher he'd ever had.

When he went to practice a suitable expression, however, he discovered the looking glass had been hung either for or by a person of considerably shorter stature. Try as he might, he could catch a glimpse of no part of him higher than the scattering of dark hair across his chest.

"Beggin' your pardon, Mr. Stanhope, sir. I've brought some hot water and come to fetch down the—oh!"

The voice, he discovered when he turned, belonged to Mary, the maid from yesterday, who had paused in her explanation of her task to ogle his bare torso.

Christ, it was as bad as having Fanny Drummond about. Well, a bit better than that, perhaps. Fanny's glances never hinted that she liked what she saw.

Though to be fair, the maid was doing more than hinting.

"Thank you, Mary," he said, gradually drawing her notice back to his face. "That will be all."

"If you're sure, sir." She set the canister of steaming water on the floor, curtsied without lowering her eyes, and backed from the room, feeling behind her with one hand to avoid hitting the door with her backside. Before she disappeared entirely, she favored him with a saucy wink.

Langley wasn't a vain man, though he knew women generally found his looks appealing. Certainly, he'd used that knowledge to his advantage over the years, both on duty and off. But catching the notice of a flirtatious maid and earning the respect of two young boys were vastly different things.

Then again...what he really wanted to inspire was their confidence, not their fear. In order to keep them safe, he needed them—and their mother—to trust him.

Perhaps a smile would go further than a scowl.

With the dull side of his razor blade braced against his thumb, he pried loose the two nails holding the looking glass in place, catching it easily on the palm of his other hand before it tumbled into the washbasin. Then, perching on the edge of the bed, he peered into the little rectangle.

*Bloody hell.*

Philip had not been far off. With that scruff and those dark shadows beneath his eyes, he looked more like a highwayman than a tutor.

Experimentally, he curved up the corners of his mouth. His lips stretched over an unfortunately lupine set of teeth. As if of its own volition, one brow bent in a skeptical arch.

Perhaps the Magpie had at last reached the limits of his gift for mimicry.

\* \* \* \*

"I must say, Amanda, when you asked me to join you in the morning room for breakfast, I did expect you might make some little effort at conversation." Mama's spoon rang against the edges of her cup, then clattered onto the saucer.

Amanda winced. How was it possible for her head to ache worse this morning than it had yesterday? Still, Mama was right. She *had* issued the invitation. Remembering Langley's words of last night, she had hoped to concoct some excuse to keep her mother from going out today. She had also dreaded the thought of eating alone. "What would you like to talk about, ma'am?"

Mama leaned forward. In her loose-fitting morning gown of rose pink, and with her fair hair softly arranged, she looked youthful and lovely, despite the unforgiving brightness of the window-filled room and the relative earliness of the hour. "You still have not told me what you and Lord Dulsworthy discussed yesterday morning."

Amanda's mind had been so filled by the conversation of last night, she had almost forgotten George's proposal.

She took a sip of coffee and grimaced when she discovered she had forgotten the sugar. "He came to talk about the boys, as I said."

"Nothing…else?" The pause was filled by an artful, suggestive twirl of one wrist. Her mother's flowing sleeve danced over the edge of the table, flirting with disaster in various guises—the butter dish, a knife handle, three neat stacks of carefully sorted correspondence—but always eluding catastrophe. At present, Amanda almost envied her ability to avoid getting into messes.

"Our conversation was interrupted by the arrival of the new tutor." *Thank God.* Otherwise, Amanda would have had to make George some sort of answer on the spot.

"Ah, yes." Mama fixed her with a look of disapproval. "The tutor. You might at least have mentioned to me that you were thinking of hiring such a person. I could have—"

"I assure you, he comes well-recommended, ma'am."

*He's a high-ranking intelligence officer,* she was perversely tempted to add, just to see Mama's reaction. *A spy sent to guard me from other spies who are desperate to get their hands on a French cookbook.*

In the light of day, it all sounded perfectly ridiculous.

And far less frightening than the cold reality of having to make a devil's bargain with George.

Perhaps her mother had been right to worry about her.

"I never imagined otherwise, my dear," her mother said coolly. "Still…" She plucked up an invitation from one of the three piles, peered at it for a moment through her lorgnette, and laid it a different stack. "I should like to meet him."

Amanda started to suggest that her mother could go up to the schoolroom at any time, knowing it was highly unlikely she would make the effort.

Two thoughts gave her pause. The first was the possibility that her mother might insist on Amanda accompanying her on such a visit. The second was Langley's imagined reaction to being observed and inspected by his supposed employer.

That mental picture of his disapproving expression, delivered over the top rim of his spectacles, sent the most delicious—and dangerous—quiver through her.

He was here, now, and entirely at her disposal, he had said.

And despite what he'd told her in the garden last night, he wanted to kiss her at least as much as she wanted to be kissed.

She blew out a breath and reached for the little silver bell on the table. "Very well, Mama. I'll ask him to join us for luncheon." Luncheon was surely safe. No one disapproved of luncheon.

When Lewis appeared in the doorway, she called for pen and paper. "A note will be less disruptive to lessons," she reasoned aloud.

It took longer than it ought to have done for her to write out the request, but when she was done, Lewis took the note with a bow and disappeared. Amanda prepared to resume her breakfast in peace.

A few moments later, Lewis returned and held out the folded paper on a tray. She had not expected a reply and did not know what to auger from it. Though she gave Lewis a searching look, his face remained impassive, as any good footman's should be.

At least as far as her mother was concerned. In the present moment, Amanda would have been glad of a hint.

Cautiously she took up the note and unfolded it. Beneath her carefully worded invitation, a bold masculine hand had scrawled

*I never eat luncheon.*

Amanda bit her lip to keep a most inappropriate bubble of laughter from escaping.

"What it is, my dear?" Her mother craned her neck slightly and fingered the handle of her lorgnette.

"He begs leave to say that it will not be quite convenient for him to join us at midday today, given the schedule he has already set."

Amanda picked up her quill, brushed the feather over her lips, smiled to herself. She knew he liked to fancy himself in charge. But perhaps he had forgotten that she was the Countess of Kingston?

She wrote a few words beneath his. "If you would, please, Lewis," she said, once more extending the folded paper to the footman.

Two could play at this game.

\* \* \* \*

For the first hour of the morning, Langley had invited the boys to show him their best work. He'd heard conjugations in three languages, listened to speeches from the great orators, watched them solve equations. Most of what he had observed had only confirmed his first impressions.

Philip was a brash, handsome lad. Impatient, and consequently a little careless. Athletic. He had boasted of his fencing ability and pranced about the schoolroom waving an imagined sword to demonstrate. At a place like Harrow, he would be chosen by his peers to lead them in mischief of all sorts. He would thrive.

Young Kingston was unquestionably the more bookishly inclined of the two and obviously well-prepared academically for school. Still, Langley could guess how the boy might fare there, and why Amanda was worried. Even the teachers could not be counted on to be kind to a lad who was slight of build, delicate of feature, and quicker of tongue than was wise. Away from home, Kingston would have only his title, and perhaps his younger brother, to shield him from the inevitable cruelties to which he would be exposed.

After the boys had had ample opportunity to boast, Langley had taken a page from General Scott and asked them about their most spectacular failures. Mistakes inevitably taught more than successes.

From what they chose to show him then, Langley learned more still. Philip was smarter than he'd first suspected. And Kingston was braver. When the boys eventually had to leave their mother's care—and it would happen, of course, possibly over their mother's objection and whether Dulsworthy had his way this autumn or not—Langley began to think that with a little help, they could manage quite well. Both of them.

Yes, there were things he could teach them. Amanda's lessons had sometimes been more creative than concrete, but on the whole, he was impressed—

*Reluctantly* impressed?

No, there was nothing reluctant about his admiration for her, for how and what she had taught her sons. Girls and young women were largely kept from the subjects that men self-servingly considered the foundation of "real" knowledge: philosophy, higher mathematics, Latin and Greek. But Amanda had somehow managed to acquire an extraordinary education, and to pass it on to the two young men seated before him.

Langley was not sure it made him feel better to discover that Amanda possessed a fine mind in addition to a fine figure. Certainly he had no business being attracted to either one.

To say nothing of both.

A footstep sounded on the stairway, and he looked up from the page he'd been pretending to read while the boys resumed work on yesterday's river map—one of their failures, they'd confessed. He frowned. This would make the second interruption of the morning.

The footman, Lewis, looked appropriately contrite as he delivered yet another note—no, the same note, Langley realized as he retrieved the folded paper from the tray in his hand.

The boys looked up too, their curiosity piqued. One quelling glance from their tutor sent them scurrying back to their work—no squabbles over the blue paint, today—and once their heads were bowed over the map, he slowly unfolded the note.

Beneath his earlier answer, Amanda had written just two words, in her delicate, feminine hand.

*Dinner, then.*

Not a question, this time. She had pressed down so firmly when making the point that the tip of her pen had nearly gone through the paper. Barely even a request. In fact, it rather looked like...an order.

Slowly he refolded the little square of hot-pressed paper and moved to slip it into the breast pocket of his coat.

"No answer this time, sir?" said the footman.

"No answer," he concurred, tucking the note out of sight.

At least, not one he meant to make publicly.

Over the course of the afternoon, he found more than one occasion to remove the note from his pocket and reread it. *Dinner, then.* Oh, but she was clever. By four o'clock, when lessons finished for the day, those words had succeeded in making Langley ravenous.

And his hunger had very little to do with food.

\* \* \* \*

Two hours later, his hair freshly combed, his spectacles polished, and his cravat rather too tightly knotted, he followed the boys downstairs to the empty dining room. His rapid glance took in the soaring painted ceiling, silk curtains, crystal chandelier, and a table that would easily seat twenty, though at present only one end was set. Young Kingston directed him to the seat beside Philip, across from their grandmother's place, as it turned out when that lady swept into the room a few moments later and introduced herself.

"I am Mrs. West, Lady Kingston's mother," she said in a voice whose warmth only highlighted its faint northern notes as she dipped into a shallow curtsy. He knew she must be fifty, perhaps even on the far side of that number. But the years had been kind to her, and Mrs. West made every effort to exploit their generosity: the arrangement of her hair, the drape of her gown, even the softening glow of the candles.

He bowed. "Lord Kingston and Master Philip speak fondly of you, ma'am. Stanhope, at your service."

They had only just taken their seats when Amanda slipped into the room—no grand entrance like her mother. In fact, she was glancing over her shoulder, her attention on something other than the assembled company, and she turned to face them all only when Langley and the boys stood and the scrape of chairs drew her startled notice.

"Oh. I had intended to—am I late?"

A general murmur of dissent went around the table, but Mrs. West said reprovingly, "It's five minutes past the hour, my dear."

"Then my apologies for keeping you waiting. Please serve the soup," she said with a faint smile to the footman who wasn't Lewis. He had pulled back the chair at the foot of the table for her, with her elder son to her right and the younger to her left.

Langley wondered selfishly whether the extra five minutes had been spent at her dressing table, preparing herself for this little match—of wits? of wills?—in which they seemed to be engaged. Unnecessary, of course. He'd not been indifferent to her loveliness when her wet hair had been plastered to her head and rain had been dripping from the end of her nose.

But if pressed, he would have to admit she looked lovelier still now. Her warm brown hair had been dressed with pearls tonight, each one on a pin, gleaming here and there from a riot of carefully arranged curls. Her bosom rose from the deep, square neckline of a pale green gown, a shade that would have made most people look rather sickly, but which set off her skin like a creamy bud about to burst into bloom.

He suspected he had been caught staring at the hint of bosom that neckline revealed when she fixed him with her dark eyes and said in a voice considerably cooler than her mother's, "It was very good of you to join us, Mr. Stanhope."

*Dinner, then.*

The slip of paper that had carried her order was burning a hole through his breast pocket.

"It would have been churlish to have refused so generous an invitation," he replied, pointedly enunciating the final word.

"And are you comfortably accommodated in the schoolroom, sir?"

Was that the twitch of a smile about her lips?

"You are kind to enquire," he said, thinking of the narrow, cluttered cupboard that passed for his bedchamber and the waist-high looking glass, "but your ladyship must already know the answer."

She resented the necessity of his presence, and for that, he could not blame her. She was smart enough, he knew, to be afraid of what it meant. She understood the danger her family could be in.

But at the same time, he suspected that she liked having him there. In part, yes, because he had given her a way to thwart Dulsworthy's authority, at least temporarily.

That wasn't all, though.

Her kiss at the ball, her words last night, her sharp, surreptitious glances at him throughout the meal, all suggested she was as fascinated—*reluctantly* fascinated—with him as he was with her.

Perhaps it was that fact she resented most of all.

The present bout in their strange little skirmish came to a draw when the first course was laid before them. Sounds of silver scraping across china filled the room.

As he ate, he thought again of her peremptory reply to his earlier refusal: *Dinner, then.* In his mind, the weight of those words shifted, and with it, their meaning.

*Dinner. Then...*

Who would make the next move?

"I find that your sons have been under most excellent tutelage, Lady Kingston," he said, breaking into the boys' minute detailing of their day for their mother.

"They are bright boys," she demurred, smiling at both of them in turn before correcting herself. "Bright young gentlemen, I should say. Promising scholars." Then she directed her attention to her plate once more, prodding with her fork at an untasted mound of creamed turnips. "Ready, I suppose, for school?"

The fear behind her question was unmistakable. Both boys echoed the word *school* with varied degrees of surprise and incredulity, the younger looking less enthused than Langley would have expected, and the elder less alarmed.

"Harrow, do you mean? Like Papa?" asked young Kingston.

"And Lord Dulsworthy," Philip reminded him.

"Your guardian and I have had some discussion of the matter, yes," Amanda was forced to admit. "It's expected of boys in your position. But I worry that your poor mother's instruction will prove to have been inadequate to the purpose." At that she sent Langley a beseeching look.

"It will require much more than a day's acquaintance to determine their level of preparation, your ladyship," he reassured her. "But as to the quality of your instruction, I confess I find myself surprised at the depth and breadth of knowledge you have been able to impart. Your own education must have been quite—"

"She attended Mrs. Plinkton's Academy for Girls, in Bath," said Mrs. West, as if that settled the matter.

"A fine institution," he agreed, though he'd never heard of it. No girls' school was entirely responsible for teaching Amanda what she knew, in any case. Of that he felt certain.

But Amanda, still focused on her sons' future, showed no inclination to solve the mystery and said nothing more.

The meal was very nearly over. He fished about for some change of subject, something that would cast off the gloom that now hung over Amanda and restore the charmingly defiant spark to her eyes.

Then Mrs. West dabbed her lips, set her napkin aside, and said, "Stanhope."

"Yes, ma'am?"

"No, no. I beg your pardon. I was only thinking of the name. There's something familiar about it." A footman replaced her empty plate with a crystal dish of custard, and Mrs. West took up her spoon. "Are you by any chance related to Sir Langley Stanhope?"

Silver clattered onto china, and for just a moment, he feared he had been the one to drop his fork. But no, the noise had come from the end of the table, from Amanda, who was looking at him now with an expression for which he had no name.

Following a sidelong glance at the commotion, Mrs. West continued, "I remember reading about it in the papers when he was knighted… something he'd done…" She waved a spoonful of custard through the air. "Oh, what was it?"

A man did not rise to his level in the intelligence service without having run the risk of exposure. But the situation in which he found himself now was somehow worse. Damn that knighthood and damn every mention of. He would not be addressed as Sir Langley by anyone, least of all the Countess of Kingston.

"I could not say, ma'am," he replied, mustering a tone of utter boredom. "No relation, I'm afraid."

"Then who are your people?"

Langley hesitated. "I have no family, Mrs. West."

Mrs. West made a noise of mild disappointment, or perhaps sympathy. The boys, knuckle-deep in their custard cups, appeared to have heard none of the exchange.

But Amanda's surprise at the mention of the knighthood had turned to narrow-eyed scrutiny. She looked as if she were trying to sort out whether he were telling the truth—about any of it.

Would she demand an explanation?

Would she be satisfied by the one he was prepared to give?

Abruptly he waved off dessert, nearly knocking the glass of custard from the footman's hand as he bent to place it in front of Langley. "Nothing for me, thank you. I've little taste for sweets. If you'll excuse me, ma'am." He pushed to his feet, bowed first to Mrs. West, and then Amanda. "Your ladyship. I'll bid you all good night."

"Tomorrow's lessons to prepare, Mr. Stanhope?" Amanda tilted her head at a slight angle, a pose at once of curiosity and challenge. For just a moment, he thought she meant to tell him he hadn't permission to leave.

*Dinner. Then...*

"That's right," he agreed.

He should say nothing more. Go upstairs to his garret and call the match between them a draw.

Instead, he boldly met her eye. "And I've just remembered I need something from the library." After all, he *was* supposed to be focused on finding a book.

With that, he turned and strode from the room.

Cheating, perhaps. But he played to win.

*Your move, my lady.*

# Chapter 10

No matter how tempted, Amanda could not very well jump to her feet and follow him from the dining room without raising suspicions.

So she finished her custard, careful to scrape every last dollop from the cup as she always did; she bid the boys goodnight and sent them upstairs with a kiss on each cheek, following the usual rounds of protest and professions of indignation; she sipped a leisurely cup of tea with her mother in the drawing room, then announced her intention to write a note of thanks to the Hursts before she retired.

Finally, she stood, hand on the library door, foolishly hesitant about what she might find on its other side.

When she entered, Langley was standing with his back to her, examining the bookshelves, a candlestick held aloft in one hand. Other candles had been lit at that end of the room, and a small, lopsided pile of the volumes he had already collected threatened to topple from one corner of the desk. At the sound of the door, he turned.

Whether his spectacles had slid slightly down his nose, or whether he had adjusted them so, the better to aide his search, he looked over their top rim at her, just as she had imagined him doing earlier that day. And just as she had known would happen, her insides went slightly wobbly at the sight, though his expression was more amused than reproving.

His dark brows lifted as he looked her up and down. "I win."

"I—I beg your pardon?" she stammered.

"The game of push and pull we've been playing all day. Cat and mouse. You've walked right into the trap I set at dinner."

Clearly, Langley imagined himself as the cat.

She mustered a tinkling laugh. "Have I? Oh, dear. Well, the boys will tell you I'm not very good at games."

Having declared victory, he seemed to expect she would accept defeat and go. He half turned toward the bookshelf again.

Instead, she glided toward the desk, squaring the books into a stack as she passed. Then she went to the bookcase next to the one on which he was ostensibly searching—he'd gone perfectly still at her approach—and ran her hand into the narrow crevice above a row of books about seafaring expeditions, exploration, and travel. The shelf on which they sat formed part of a ledge across that end of the room.

With the soft *snick* of a lever being pressed and the mechanical *cre-e-eak* of infrequent use, the entire shelf, books and all, swung forward to reveal a hollow space behind, filled with crystal decanters and matching tumblers. She picked up a tumbler, blew away the dust—not even Mr. Matthews or Mrs. Hepplewythe knew of the existence of her late husband's secret liquor cabinet—and turned toward Langley, who was, as she had intended, now watching her every move.

"May I offer you a drink?"

With unnecessary force, he thumped down the candlestick he still held. "No. Thank you."

She shrugged. "As you wish." She trailed one fingertip over the collection of stoppers, at last pausing to pluck one from its bottle. Lifting the decanter, she splashed a generous swallow of amber liquid into the glass she still held. After returning the bottle to its place, she nudged the cabinet closed with her hip.

Langley watched that movement too—or so she thought. The gleam on his spectacles made his eyes impossible to read.

With exaggerated slowness, she carried the drink back to the desk and leaned against its solid bulk. "No luncheon. No dessert. No French brandy." She lifted the glass to her mouth, let the liquor's warmth coat her lips, licked it away. "Haven't you any vices at all?"

By the flickering candlelight, she watched his throat bob in a hard swallow. "Vices? I'm sure I do. Let me see…" He mirrored her easy posture, propping himself against the ledge, crossing his feet at the ankle. "I drink entirely too much coffee, for one. I don't sleep particularly well, you see. Haven't for years—though perhaps the coffee is as much the cause of that problem as it is a solution for it."

"I daresay I could make a similar confession." She smiled around the tumbler's edge. "Lately, something has been interfering with my sleep as well."

His brows rose above the rim of his spectacles.

After another moment, he carefully passed the palm of his free hand over the light of the nearby candle. Almost, but not quite, touching the flame. "I deliberately seek out adventure, excitement, danger. A more serious vice, certainly." And a warning? When her lips parted to form a retort, he shook his head. "Pray do not try to convince me it is one we also share."

For just a moment, she doubted herself. Perhaps she ought not to have come tonight.

But no. She had made up her mind. She knew what she wanted from him—and she thought she knew how to get it.

She lifted one shoulder, set the tumbler on the desk beside her. "Well, I *am* here with you, at your...*invitation*, shall we call it?"

He pushed his spectacles into their proper place and looked from her to the liquor cabinet and back again. "I believe I underestimated you, your ladyship. Nevertheless, I'm certain it would be a better use of your time to take a solitary stroll through the garden."

"There's a chill in the air tonight."

"Then fetch a shawl."

"Skitter off like a good little mousie, glad of my narrow escape, you mean?" She straightened. "Seems rather a hollow victory for the brilliant... what *am* I to call you, now? Magpie? Major Stanhope? Sir La—?"

With a catlike spring, he closed the distance between them, his hard body almost pinning her to the desk. "Not that."

His sharp denial, the way he bit off each word, reminded her of the way Philip sounded when he had a scraped knee he was determined not to let her probe—"don't touch!"—but which nonetheless required tending.

Resolutely, she continued. "Why did you lie to my mother?"

"Did I?" He tore his spectacles from his face and tossed them onto the desk. They slid across the polished wood, stopping when they struck the crystal tumbler with a quiet *clink*. His darkened eyes searched hers. Nothing between them now.

Her heart pounded, though not with fear. "Yes. You denied being..." The name was on the tip of her tongue, but she hesitated, not worried about how he would react if she said it, but wary of her fascination with his volatility. "The man of whom she'd read in the papers."

"Go on. A woman like you doubtless craves the feel of a title on her tongue. All right, then," he conceded when she shook her head. "Yes, I'm Sir Langley Stanhope, K.B. Does that string of letters invest a fellow with sufficient pomp and ceremony to suit a countess?" He lowered his lips to her ear, and she shivered as his hot breath skated over her skin. "Were you relieved to discover that the man you're passing off as your sons' tutor is in fact a gentleman?"

Closer still, his body, his breath, until every inch of her was aware of every inch of him. He nipped her earlobe with his teeth, and to her shock, a moan of surrender rose in her throat. "Or..." Another nip, this time along her neck, sent a shudder of longing through her. "Were you disappointed to think I might not be a rogue after all?"

When still she did not answer, he soothed the sting of the bite with a flick of his tongue that made her go weak at the knees. "Ah, well, don' fret yerself, luv," he reassured her in a coarse accent, like nothing she'd ever heard. "I kin still play rough, since it's clear as it pleases ye."

She struggled to bring her ragged breathing under control. "That's not your voice."

"Are you quite certain, ma'am?" Those words, still whispered dangerously close to her ear, might have belonged to the foppish aristocrat at the theater.

"Stop it." Her head spun at this dizzying display of his strange gift. "Who are you, really? Just—just tell me the truth."

"The truth, your ladyship?" A bitter laugh gusted from chest, but after a moment, he obligingly levered his body away from hers, snatching up the tumbler and draining its meager contents as he threw himself backward, into the desk chair. "Nobody knows who the hell I am."

Freed of his weight, his touch, she considered taking his earlier advice and leaving. Yet he exerted an inexplicable pull, like the cold moon drawing the warm tide.

In another moment she found herself perched on the edge of the massive desk, her left leg almost resting against his. "I don't...understand. You're an intelligence officer." With uncertain fingertips, she plucked at her skirt. "If there's some mystery, couldn't you—clever as you obviously are, and with all the resources at your disposal—couldn't you...solve it?"

"Who's to say I'd want to?" His gaze shifted to a point beyond the desk, where the shadows of the room grew deeper, out of reach of the candles he'd lit. Whatever it was he seemed primed to tell her, she was no longer certain she wished to hear.

Still, she did not leave.

"I can't tell you where I was born," he began, in that distant voice she did not recognize, "or who was responsible for bringing me into the world. Is Langley my mother's name? My father's? The word stenciled on the side of the butcher's crate in which I was found?" His shrug of apparent indifference pinched her heart. "My first memories are of the alleyways around Newgate, begging, stealing. Whatever it took to get a mouthful of bread."

She flinched at his almost emotionless retelling of his childhood. This was no mere scrape, to be healed with a jar of salve and a pat on the head, but a wound, deep and bloody.

And he was not the sort of man to welcome a display of pity, she could guess. Carefully, she shifted her weight onto one hip, so that her knee fell softly against his, a silent reminder he wasn't alone now.

What sort of reaction she had expected to her movement, she couldn't say. But not what followed: his strong, warm palm settled on her calf, absently caressing its curve through the thin silk of her gown and stocking. His gaze, his thoughts were still far away. She wasn't even certain he realized he'd done it.

"The last pocket I ever picked—well, almost," he corrected himself with a sort of laugh, "I've lifted a few valuables since then, I suppose—belonged to General Zebadiah Scott. *Colonel* Scott, at the time. Being sharper than most men, he caught me in the act of relieving him of both watch and chain." A slight smile lifted one corner of Langley's mouth. "I'd have had a few of those mother-of-pearl buttons off his waistcoat, too, if he hadn't—" The smile deepened, but he shook his head. "He caught my wrist and said, 'I shouldn't do that if I were you, lad.'

"I—I tossed his words back in his face, intending to mock him. But I managed to catch his voice, his accent…well, it was a knack I had, imitating people. It surprised him. Almost seemed to…to delight him. He tipped his head to the side and said, 'What's your name, boy?'

"'Magpie, ye daft nob,' I told him. It was what the other street urchins called me, because I had a sharp eye for shiny things. That amused him too. He repeated it two or three times before asking my Christian name. I hardly knew what he meant by that, but eventually I came up with Langley.

"'Well, Langley,' he said, taking me by the elbow, 'why don't you come with me?'

"That meant prison, I figured. The hangman's noose. I tried to run, but his grip was firm." As Langley spoke, his fingers curled more tightly around her leg, almost to the point of discomfort. She did not pull away.

"He tried to tell me I had naught to fear from him. And I told him…" He tipped the glass to his lips again, searching out the last drops. "I told him a chap in my line liked to feel a jolt of fear now and then. How else was I to know I was still alive?"

The desire for danger that was so new and forbidden to her—he'd carried it with him all his life.

"Well, at that, he got a strange look in his eye and said…" A slow movement of Langley's head followed, not quite a shake. "I don't remember what he said in reply."

The first untruth he'd told her tonight. She hesitated to call it a lie. She didn't think he'd meant to do it. Perhaps he didn't want to remember.

"He bundled me off down the street, into his carriage, all the way to his house. Scrubbed the dirt from my face and my neck with his own hands, he did." The very rhythms of his speech changed as he slipped between the boy he had been and the man he'd become. "He and his good wife tried their best to make me less feral, though it was a thankless task. Eventually he told me I was going to live with some friends of his, who had a grand big house, practically in the country, he said, but sadly no children to share it with. My first real home. I was—oh, younger than Philip, certainly," he said, and she jerked in surprise at the mention of her son, so certain she was that he had temporarily forgotten her existence.

Absently, his hand smoothed up and down her leg, intending, she supposed, to soothe away her skittishness, though the heat of his touch produced quite another reaction, burning through her veins with the sinful liquid warmth of a whole tumbler-full of contraband French brandy.

"The Stanhopes were an elderly couple—or so it seemed to me at the ripe old age of seven or eight. Good people, whose goodness I rewarded by running away…oh, a dozen times at least. Usually with a sack full of their silver bits and bobs, candlesticks and the like. Any man of sense would have let me go, or at least tried to beat the impulse out of me. Benjamin Stanhope gave me his name. Sent me to Rugby when I outstripped his teaching. To Oxford after that. And bought my first commission, too. Sent me back to General Scott at the last, I suppose you might say. Sometimes I wonder whether it wasn't always the plan between them."

With a noise somewhere between a laugh and a sigh, he thumped the tumbler onto the desk. "And that, your ladyship," he finished, giving the fleshiest part of her calf a squeeze before releasing her to set both hands on the arms of the chair as if preparing to rise, "is the mostly true tale of how I came to be Major Langley Stanhope, intelligence officer and master mimic known as the Magpie."

He had skated over a great number of incidents, she felt sure, as well as a promotion or two. But she dared just one question. "And the matter of the knighthood?"

At that, he stood so abruptly, she nearly lost her balance. "A mistake. A misunderstanding on His Majesty's part."

"Surely you would not have me believe you so modest as to deny your own heroism?" she said lightly, doubting even as she spoke the words whether it was wise to tease him just now.

"If I've ever done anything worthy of being called a hero," he demurred, shaking his head, "it certainly was not on the occasion in question." Then another bitter laugh huffed from his chest. "I'm sure old Ben would have liked to hear me called Sir Langley Stanhope, all the same."

"He's gone?"

"A little more than three years ago."

About the same time she had lost her husband, Amanda noted with a strange pang of something like sympathy, though their pain had sprung from such different sources.

"Sophia went first, of a fever. Ben died a few weeks later, of a broken heart—and now I'm spouting sentimental nonsense, aren't I?"

Slowly, she slid from her perch on the edge of the desk and stepped closer to him, laying a hand on his arm. "No."

His gaze settled on the place where she touched him. "You're a smart woman," he said softly. "And a lady. Surely that story was sordid enough to send you scampering away?"

Her fingers curled tighter, pale against the dark wool of his coat. She made no move to go.

"Amanda." More plea than warning. Oh, yes. He wanted her.

And she wanted him. Surely a discreet widow might take a lover? There was no great scandal in that.

Well...*some* scandal.

Recalling her mother's endless cautions and reprimands, Amanda feared scandal might be part of the appeal.

Her pulse fluttered like a bird in a snare as he trapped her beneath his steady, stern regard. Resistance flared in her, along with a forbidden tingle of anticipation.

For what seemed an eternity, they stood at a silent impasse: cat and mouse, just as he'd said, his eyes raking over her, that hint of a sardonic smile curving his lips. When she could bear the weight of his imperious stare no longer, she lifted her chin, drew back her shoulders, and said, "Well?"

With one swift movement, he switched the position of their hands, so that he now gripped her arm. His other hand settled over her ribs, just beneath her breast. Could he feel her heart race?

"Right now," he murmured against her ear, his breath stirring the curls clustered there and shooting sparks of awareness across her scalp, "you seem to imagine that you may flirt with danger, dally with it, and still escape unharmed. But the life I lead is not for you. *I* am not for you." Once more, he nipped her earlobe, sending a bolt of lust to her core. "What must I do to make you understand?"

"You're the tutor," came her impudent reply.

At least, that was what she had intended to say. She rather feared that her words had been lost in an incoherent groan of pleasure as he nuzzled at a particularly sensitive spot beneath her ear.

"That's right," he growled. "I am."

And with that, his lips trailed over her throat, along her jaw, and found her mouth at last, his kiss just as rough as he'd threatened.

Or had intended to threaten.

To her mind, he was merely keeping a promise, a promise to reveal something of her, something to her, something she could not otherwise have discovered. The way the scrape of his bristly jaw along the delicate skin of her neck, followed by the press of sharp teeth—sensations she once would have dismissed as discomfort—made all her skin come alive. She was pure sensation, drunk on his touch.

And perhaps that was his object, to overwhelm her senses, the way one let a child have too many sweets, until he was heartily sick of them.

But her appetite had gone unsated for so long—had *never* been sated— she could only press hungrily against him, willingly supplying the answer his kisses demanded. She hid nothing from him as he plundered her pliant mouth, whimpered with pleasure when his teeth snagged the plump curve of her lower lip. Nothing gentle, nothing coaxing. Just scorching heat and salt and a hint of brandy.

*Oh, sweet heaven.* Who could have imagined that amazing range of voices and accents were not his mouth's greatest skill?

Nor were his hands still. The palm at her ribs rose higher, skating over her breast to the bare expanse of her décolletage. He hooked two fingers in her bodice and tugged. The sound of popping threads only ratcheted her need higher.

She threw back her head, craving the torment of his hot mouth on the nipple he'd freed, and then...

Out of the corner of her eye, she glimpsed the library door.

Had she locked it?

No, of course she hadn't. To have done so would have made it seem as if she had been expecting—

*Oh, God.*

He pinched her nipple between the knuckles of his first and second fingers, bringing it to an urgent peak as his lips drifted lower, lower....

Her back arched again as the decadent pleasure of his tongue consumed her. So good, so—*oh.*

Once more the door caught her eye.

She squeezed her eyelids shut, trying to focus on Langley's mouth and the pleasures yet to come.

Still, the mental image of the unlocked door intruded. What would happen if someone, a servant, her mother, came in and caught them in… in…? She couldn't think of the proper words, or rather the improper ones, to describe their current situation. In—*something…*

His other hand slid up her arm and settled at the base of her throat, its pressure yet another sensation she had not known to crave, yet impossible to ignore. "Is something distracting you, Amanda?" he whispered coolly across her wet nipple.

She could hardly catch her breath to explain. "The—the door isn't locked. We could be caught in—*in flagrante delicto!* That's it, that's the phrase I was trying to remember. Though it hardly seems adequate to the purpose, does it?" she added with a nervous laugh. "Well, perhaps the *flagrante* part. *Delicto,* too," she added reassuringly. *Oh, what was the matter with her?* This was no time to be showing off her knowledge of Latin—

He lifted his head from her breast and favored her with a smile that sent a shiver up her spine. "You said you wanted to live dangerously, did you not?" As he spoke, he brushed the pad of his thumb over the pulse thrumming in her neck.

"Yes," she confessed breathlessly. "I want a night with the rogue. But if we're caught, you may be compelled to act the gentleman."

"And you wouldn't want that." Was it her imagination, or did he sound disappointed? "Then I suppose you're right," he said, straightening. "We'd best not risk it."

Despite the fact that she had been the one to point out the perils of their present position, a wail of protest rose in her throat. Before it could escape, however, he was kissing her again. His arms came around her as he stepped forward, propelling her backward, until her hip struck not the immoveable bulk of the desk, as she'd expected, but the door itself. One *thunk,* as the panel settled against the frame beneath their combined weight, recalling the illicit, eager lovers the night of the ball.

"There. Now no one can get in."

And then the torment began anew: lips, tongue, teeth, fingers, each sensation sharper, sweeter than the last. With one hand, she gripped his shoulder, while with the other she blindly groped behind her back to steady herself, dragging her fingernails over the cool, painted wood.

Unrelenting, he gripped one of her thighs, lifting it, hooking it over his hipbone. Then, dropping his hand to her ankle, he swept up her leg, not over her skirts this time, but beneath them, her stockings the only thing separating her skin from his palm. Higher…higher…his fingertips pausing to toy with her garter, then dancing across the back of her bare thigh.

At long last, he dragged his knuckles through the crisp curls that guarded her mound, stirring those sensitive hairs. The pleasant throbbing between her legs swelled to an ache. Then his questing fingers grazed higher, over the damp folds of her sex, and his thumb began to lightly circle her nub.

"Ahhh…" A sigh shuddered from her as she chased a release that still shimmered on the distant horizon.

He settled his mouth once more near her ear. "Such a willing pupil," he coaxed, stroking deeper into her wetness. "But just how far must I go to drive home the point that I'm no gentleman?"

She couldn't frame an answer, just lifted her hand from his shoulder to his head, driving her fingertips against his heated scalp. Desperate for something she couldn't put into words, she resorted to his own methods, tangling her fingers in his damp, dark hair and tugging sharply.

With a grunt, he cupped her bottom in both hands, lifting her effortlessly. She wrapped both her legs around his waist. His erection, still encased in his breeches, rubbed against her mound and made her pant with need.

At two and thirty, a wife and a widow, she could hardly be considered an innocent. But her late husband's infrequent visits to her bed, candles doused, nightshirt raised, nothing to alarm, offend, arouse her…what had they to do with this? With Langley's clever mouth, his strong hands, teaching her things she would never forget?

Eagerly, she reached between them, shoving her bunched skirts out of the way, fumbling for the buttons of his fall. Once she had freed his manhood, she paused only for a moment, a single stroke of its velvety length with her fingertips, before sheathing him inside her.

*Oh, God.* Each nudge of his hips forced a gasp from her lips, her body caught between the unyielding door and his hard body as he drove her closer and closer to the edge of madness.

"Come for me, Countess," he demanded.

And she did, powerless to hold back the crashing wave as he thrust upward, a last perfect stroke, and his hot seed spilled into her.

Afterward, she slumped, satisfied and boneless, against the well-made door. It creaked softly once and was silent.

He tipped his head forward to rest against hers. "I hope you found that instructive."

Her breath burned as it sawed in and out of her lungs. "Oh, I did," she readily agreed when she could speak again. She hadn't even imagined such a thing was possible.

But she was equally certain that, when it came to the dangers of Langley Stanhope, she had not learned her lesson.

# Chapter 11

Sometime after Amanda had said good night, Langley had crept up the stairs to the schoolroom, the paltry excuse of the stack of books long forgotten, fully intending to spend the rest of the night wallowing in his guilt for having taken the Countess of Kingston up against a wall like some tuppenny whore. For having taken her at all.

Had he entirely forgotten his mission? He was here to help uncover what Dulsworthy had done with the codebook. He was supposed to keep her *safe*.

Dutifully, he'd scrubbed away all traces of their encounter, the lingering scent of her perfume, of her. Then he'd laid himself on the uncomfortable bed, prepared to stare at the ceiling for hours.

He was not supposed to have fallen asleep.

He certainly was not supposed to have had the audacity to awake refreshed.

God, he had never dreamed—no. That was precisely the problem. He *had* allowed himself to dream of her, allowed his mind to concoct some foolish fantasy in which Amanda was a sweet, sensual, adventurous lover. *His* lover.

But he had not dreamed that it might be the truth. Or that—despite the nature of his duty here, despite his past—he might not be able to summon the necessary guilt to regret the discovery.

With a noisy, satisfying stretch, he hoisted himself from the bed, splashed cold water on his face, dressed. The aroma of coffee filtered in from the schoolroom and his belly rumbled. Smiling to himself—he'd certainly earned his appetite, along with the pleasant tightness in his biceps and across his shoulders, a sign of muscles well-used—he opened the door and stepped into the schoolroom.

Kingston and Philip were seated at the table, and by the looks of the breakfast tray, had been there for some time. Langley squinted at the mantel clock, which sat atop a bookshelf on the far side of the room, trying to bring its face into focus.

The boys scrambled to their feet. "Good morning, sir," Kingston said. "I hope you found what you were looking for in the library last night."

Philip tipped his head to the side. "Where are your spectacles?"

Silence hung in the air for a moment as a twinge of something—still not precisely guilt—passed through Langley. He generally managed his affairs in such a way as to avoid any awkward mornings-after. But there was no avoiding this one. At least, not entirely.

"In answer to your question, Master Philip," he said, crossing the room and drawing back the remaining chair from the table, "my spectacles sometimes interfere with close work. I laid them aside while I was working last night, and I must've forgotten to pick them up. I did, however, find several items of interest in the library. So many, in fact, that I decided it would be more convenient for us to go down to them later this morning."

The young earl politely poured a cup of coffee and handed it to him. "The fencing master comes this morning, sir. At half past ten."

"Shall you come down and watch, sir?" Philip asked, with more enthusiasm than he had previously shown for anything. "In the drawing room. Jamie and I always have a little touch at the end, and sometimes Mama and Grandmama look on."

Langley glanced toward the clock. Nine, now. He very much doubted that an hour and a half would be enough time to prepare himself to face Amanda with anything like composure. A year and a half might prove insufficient.

Yet he was undeniably impatient to see her again. And to see how she looked at him.

"Yes, of course," he told Philip as he reached for a piece of toast and smeared it liberally with sweet, sticky jam. "I should be most interested to observe."

A few minutes shy of the appointed hour, he dismissed the boys to their fencing lesson with promises to join them in the drawing room shortly. As soon as they were gone, his thoughts threatened to return to last night and Amanda. He dragged them instead to the codebook. The fact that he had heard nothing from Millrose meant that it had not been found.

As he made his way downstairs, he pondered his next move. Could he use his newly created role as the boys' tutor as an excuse to call on

Dulsworthy and have another look around? Could he manage to work his way into the man's confidence?

Or would Dulsworthy take one look at him and know what he and Amanda had done?

Langley found the library empty, as he had hoped he would, and the books he had collected still stacked on one side of the desk—not returned to their shelves, he was glad to discover, for a few of them actually might be of use in the boys' lessons.

On the top of the books sat his spectacles, neatly folded and gleaming—rather accusatorily, to his mind—in a shaft of morning light. Wondering who had laid them there, he plucked them up and put them on to take a better look around. To his relief, he saw no further evidence of what had taken place in the room the night before. The dirty tumbler had been whisked away. The door stood, blank and impassive.

The door...

He shook his head briskly. If he let himself stay a moment longer here, let himself dwell on pleasant memories, he'd soon be harder than that mahogany desk. Immediately discarding his earlier plan of bringing the boys down to the library for their lessons, he gathered up the books in one arm and directed his steps to the drawing room.

Only the two boys and the fencing master were within. Stifling his disappointment, Langley crossed the threshold and made his way to a chair on the far wall, depositing the armload of books on the sturdiest-looking table within reach. Although he'd not previously seen the drawing room, it was easy to guess it did not typically look thus, with its expensive furnishings pushed to the edges and packed tightly together. The carpet too had been rolled up and laid to one side.

He had a moment's flash of pity for the servants who were tasked with taking the room apart and putting it back together, time after time, all for the amusement of two young boys. Though to be fair, Lady Kingston's servants appeared to be generally well-treated. He'd also been glad to see signs of their sympathy to the countess. Disgruntled household staff could be a point of easy entry for someone with ill intent.

"Ah, sir, there you are," cried Philip, coming toward him, with the other two trailing in his wake.

"You must be the new tutor. A pleasure to make your acquaintance," the fencing master said with a willowy bow. "I am Jacobs."

Langley, always attuned to patterns of speech, caught a slight French accent, despite the English name. The discovery didn't surprise him—not exactly. In London, one might always find men from every part of the globe, and since the revolution, Britain had been playing host to many displaced people from the nation across the Channel.

The war had not diminished English passion for all things French, so much so that certain tradesmen had been known to assume a French name or mimic a French accent to increase their business. The elegant art of fencing would surely not be immune to the whims of fashion. So, was Jacobs in fact English, and merely playing at being French to attract more customers?

Or was he a Frenchman trying to hide the fact?

Langley's skills of perception had been honed from childhood, in the dank, crooked East End streets he'd called home. He had not needed years of army training to teach him to regard every person he met with suspicion. Suspicion came naturally to him.

"Stanhope," he said with a bow, forcing himself to unbend, despite the distrust that prickled along his spine. Sometimes appearances were *not* deceiving. Jacobs was likely just some poor chap who earned his coin by teaching the sons of nobs to fence. Langley wasn't here to stand in his way.

However, the fencing master's presence was a useful reminder that Bartlett House was porous, hardly an impenetrable fortress, despite the men standing guard outside. Even within its walls, Langley must stay on alert and focused. Yesterday's games, last night's…amusements, were a distraction in which he could ill afford to indulge. Becoming Lady Kingston's lover was not part of his mission.

And becoming something more than that was out of the question.

"I'm glad you've come, sir," Philip enthused.

His elder brother sent him a sidelong glance. "Of course you are, Pip. How else is Mr. Stanhope to discover you're a *prodigy*?" The label, it was easy to guess, had not come from young Kingston originally, and its application was clearly a bone of contention.

"We shall endeavor to provide you with something worth seeing, Mr. Stanhope," Jacobs said, though the modesty of the words was undercut by the man's rather pompous air. "Come, young sirs."

Philip and Kingston returned to the far end of the room and stood two arms'-lengths apart, facing their audience of one, bodies straight, swords up, toes out. Then Jacobs shouted, "En garde!" The thin, flexible blades of their foils sang as the boys whipped them through the air, moving through a series of poses, pausing on each at the fencing master's command.

Langley saw very little either to impress or dismay him. Philip, the more naturally athletic of the pair, held his sword with greater comfort and moved with greater assurance, though not necessarily demonstrating more true skill. Young Lord Kingston, on the other hand, showed no sign of realizing that his lightness could have its advantage. On the whole, it seemed to Langley that either the lessons could not have been going on very long, or the fencing master was overpaid for his efforts. Had an unsuspecting Lady Kingston been taken in by the man's dramatic flair and subtle French air?

Eventually, Jacobs ordered the boys to face one another for a bout, "a little touch," as Philip had promised in the schoolroom. Langley caught himself looking expectantly toward the doorway, awaiting the arrival of their mother. But the threshold remained empty. Reluctantly, he dragged his attention back to the match.

"Pret," warned Jacobs, then "Allez!"

The foils clashed, the blades chattering against one another as both boys lunged, eager to gain the advantage of attack. What followed was a good deal of sword-waving and showy footwork, none of the deliberate, careful movements that might reveal an opponent's weakness or create an opportunity to score. Parry met thrust by luck, rather than design. Neither boy seemed willing or able to defend.

After watching for a few minutes, Langley came to his feet and called, "Arrêt," not disappointed by the performance—he had expected little, despite Philip's braggadocio—but unsettled. "What," he demanded of Jacobs, whose face had gone slack with surprise, "can you have been teaching them?"

"Ah, Mr. Stanhope," he said, with a visible effort to collect himself, tugging his coat into place. "So you understand something of the subtle artistry of fencing, do you?"

"Something, yes. It would appear you have worked very little on defensive maneuvers."

Jacobs stepped closer. "Indeed, sir, we have," he insisted. "But they are only beginners."

Out of the corner of his eye, he saw Philip's mouth pop open to protest the description. Kingston's foil twitched, the movement echoed by a swift shake of his head to stop his brother from speaking.

"And of course," the fencing master continued in a confidential tone, "as a tutor you must know that what one may teach, pupils sadly do not always learn."

"Then one must modify the instruction to suit the student," Langley countered, trying hard not to think of last night.

"With no sparring partner of my own skill, it has been difficult to demonstrate proper technique." Jacobs's small, dark eyes traveled assessingly over Langley. "I would invite you to engage in a little bout, sir. For demonstrative purposes. But alas, you are not properly attired."

Langley did not need to see either the flash of enthusiasm in the boys' faces at the idea, or the wave of disappointment that followed the observation about his clothes, to know how to answer the fencing master's challenge. Wordlessly, he slipped off his coat and tossed it onto the seat of the chair from which he had risen. "I'll make do," he said, unbuttoning the cuffs of his sleeves and rolling them over his forearms in precise folds.

Kingston hurried to his side. "You may use my foil, sir," he said, proffering the weapon on both palms.

Langley took the sword from him, tested its heft and balance with a few experimental flicks of his wrist. "Thank you."

Jacobs removed his own foil from a long case that had been tucked away beneath a sofa. Langley observed the other man's technique as he warmed up: sound enough, but prone to the same sort of extraneousness he'd noted in the boys' movements. At last he nodded to Philip to indicate he was ready.

"En garde," Philip almost shouted in his eagerness. Both men raised their arms. "Allez!"

"In fencing," Langley explained, as he easily parried Jacobs's first thrust, the blades singing as they slid along one another, "your most important weapon is your mind. Like a chess match. Even in a defensive pose," he said, shifting his weight onto his back foot, "you must always be anticipating, watching for an opening. The tide can turn in an instant."

The fencing master stumbled as Langley lunged, driving him backward. "Any sign of weakness becomes an opportunity for attack," Jacobs agreed, trying to disguise his misstep as deliberate. "It may also be a trap, into which an unwary opponent may fall."

The boys rewarded each maneuver with cheers and gasps. Philip, who still had his foil, occasionally attempted to imitate a clever move, demanding of his brother, "Did you see that?"

In truth, though, the men's blades were little more than a blur. Despite the bout having been billed as instructive for the boys, it was almost immediately clear that Jacobs intended to clear his honor with the challenge.

Besides that, he was soon too out of breath to pretend to teach.

Langley was not surprised to discover himself more fit than the fencing master, who must rarely or never have had to defend against actual, life-threatening attacks. Nevertheless, even with Jacobs's ripostes limited to the fencing variety, it was no easy victory. The man had an appetite for violence far beyond what his flourishes and his feeble instruction of the boys suggested.

Back and forth they moved, their footwork more intricate than the most complex country dance. Jacobs had the first hit, but Langley took the second and would have been ready after several scoreless minutes to call the match a draw, when the young earl shouted, "Look, Mama!"

For just a fraction of a second, Langley's attention shifted from his opponent to the figure in the doorway. Jacobs, his face contorted in a rictus of triumph, seized the moment and lunged.

# Chapter 12

Amanda shrieked—then immediately chided herself for her foolishness.

She understood that Langley was in no real danger, no matter the fierceness of Mr. Jacobs's expression. First, because the foils were blunted and could inflict no wound more serious than a welt.

And second, because she had been watching silently from the threshold for several moments before Jamie had spotted her. She knew almost nothing about the sport, but even she could tell that Langley was the more skilled fencer of the two.

She rather suspected that her first glimpse of him today would have brought memories of last night rushing back to the forefront of her mind, no matter how he looked or what he had been doing.

But the sight of him now—his shirt slightly damp with sweat, sleeves rolled up to reveal corded forearms dusted with dark hair, the flex of muscles in his back, his legs, his buttocks as he...*thrust* (it was, after all, the technical term; she knew at least that much) again and again—made the remembered pleasures of that hour in the library wash over her with a wave of heat, as if someone had stoked a pile of glowing coals in her belly to roaring flame.

Belatedly, she clapped a hand over her mouth, the flush of her cheeks almost scorching her fingertips. "I'm so sorry, Mr. Stanhope," she began, the words muffled by her palm.

Rather than turn toward her, Langley redoubled his focus on his opponent. With a quick, subtle movement of his blade, too fast for the eye to see, he first countered Jacobs's thrust, then swept the man's sword from his hand. The fencing master was still attempting to parry before he realized his weapon had clattered to the floor.

"Well done, sir, well done!" Pip came rushing forward, his foil tucked beneath his arm, to congratulate his tutor. Amanda could not help but share in her son's admiration.

Jamie, on the other hand, hurried to her. "Wasn't it thrilling, Mama? Were you worried? Your face is red."

"Oh, I—you know. Just your dear old Mama's silliness. I do apologize, Mr. Stanhope," she said again, for he was striding toward her, or rather toward Jamie, the boy's foil held out to him, grip first. "I am relieved that my crying out did not cost you your victory."

Langley swept a hand through his sweat-dampened hair, making it stand on end, and her fingers tingled at the remembered sensation of driving through those silky waves. Not just her fingers—every part of her was too aware of every part of him. His strong arms. The satisfied breathlessness of exertion. The gleam of triumph in his eyes. All of it took her back to last night, in the library—even the color that rose to streak across his cheekbones when he met her gaze, a hint that perhaps he too was remembering.

"It would have been my fault," Jamie corrected, eyeing his foil as if it were some newfound treasure. "It was I who called out first."

"A swordsman worthy of the name must be able to maintain his concentration at all times. Is not that right?" Langley asked, turning back to his opponent, who was bending stiffly to retrieve his foil from the floor.

"Indeed," admitted Jacobs rather sourly. Defeat was almost always a bitter pill to swallow. "The feint is one of a fencer's most valuable tools." He withdrew a spotted silk handkerchief from his pocket to polish his foil, then mopped his brow with it instead. "Clever of you to use the opportunity to show them how effective such a maneuver can be."

"Can you teach me?" demanded Pip with an erratic-looking flourish of his blade, so close she felt the air stir.

Amanda parted her lips to reprimand his carelessness, but Langley reacted first, catching the tip of the foil in the V between his thumb and forefinger. He wore no gloves and it must have stung, but he did not flinch. "I'm certain your fencing master must have trained you better than that," he said sharply. "And it is for him to determine when you are ready for more advanced techniques."

Though obviously crestfallen, Philip nodded his understanding. "Sorry, sir." Langley released the blade.

Amanda had a mother's heart, soft and easily broken. She gave in too often, she knew. And though it pained her to see Philip's disappointment, at the same time she marveled at how quickly Langley had managed to earn her sons' respect. Even they, it seemed, recognized the occasional benefit of a firm hand.

"I see no harm in a little additional practice with your tutor," Jacobs offered magnanimously. "Having observed Mr. Stanhope's swordsmanship today, I do not think you will pick up many bad habits from him."

Both boys pressed forward with eager, pleading faces. "After luncheon, sir?" Jamie asked.

Langley wore his habitual stern expression, but pleasure at the request twitched up the corners of his lips. "Perhaps," he conceded, "after luncheon. *And* after I hear your Latin."

Pip groaned. "I don't see why we should have to go on learning that old stuff."

With a philosophical shrug, Langley set a reassuring hand on the boy's shoulder and said, "You never know when a phrase or two might come in handy." And then he lifted his face to Amanda and winked.

*No, surely not.*

Surely he was not making a teasing reference to last night? Surely what she had imagined to be a wink was simply light glancing off the steel rims of his spectacles?

"I don't suppose you will join us for luncheon today, Mr. Stanhope?" she ventured, despising the girlish, hopeful note in her voice.

She would never be so foolish, so selfish, as to hope the book stayed missing, just to keep him here. She wanted it to be found. Of course she did. For everyone's sake. For the poor soldier being held captive over it. For the welfare of the nation.

For her own peace of mind.

Because it wasn't only Langley's handsome face and strong arms that drew her. Because the risks of wanting him for more than those superficial charms were too great.

Before he could make his answer, Jamie interrupted. "I'm not hungry, Mama. If it's all right, I'll stay in the schoolroom with Mr. Stanhope." He sent a questioning glance between the two of them. It could not have been clearer that he had something he wished to say to—or ask of—his tutor.

Amanda understood that a boy of almost twelve might have concerns he would prefer to share with a man, and unlike his brother, Jamie had never warmed to Lord Dulsworthy as a sort of friend. She could hardly protest that the boys' *tutor* was not an appropriate confidante, could she?

It seemed that intimacy was one of the dangers of which Langley had tried to warn her.

As she stood in the bright light of day, watching him with his hand on the shoulder of one of her sons and his head bowed earnestly toward the other, she understood anew, with painful clarity, that her craving for adventure and excitement had put all of them at risk.

Risk of heartbreak.

Because when his mission was over, Langley would leave.

"Yes, of course," he was saying to Jamie, surprise and uncertainty wrinkling his brow. "With your mother's permission."

She started to nod her assent, then clawed back the gesture by twisting her neck in an awkward manner. She had reassured herself with the knowledge that his presence in their lives was only temporary, had seen it in truth as an advantage. By design, theirs could be nothing more than a temporary liaison. Her heart need not be involved.

But her sons' hearts were another matter....

She shook her head. "I don't want you to miss luncheon, Jamie. A growing boy needs food." That stubborn lock of hair fell over the boy's eyes, not quite soon enough to hide his frustration at her answer. Langley's frown deepened. Her heart gave a fearful twinge. "I will tell Mrs. Hepplewythe to hold the meal until you arrive." A compromise—the best she could offer.

She'd given Langley her body. She could not afford to give him everything.

"All right, Mama." A rare smile lit Jamie's face. "I shan't be long."

He turned toward the door, while Philip slipped from beneath Langley's hand to say something to a departing Mr. Jacobs.

For just a moment it was only the two of them again, meeting one another eye to eye, standing closer together than was wise. Awareness zinged through her like the flash of a fencing foil, and when he drew a sudden, sharp breath, she knew he felt its danger too.

"Amanda," he murmured, so quietly that she saw her name on his lips rather than heard it.

Before either of them could say more, however, Jamie called over his shoulder. "Are you coming, sir?"

Just like that, the Magpie's bright eye darted to focus on a new object. He shook out his feathers, smoothing them into their usual order, and spoke in the tutor's clear voice to her elder son.

"Let me fetch my things, and I'll be right behind you."

But for just a moment, she had caught another glimpse of the man who lurked behind all those layers of masks. The vulnerable one. The passionate one.

The man she'd met last night.

The man, God help her, she longed to have an excuse to meet again.

\* \* \* \*

*At least I didn't kiss her.*

Small consolation, given how close together they had been standing, how easy it would be for even two not-so-young boys—to say nothing of the fencing master—to notice the hungry way they'd been eyeing one another.

No consolation at all, given how much Langley had wanted—still wanted—to cup the back of her head in his palm and bring her lips to his to put the seal on his victory.

Instead, he found himself dutifully following the young earl up two flights of stairs to the schoolroom, trying not to imagine the sort of questions a boy of that age might have for him.

He very much doubted they involved either algebra or Latin.

"Well, Lord Kingston?" he asked when he reached the top step and found the boy staring out a window overlooking the front of Bartlett House and the green promise of Grosvenor Square beyond.

Kingston said nothing for a long moment. Langley was just on the point of repeating his question when he noted the inward curve of the lad's shoulders, a familiar, self-protective hunch. So, instead of speaking, he merely stepped forward to take in the same view, crossed his arms behind his back, and waited.

"Is it awful, sir, that I don't like to be called 'Kingston'?" he asked a few moments later, without turning. "I always knew the title would be mine, one day, of course, but…"

"But you didn't expect to inherit it when you were only—"

"Nine. No, sir. And even after all this time, when people speak to 'Lord Kingston,' I find myself hoping my father will answer them." He shot a sudden glance Langley's way. "Don't, please, think I'm mad. It's only—"

"Only natural, I should say," Langley reassured him. "And even if it isn't, you'll get no judgment from me. Names are a tricky business."

The boy's shoulders eased into a more natural posture, as with the exhalation of a long-held breath, relief at hearing words of understanding. "Yes, sir."

"How do you wish to be addressed? In private, I mean. In public, I'm afraid, I will be bound to observe the usual proprieties."

A wry sort of smile lifted the boy's mouth. "That's all right, then. We never go anywhere." He turned and extended a hand, as if they were meeting for the first time. "I'm James, sir. Mama and Pip call me Jamie, and you may too, if you'd like."

Langley wasn't sure whether the invitation to use a familial nickname was precisely a gesture of trust, not when the lad's title so obviously pained him. Then again, perhaps it was only Langley's own occasional twinges of guilt that made him hesitant to claim something he'd not earned.

After all, he *had* tupped the boy's mother against a door last night.

But whatever it was, the lad seemed to have overcome his initial hesitation toward Langley, and Langley was prepared to return the feeling. He accepted the handshake, then waved an arm toward the table in a silent suggestion they sit down for what came next. "Well, then, *Jamie*. What was it you wanted to talk with me about?"

As Langley pulled back one of the unforgiving, undersized wooden chairs—whatever the subject, this was destined to be an uncomfortable conversation—Jamie swerved past him, to the door of his bedchamber. "One moment."

If Langley angled his head just so, he could see into the boys' room. Beside his neatly made bed, Jamie dropped down on one knee and fished his arm beneath the mattress, withdrawing a small, flat package. With his chin tucked too low for Langley to meet his eye, he returned to the schoolroom and laid the paper-wrapped package on the table. "It's this, sir."

"And what is this?"

"A book."

It could, of course, have been any book at all. An adventure story the boy had been forbidden to read. Or something more salacious still.

Nevertheless, Langley's thoughts darted in another direction. Anticipation vibrated through his chest, like a bell that could not be un-rung. But how ridiculous of him to imagine...

"What sort of book?"

"You can see for yourself, sir," the boy said, poking the package toward him with a fingertip. "The wrapping's torn."

Slowly, Langley drew it the rest of the way across the table, afraid to hope. As he peeled back just enough of the paper to reveal what was inside, he fought the impulse to close his eyes. It was extraordinarily unlikely for Jamie to have somehow laid his hands on...

"A—a cookbook?" He struggled for something like a tone of mild curiosity. "How did you come by this?"

"I found it in Lord Dulsworthy's phaeton. The other day, when he took us for a drive. Before—before you came."

Certain his hands would tremble if he dared to thumb through the codebook, Langley carefully laid it on the table in front of him. *Think, think.* What did he most need to know?

"And you were so…alarmed by the discovery that your guardian had purchased a, a cookbook that you"—*thank God*—"took it from him?"

"Well…it isn't just any cookbook."

Langley's heart stuttered and nearly stopped. "Oh?"

"No. The man—the one who came to the house, asking for it—he said it was quite valuable. Oh, I'm not doing a very good job of explaining, am I? You see, not quite a week ago, my mother went out and bought a book. I'm not sure what it was, but later that day a chap came from the bookshop and said her package had got mixed up with another customer's. She'd brought home some rare book that belonged to someone else, and could he have it back, please?"

"And you saw this exchange?"

"Well, overheard it, really. Pip and I were in the library. I wasn't trying to listen," he insisted earnestly. "Anyway, Uncle George—Lord Dulsworthy, I should say—was there too, and he told the man to come back another time. And then that afternoon, when we were all sitting down for tea, Mrs. Hepplewythe, our housekeeper, brought in a cookbook and said it was French and no good—it was the book Mama was to have returned to the bookshop, as it turned out—and so Lord Dulsworthy took it and said he would see to the matter. But"—Jamie sent the package a wary glance—"he didn't."

Langley toyed with a loose end of the twine that held the wrappings in place, trying to sort his thoughts. "Surely that's why Lord Dulsworthy had the book in his carriage? To return it?"

The boy gave an uncertain nod. "That what I thought at first too, sir. Or that he'd meant to do it, but forgot. It had slid quite far underneath the seat. I picked it up and started to ask him, and that's when I happened to notice the direction written on the wrappings. I—I'm quite sure the man said he came from Porter's."

With his thumb, Langley lifted the package and flipped it over onto his palm, displaying an unfamiliar name and address, scrawled across the paper in what he could only assume to be Dulsworthy's hand.

"A strange affair, certainly."

"I don't want Mama to get in trouble. The man from the shop said it's worth a lot of money. Uncle George shouldn't've…" As the words trailed off, he shook his head, his gaze distant, as if envisioning his guardian's displeasure when he discovered the book missing. "Anyway, now I've got it, but I don't know what I should do with it," he finished simply, bringing his eyes back to the table, looking first at the book, and then at Langley. "Can you help?"

Langley still wasn't sure whether it would be fair to say that Jamie trusted him. But the boy's distrust of Dulsworthy was palpable—and evidently, not misplaced. Could the man somehow have discovered the true value of what he'd had in his possession?

"Would you like me to see that it gets where it belongs?"

Jamie hesitated. "Will you tell Mama?"

"Are you worried she will be unhappy with you for taking it?"

He shook his head, causing his hair to fall into his eyes. "She would be more unhappy to know Uncle George didn't keep his promise."

The boy's heartfelt impulse—instinct, perhaps; Langley hadn't any experience with the matter—to protect his mother from a scoundrel skewered through him like an expertly wielded lance. *Christ.* He needed to get out of this house before he did any more damage.

And the book in his hand was his ticket back to the world in which he belonged.

His grip on it tightened almost convulsively. The movement caught Jamie's eye. Again the lad hesitated. Then, "Yes. You take it, sir." As if relieved of a burden, he shoved away from the table and leaped to his feet. "Mama will be wondering where I am."

"You wouldn't want to keep her waiting."

A quick nod, another glance at the book. "Thank you, sir."

"Of course."

He had every intention of letting the boy go. He had work to do, now. But while Jamie was still on the stairs, some contrary urge made Langley call after him to ask, "Did you see the man from the bookshop? When he was here, I mean."

Jamie turned, a frown notched into the space between his eyes at the unexpected question. "Only a glimpse, sir. He was a dark-haired, older fellow. Like yourself," he added, studying Langley's face, his brow still furrowed. "Only not so tall. And no spectacles."

"Good to know." Langley managed a crisp nod, then gestured with the book. "I want to make sure it gets into the right hands."

Jamie turned toward the stairs, then paused again. "Are you sure you won't join us for luncheon, sir?"

"No, thank you, Jamie. I've a Latin lesson to prepare, remember?"

Another quick nod of understanding and the boy was gone.

Langley sat at the table and marveled at the object in his hand, at his fortune. He'd imagined quite another outcome. He'd expected his stay at Bartlett House to go on much longer.

Better, of course, that it did not.

Better for everyone.

He reached across the table for paper and pen, scratched out a quick note. Then he got up, tucked the book inside his coat, and donned his greatcoat. "Going out for a breath of air," he explained to the indifferent footman as he strode through the entry hall and out the front door. With quick eyes, he found Lieutenant Eggleston standing guard across the way, dressed after the fashion of one of the square's older residents, pretending to watch the birds on the green.

He approached the other man with an impersonal nod of greeting, feigning interest in a pair of doves. "Take this to General Scott," he muttered under his breath a moment later, handing off the folded note. "I'll wait here."

For three-quarters of an hour, Langley strolled leisurely back and forth along the square, the book heavy against his ribs, glancing only now and then, and always with perfect indifference, toward the row of houses across the street.

He'd slipped into and out of so many roles, so many disguises in his life, never pausing, never looking back. Why should the present occasion be any different? Success at one mission meant moving on to the next. Scott's best agent had got exactly what he'd come for.

Oh, yes. And a little more besides.

Lost in his thoughts, he nearly missed Eggleston's return, as the man strolled by and a slip of paper fluttered from his kid-gloved hand to the ground. Langley pinned it with his toe, then bent to retrieve it. Just a few words, in General Scott's improbably elegant copperplate.

*My office, without delay.*

Like any good soldier, Langley would accept his commanding officer's order, of course. He would stop for nothing.

Not even goodbye.

Zebadiah Scott had never been a man of sentiment, not even when he'd rescued an urchin from the streets. He moved with deliberation, kept his mind on the endgame, and now Langley must do the same. From a few yards away, Eggleston had already resumed his guard duties, meaning Amanda was safe inside Bartlett House. Far safer, now that the codebook had been found.

Far safer without him.

As he crumpled the note, his eye caught another line of print, hidden at first beneath a fold. A sort of postscript. He had to read the words through twice to make sure he had not imagined them.

*And bring the countess with you.*

As he marched back toward the house, the note clenched in his fist, an uneasy breath shuddered from Langley's chest. He did not dare to call it relief, not even to himself.

He was grateful, yes, for the chance to see her one last time.

But what could General Scott want with her? What did the old man have up his sleeve now?

# Chapter 13

As the battered old coach jerked and swayed over cobblestone streets, Amanda's fingers plucked anxiously at the long, jagged slit in the skirt of her favorite sprigged muslin.

When Langley had stepped into the morning room, where she and Mama and the boys had just been finishing luncheon, and begged leave to speak with her, she had known instantly that something had changed. Oh, he'd moved with the same confident, easy grace as always, though his greatcoat had been draped over his arm, which had struck her as odd, as he had been upstairs, not outdoors. With a few words, he'd sent the boys to the schoolroom to read and translate a passage from Cicero. Mama had declared her intention to ready herself for her morning visits and followed them out.

Once he'd bowed the three of them on their way, he'd turned to Amanda, radiating a peculiar energy that only seemed to intensify her earlier awareness of him. "Order your carriage around to the front," he'd said. "Have the driver wait five minutes and then be off, headed west."

Aghast at the strange request, Amanda had nonetheless managed to ask, "And who is to be the passenger inside that carriage?"

"No one. We'll be leaving this way."

"I beg your pardon?"

But he had already opened the glass-paned door and stepped into the garden.

"I can't go out without a pelisse and bonnet," she'd insisted.

"There's no time to waste. Can't you make do with—with that?" He'd gestured toward the rather worse-for-wear broad-brimmed straw hat she kept hanging on a hook near the door for the time she spent in the garden with her sons.

A laugh had burst from her. "Not unless you can promise me I won't be seen."

"Not by anyone who gives a damn about ladies' fashions. Come."

Just as it had the night before, her body had responded to his command. As if under a spell, she had let the ribbons of the straw hat trail through her fingertips, abandoned, and followed him into the garden, to the fence, just as a hackney coach rumbled into the alleyway.

"The gate latch is still broken," she had reminded him.

"Then," he'd said, lacing his fingers together in the form of a stirrup and bending to hold them at about the level of his knees, "we'll have to go over."

"You can't be serious," she'd gasped.

But he had been. Hence the tear in her skirt. And a scrape on one ungloved palm. And the lingering awareness of where his strong hands had been—cupping her bottom, the underside of one breast—as he'd helped her awkwardly scale the wrought-iron palings, hoist her legs over the top, then perch there like the world's worst burglar, while he ascended seemingly without effort, dropped gracefully into the alleyway, and waited to catch her when she at last worked up the nerve to let go.

She plucked nervously at the ragged threads, knowing she was only making matters worse. Martha might be a miracle worker with a needle, but even she had her limits.

Langley, sprawled on the rear-facing seat, must have been watching her, for after a moment, he said in a decidedly sardonic voice, "Sorry about that. But you did tell me you were willing to take risks."

"Yes, well." She jerked her gaze to the window and the buildings spinning past. "I assumed I would be risking the ordinary sorts of things: Life. Limb. Reputation." At that last, she darted a glance toward him, not quite meeting his eyes. A muscle twitched along a firmly set jaw that did not appear to have been shaved that morning. "Not three dresses in as many days."

"Three?"

"First," she said, ticking off the list on her fingertips, "Lord Penhurst trod on the hem of my gown at Lord Dulsworthy's ball. Which wasn't all bad, I suppose, as it gave me an excuse to leave the dancing and sneak off to the study, where we—well, you remember, I'm sure. Then last night—" Heat rushed into her face, first at the memory of Martha's raised eyebrows as she'd wordlessly examined the strained seams in the bodice of her mistress's dinner dress, and then at the remembered feel of Langley's hand against her bare breast.

"And now this…" With a flick of her wrist, Amanda gestured helplessly at her skirts, suddenly wondering where the injury to the sprigged muslin might be leading. "That's three."

Something like a smile softened the angle of Langley's jaw. "I cannot fault your arithmetic, Lady Kingston."

"What's going on, Major Stanhope?" she demanded, and with that question came a rush of others, all of the questions she should have asked while standing in the morning room of Bartlett House. "Why all this subterfuge—ordering the carriage out front, while we sneak out the back? Where are you taking me?"

He straightened his spine against the hackney's worn squabs, then leaned forward, elbows on knees. She could not escape his gaze now. "Your carriage was a red herring. In case anyone might be keeping an unusually close eye on your comings and goings, I wanted to put them off the scent. A casual observer, or even a dedicated one, will have watched that highly polished, crested coach with a liveried driver headed one way and paid no attention at all to the ancient hackney cab that emerged from the mews at approximately the same time, going the opposite direction."

"You—you think s-someone is watching me? Following me?"

"Several someones have been watching you for days. Whether anyone will attempt to follow you remains to be seen."

"But why? I haven't got—oh."

As she spoke, he reached into his coat and withdrew a parcel, and she knew without any closer inspection that beneath its paper and string lay a French cookbook bound in green leather.

"Where did you get that?" she whispered, as if fearful of being overheard.

"Jamie found it," he answered in a perfectly normal voice, despite the utter abnormality of the situation. "Beneath the seat of Lord Dulsworthy's phaeton. It seems he overheard enough of our conversation on the day I first called to be concerned by Dulsworthy's failure to return it to the shop when he saw it there. He was worried you might be in trouble."

She could not help but notice Langley's use of her son's given name. She did not think he would have done so if Jamie himself had not invited it. And if Jamie *had* invited the familiarity, then…

Something fluttered in her chest, in the vicinity of her heart. "He has always been a worrier," she said. "But why hadn't Lord Dulsworthy returned it?"

"That I cannot say." Langley turned the book in his hand once before tucking it back into its hiding place against his chest. "But I intend to find out."

"Surely you don't think he—?" She couldn't even finish the thought. The very notion of George mixed up in the affair of the codebook was more than she could make herself imagine.

And of late, she'd been imagining a great many impossible things.

"I don't intend to speculate. Besides, we've nearly reached our destination."

He turned his attention to the window, so she did too, though everything beyond it was unfamiliar and had been since they'd left St. James's behind. They must be near Whitehall, she thought, which meant...

"This is the Horse Guards." He nodded toward a Palladian-style building of white stone as the carriage crossed the nearly empty parade ground and paused beside an arched doorway for them to disembark. "Which among many other things houses the headquarters for several divisions of the British military." Now she observed the greater than usual number of red-coated officers about, and when she glanced up at the driver of their coach, she noted that he was sitting on his perch with a considerably straighter spine than any cabby she had ever seen. Almost like a soldier.

"This isn't an ordinary hackney, is it?"

"Of course not." Langley had been speaking to another officer in a low voice, but turned now toward her and held out an arm.

She hesitated before taking it. "And why have you brought me here?"

His expression was impassive. "Just following orders, your ladyship."

"Whose orders?"

"The only man whose orders I'm obligated to follow." And with that, he began to walk away, evidently having grown impatient of waiting. "We mustn't keep General Scott waiting."

*General Scott.* The gentleman who'd rescued Langley from the street some thirty years ago. She had not considered that when Langley had spoken of being "returned" to the general when he'd joined the army, he had meant the connection quite so literally.

She hurried to keep up with Langley's brisk clip down endless miles of corridors, deeper and deeper into the warren of offices, into the heart of military intelligence.

Or, when speaking of intelligence, would it be a more accurate metaphor to describe General Scott as the brain...?

"Here." Langley rapped his knuckles on the surprisingly plain oak door before which they had stopped and did not wait for a reply before opening it. The room into which it led was smallish and practically empty, containing little more than a desk from which a uniformed soldier was rising as they crossed the threshold. Langley nodded. "Captain Collins."

The officer dipped his head in acknowledgment. "He's expecting you, Major Stanhope."

Langley led her across the room to an unobtrusive door, and reached out a hand to open it, this time without knocking at all.

The door swung inward before he touched it. "Ah, Magpie. Good, good. And you are Lady Kingston, of course," said the older uniformed man behind it with a surprisingly showy bow for her.

Amanda hadn't really had time to form any expectation about the office of the head—heart?—of British military intelligence. But if pressed, she almost certainly would have used words like *spacious* and *orderly*.

General Scott's office was neither of those things.

Dark blue curtains had been looped back haphazardly to one side of a large, open window, inviting in the light along with a soft breeze that swirled through a cloud of pipe smoke and ruffled the papers on the man's desk. Disorder reigned across its top: slipping and sliding piles of letters, maps, documents with important-looking seals, those stacks interspersed with books and ledgers, small and large, open and closed. If Langley handed over the codebook, she felt certain that in short order, it would be lost amid the clutter, never to be found.

Then again, perhaps that was the general's strategy for safekeeping?

Nor was the man himself quite whom she would have envisioned in such a role. Langley towered head and shoulders above General Scott's slight form, which moved with a peculiarly childlike rapidity as he gestured them to chairs. Someone evidently saw to it that his uniform was pressed and his linen crisp at the start of the day, but the mother in Amanda recognized the futility of the effort. The ash of pipe tobacco speckled his white breeches, and ink smeared both cuffs of his coat sleeves. A pair of wire-rimmed spectacles, the lenses smudged with fingerprints, had been pushed onto the top of his head, almost lost in a wild tangle of white hair.

But his blue eyes were bright and clear, and they had evidently been watching her assess the state of both his office and his person. "Don't let appearances fool you, Lady Kingston," he said with a smile as he sat down across from them, behind his desk, almost hidden by its contents. "Though fooling people with appearances is rather our stock in trade, eh, Magpie?"

Langley's answering expression might accurately have been described as a grimace. "You could say that, sir."

"Now, Lady Kingston, do you remember our last meeting?"

The crease in Langley's brow grew more severe, directed now at her. "You've met?"

"I really don't..." Amanda began. General Scott gave an eager, prompting nod. "Oh." For she did remember, then. Just a vague, shadowy recollection. "Why, it must have been..."

"More than ten years ago. Yes, sadly. Lord Kingston was, shall we say, a friend to my service," he explained to Langley. "Lady Kingston organized a ball to benefit the Widows and Orphans Fund, one of those charity galas the *ton* so delights in throwing. You were just a bride, then," he said, favoring her with a fond smile that gradually softened even further, almost to melancholy. "May I offer my condolences? Your husband was a most excellent man."

"Thank you, sir. Yes, he was." She dipped her chin, aware suddenly that she was blushing. "I apologize that I forgot our having met."

"No matter," he smiled benevolently. "A countess must inevitably have a large acquaintance—easy enough to lose track. Rather like a military man, I suppose. Poor Mrs. Scott has quite given up trying to remember the name of everyone I know well enough to tip my hat to."

Amanda managed to nod. The point had been neatly made.

Despite the clutter on his desk and his air of helpless befuddlement, General Scott forgot nothing. Missed nothing.

Surreptitiously, Amanda folded her hands across her lap, doing her best to disguise the ever-lengthening rip in her skirts.

With a gruff noise in his throat, Langley reached into his coat and withdrew the paper-wrapped parcel. "Ah, yes," General Scott said, something that wasn't quite a smile creasing his face. "How good of Major Stanhope to recall me to the business that brought you both here." He took the still-wrapped book from Langley, laid it on top of one of the sloping piles on his desk, put his unlit pipe between his teeth, and began to search for his spectacles. "Here we are," he chortled around the pipe stem when he patted the top of his head, then nudged them into place.

When he once more picked up the package and began to examine it, Amanda turned her attention to Langley, who was watching the general with a strained sort of hopefulness. "Are you thinking the same thing I am, sir? That direction could lead us to Lieutenant Hopkins."

"It could," General Scott agreed after a moment, running a fingertip over the print. "But it's just as likely to belong to yet another party who's willing to pay handsomely for what's inside." With finger and thumb, he reached inside the torn paper and eased the book from its wrappings, then flicked them aside. As he turned the codebook over in his hands, he again wore that smile that wasn't amusement, that glimpse of quite another sort of man from the jovial, grandfatherly gentleman she'd first imagined him to be. "Well, well, well. At last…"

A shudder chased up Amanda's spine. "What I don't understand is—" Both men looked sharply at her, as if they'd momentarily forgotten her presence. "Why didn't Lord Dulsworthy return it to Porter's?" she continued, quieter. "You…you can't really be saying that he's involved in—in *espionage?*" The last word came out as a whisper, pushed past suddenly dry lips. "If you'd ever met him, you'd know—why, Major Stanhope *has* met him, of course. You tell the general," she pleaded, turning toward Langley, "how ludicrous it is."

A muscle twitched along Langley's jaw, and he did not meet her eye. "Appearances can be deceiving."

"Oh, bother that," she snapped, startling herself almost as much as the two men. But she was heartily tired of the phrase, *appearances can be deceiving.* Didn't she know full well how true it was? "He's my sons' guardian. I deserve to know if he—if he—"

"Indeed, your ladyship," General Scott said soothingly. "Your concern for your children is both understandable and admirable. And you *shall* know, as soon as we do. It's possible, of course, that there will be an innocent explanation. A simple mix-up. Or…" With a circle of his wrist, he waved the book through the air, as if conjuring the truth. "Perhaps less innocent, but still hardly dangerous. Lord Dulsworthy, in possession of what he believed to be a valuable old cookbook, might have seen an opportunity to make a few pounds and found another bookseller. Until we know for certain, however, I don't intend to let it be known that this"—he returned the book to the top of the pile and thumped it with his first finger—"has been recovered."

"Then the ones looking for it will still believe it to be in Lady Kingston's possession," said Langley. "She will still be in danger."

Amanda had been eyeing the codebook, wondering how soon it would be hopelessly buried beneath an avalanche of important papers on the general's desk. An archeological expedition would be required to recover it. At Langley's words, the sharpness of his voice—impatient, incredulous— she started.

"Unfortunately, yes," agreed General Scott, eyeing her. "It's good that you have Major Stanhope with you. For your protection, as well as your sons'."

"Sir?" Out of the corner of her eye, she saw Langley's fingers curl into the arms of his chair. "I expected you to reassign me to the search for Hopkins, now that the codebook has been found."

A breath caught in Amanda's throat. She knew Langley would leave eventually, be assigned to his next mission, though she had not considered that it might happen so soon. Did his reaction suggest he was eager to go?

Or just the opposite?

"No," General Scott answered after the briefest consideration—the sort of hesitation Amanda herself sometimes employed when she wanted Jamie and Philip to think she'd weighed some outlandish request before refusing it. "Colonel Millrose told me you'd appointed yourself Lady Kingston's private guard...by claiming to be her sons' new tutor, wasn't it?" He didn't wait for—obviously didn't require—an answer. Amanda couldn't decide whether he sounded displeased by what Langley had done. "Under the circumstances, I think you'd better stay in that role a while longer."

"Stay?" Langley echoed hoarsely, disbelief etched into his face. "At Bartlett House?"

From the moment he had interrupted her luncheon, Amanda had been aware of a subtle change in his demeanor, his mood. Last night, even this morning, sparks had crackled between them. Dangerous, just as he'd said. A spreading fire that would consume them both if they were not careful.

But somewhere between the drawing room and the morning room, once Jamie had given him the codebook, he'd raised a sort of leaden shield between them, through which those sparks could not travel. To protect her, she'd thought.

Now, however, she wondered whether he had not been trying to protect himself.

"Oh, goodness no," General Scott said with a laugh, plucking his pipe from his mouth.

Langley's posture shifted. Not relief, precisely, but she did not know how else to read his response.

Then the general returned his pipe to his lips and added, "Not Bartlett House. I think it would be best to get all of you quite away from town."

It was Amanda's turn to stiffen with surprise. "Leave London?"

"For a time, yes. The hustle and bustle of city life makes it easier for someone with ill intent to disguise his movements, his intentions. In the country, though, all is out in the open. Watchers are everywhere. Suspicions are more easily raised."

"The country," she repeated. "You would have us go down to Foxhaven, then?"

"In Hampshire, is it not?" General Scott appeared to ponder this option for a moment before shaking his head. "Charming, I'm sure. But a bit too remote for our purposes. And a bit too obvious, as well. There must be somewhere else, somewhat closer to hand…"

All three of them thought in silence. Or rather, Amanda thought. Langley's expression was distant, wooden, slightly alarmed. And General Scott made a show of trying to stir his brain, once more propping his spectacles atop his head and occasionally tapping his temple with the stem of his pipe.

Rather like a schoolmaster giving his wayward pupils time to come up with the proper answer.

Amanda wound a loose thread around her finger, making a slight pucker in the delicate fabric of her ruined skirts. "Would Richmond suit?"

"Richmond?" To her surprise, General Scott directed his gaze to Langley. "An interesting suggestion, don't you agree?" Langley's mouth popped open, but no words came out. The general's attention shifted back to Amanda. "Did you have a particular house in mind?"

"A few nights ago, at the theater, my friends the Hursts extended an invitation to visit them this summer. But I've already refused…"

"I'm sure your friends will be overjoyed to discover you've reconsidered their kind offer." The general leaned toward her and gave an encouraging smile. "From what the Magpie has told me, you're an inordinately clever woman, Lady Kingston. The sort who won't have any great difficulty managing to finagle a renewal of that invitation. Why, you'll soon have them believing it was all their idea to have a houseful of guests this afternoon."

"This afternoon?"

"Best not to delay," said the general, rising. Amanda followed suit, as did Langley, albeit a beat later, as if he was still a little stunned by developments. "Captain Collins will help you to pen and paper. You can write at his desk." He strode to the door and opened it. "Dash off a note to your mother, too, to prepare her for the change of scenery."

"My mother," Amanda murmured, moving toward the door. Then, "My mother! Oh dear, what if it's too late? Something might already have happened to her. I managed to keep her at home yesterday, but when I left, she was determined to pay calls today."

"And she might have done," Langley reminded her quietly, "if I hadn't had the foresight to send your carriage away."

"Oh, yes. That's right. You did." Her heart still raced, but she was determined to present an outward appearance of calm. She rather thought it might be easier if Langley would look at her. But then again, perhaps not.

"You stay here, Stanhope." General Scott nodded him back toward his chair as Amanda crossed the threshold into the outer office. "I'm sure Lady Kingston won't write faster with an audience."

She entered the outer office to find Captain Collins standing beside his desk, its neatness a stark contrast to the general's. At present the only things on its surface were two quills, a pot of ink, and a thin stack of little sheets of hot-pressed paper, the sort ladies—but probably not the British army—used for correspondence. Had he anticipated the general's order? Had the general somehow already known about the Hursts?

She offered Captain Collins a weak sort of smile as she approached. With a slight bow, he pulled out the chair and gestured for her to sit down. The scrape of its legs across the floor further disguised the sound of the general closing the door to his office. As she picked up a pen and weighed the proper words for inviting herself and her family to someone else's home on absurdly short notice, she could hear the muted sounds of masculine conversation from the other room. Though she could not make out a single word, she could not help but wonder what they discussed.

What, exactly, had they not wanted her to hear?

\* \* \* \*

Langley swung himself back into his chair without waiting for the general to sit first. "I wonder, sir, if this is really the best course of action with respect to the Countess of Kingston."

Scott eased into his chair, turning it slightly, so that his gaze was directed at something beyond the window. Without looking, he swept a hand over his cluttered desktop until his fingertips collided with his pipe, which he once more brought to his lips. "Do you object to spending a little time in Richmond, Magpie?"

The tightness in Langley's jaw made it difficult to speak. "Not if you order it, sir."

"I'm glad to hear you're back to following orders. I'd prefer not to have to add 'dealing with a rogue intelligence officer' to the rather lengthy list of things that are currently occupying my time." Once more, he fished beside him, this time retrieving the codebook. "Mrs. Scott is determined to spend a few weeks at the seaside this summer, you see. I'd like to be at liberty to accompany her."

"Yes, sir." Langley leaned forward, propping his elbows on his knees, speaking more softly, though he knew that nothing of what they said could be heard from the outer office. "But why did it have to be Richmond?"

"Because the friends who issued an invitation to Lady Kingston don't live in Bath, Major Stanhope," the general explained with a hint of good-natured mockery before becoming more serious. "Because if we're to keep this innocent family safe, then Mrs. West needs to be somewhere she knows fewer people on whom to call, and Lady Kingston's sons need to be farther away from their guardian."

"So you think Dulsworthy is involved?"

"Obviously, he's involved. The question is, on which side? Too many people are eager to get their hands on this." Scott thwacked the codebook against his palm. "Maybe you'll turn up the answer, eh?"

Langley dropped his head into his hands. Yet another assignment, but never the one that could help restore him to his fellow agents' good graces. Clearly, his retrieval of the codebook hadn't been enough to renew General Scott's faith in him, either.

"Your intimacy with the family could be a great benefit to us," Scott continued.

"Intimacy, sir?" He jerked his chin upward to discover the general fixing him with a piercing blue gaze, as if he could see into Langley's innermost thoughts.

"Yes, yes," he murmured, his eyes narrowing slightly. "Very clever, to present yourself as the tutor. Ideal for intelligence gathering. A trusted confidante within the household. Can mingle with ease both upstairs and down."

Langley nodded at the general's description, though in truth, claiming to be the boys' tutor had been more impulse than calculated disguise. "I decided upon it when Lady Kingston let slip that Dulsworthy was being rather high-handed about the boys' education. He intended to send them away to school without her approval."

Despite the grim picture Langley's words painted, a smile twitched at one corner of the general's mouth. "And you saw an opportunity to aid both country *and* countess, so you took it."

"I suppose so, sir. Yes. But I don't see how Dulsworthy's plans for his wards could explain..." He darted a glance to the codebook.

"Time will tell if there's a connection or not."

"Time Lieutenant Hopkins may not have," Langley countered.

General Scott carefully set the codebook atop a precarious mountain of paperwork. "Leave that to me. You stay focused on Lady Kingston."

Langley hadn't any doubt the man could rattle off the contents of every piece of parchment on his desk, even lay his fingers immediately on whatever he needed, despite the apparent disorder. It was all part and parcel of Scott's performance, the role of a rather muddle-headed old man who in fact commanded a regiment of spies with the snap of his fingers. The chess master who foresaw his unsuspecting opponent's every move before either of them had touched the board.

Somehow, Langley had not understood until just that moment that for all his training, his responsibilities, his promotions, he was still only a pawn.

"Sir, when exactly am I to have told you that the countess is 'an inordinately clever woman'?" he demanded, repeating the general's earlier description of Amanda.

Scott's smile deepened. "Isn't she?"

"That's beside the point."

"Is it?"

Langley's shoulders sagged with something like exhaustion. His life as an intelligence officer defined him. He'd always thrilled to the chase, the cat-and-mouse, as he'd told Amanda. But he was growing tired of playing games he couldn't possibly win. Not today's.

Definitely not last night's.

"Perhaps I was mistaken," Scott began, with all the assurance of a man who was never wrong, "but when you entered this office, I thought I sensed…something between you and Lady Kingston?"

Langley had expected to be met with annoyance, anger, maybe even disappointment if the general ever discovered that he had slept with the woman he was supposed to be guarding.

Instead, Scott looked…hopeful.

Sharply, Langley shook his head, partly to deny the general's insinuation, partly to drive such a thought from his head. He couldn't afford to let what happened last night raise his expectations. It was ridiculous to imagine the general matchmaking at all, let alone between Langley and the Countess of Kingston.

Anyone must see that Amanda deserved better than a street urchin turned spy.

"You've never shied away from a risk, Magpie," the general continued. "Not in the thirty years I've known you. Have you made mistakes in all that time?" Impatiently, Scott waved aside his own question with his free hand. "Of course you have. We all have. But you've also earned both my gratitude and your country's." His gaze softened, though somehow without losing its intensity. "Stop telling yourself you aren't worthy of the rewards."

"Is this about that damned knighthood again?"

"The knighthood." Scott shrugged. "Also a not-insignificant inheritance from the man who was proud to call you his son, though you resisted the label."

"It would have been a lie," Langley insisted.

"Would it?" Scott shook his head, dismissing Langley's objections. "Nevertheless, you now have a title and a home. Perhaps it's time for..." His brows rose once, suggestively, as his bright eyes drifted toward the outer office.

Langley jerked to his feet and strode toward the door without waiting to be dismissed, eager to put an end to this conversation. "I will claim nothing I have not earned."

And a man like him did not deserve a woman like Amanda.

No matter how much he wanted her.

Just as he reached for the knob, Captain Collins tapped on the door from the other side. "Lady Kingston's letters have been sent, sir. She's awaiting your further instructions."

General Scott motioned for Langley to open the door, as if his leaving had been the general's plan all along. "Tell her Major Stanhope will be right out."

In the outer office stood Amanda, her gaze focused on Collins's empty desktop, an expression of stunned disbelief on her face. Hardly had Langley crossed the threshold when her chin lifted and her dark, worried eyes came to rest on him. "When she gets that note, Rebecca Hurst will think I've gone mad," she said, hurrying toward him. Her voice dropped to a whisper. "H-have I?"

*Yes*, he wanted to say when she stretched out her hands for reassurance. *His* reassurance.

Instead, he caught her fingers in his and drew one hand through his arm, so that he might keep her close to his side without raising suspicions. Including hers.

"I for one am quite used to my schemes being thought mad," Scott declared as he came around to stand in front of them, his quick gaze taking in Amanda's fingers curled around Langley's arm, Langley's hand covering hers. "But I know good sense when I see it. And you, my lady, strike me as eminently sensible."

Something—a laugh, a cry of protest—rose in Langley's throat. Amanda must have sensed it. She sent him a look from beneath her lashes, as she'd done that night in the garden, scolding and defiant and vulnerable all at once. He swallowed the sound with an audible gulp.

Scott chuckled, damn him. "Collins, please make the necessary arrangements for Major Stanhope to escort Lady Kingston back to Bartlett House. If she's anything like Mrs. Scott, I'm sure she will wish to oversee the packing." Then he turned to Amanda with a bow. "Enjoy Richmond, my lady. And you, too, Magpie."

Langley made himself nod. Since when did Scott's assignments involve enjoyment?

# Chapter 14

Amanda lay on her back, staring upward, feeling the walls of Charles and Rebecca Hurst's smallest bedchamber pressing in upon her, imagining that she could make out the edges of the carved medallion at the center of the bed's high canopy, though darkness hung thickly all around her. Or perhaps she had been lying there so long, the sky outside the windows actually was beginning to hint at the approach of dawn?

No. Still fathomless, featureless black. Hours to go before morning. She drummed her fingers on the coverlet and sighed.

The Hursts' house possessed lovely gardens at the rear, sloping down through sparse woodlands to the river. Rebecca had made a point of inviting Amanda to stroll in them at any time. But she did not think Rebecca had really intended for her to wander outside in the middle of the night. Besides, it seemed a particularly foolhardy thing to do when someone out there in the world meant her harm.

The same had been true in London, of course, and the abrupt relocation to Richmond was meant to keep her and her family safe. Somehow, though, the unfamiliar surroundings, the oppressive quiet of the country, only made her more ill at ease.

Or perhaps she was just overtired. The muscles of her cheeks ached from maintaining a smile of reassurance, from laughing at herself again and again as she explained to her family that she had been so scatterbrained as to have forgotten to tell any of them about the Hursts' very kind invitation, forgotten even to order the servants to pack. Mama had been most seriously displeased by the turn of events and had spent the majority of their hour-long carriage ride peppering Amanda with questions to which the boys, too, had demanded answers. Answers she had struggled to give.

Langley might have been some help, but he had conveniently elected to go on horseback.

The envy with which she had watched him trot alongside the question-filled carriage had been somewhat muted by the discovery that he would be sharing the hastily made-over attic space with the boys, as the small house's only available guest quarters had been reserved for Amanda and her mother. She imagined him there now, two floors above her, sleeplessly staring at the ceiling too.

General Scott's insistence that he stay with her—with them—had caught Langley off guard. That much was certain. She still could not decide, however, whether he had resented the order. The ride back to Bartlett House from the Horse Guards ought to have given her an opportunity to discover his feelings about the matter, perhaps his feelings about a great many things.

Then again, perhaps his businesslike brusqueness *had* been the answer to her questions and her heart simply refused to accept it.

Not that she had been forming expectations about him, or imagining that Langley being ordered to continue the ruse of tutor might provide an opportunity to repeat last night's activities. The general would be astonished to think his instructions had been interpreted thus!

But surely, that morning, there had been a moment—a moment before Jamie had revealed how the codebook had come into his hands and the day had taken such a strange turn—when she had seen longing in Langley's warm, whisky-colored eyes?

The bed's linens whispered an admonition as she restlessly shifted her hips. *Mind your step.* When exactly had she become a merry widow, not just intrigued by but actually lusting after a devastatingly handsome, entirely unsuitable man?

This was carrying her desire for adventure too far.

Determined to put a stop to such nonsense, she squeezed her eyes shut and drew several deep breaths. Her family was in Richmond under the protection of an officer of the British army because they were in danger. She needed to keep her mind on what was important. And if she hoped to stay alert to threats, she needed rest.

She would not let her thoughts wander to the dark attic, where the air was doubtless so stifling on this early summer night that Langley's nightshirt must be clinging damply to the muscles of his arms and chest—if he had not been forced to shed it entirely.

She absolutely would not let her thoughts wander back to last night....

"Amanda." Mama's groan rose from a mountain of pillows on the opposite side of the enormous bed. "No one is more aware than I that these are hardly ideal arrangements. If I had realized that the Hursts were in the midst of redecorating and could spare just one room—and one bed—for the two of us, I would surely have stayed in London. But as I *am* here… please. Go. To. Sleep."

"Yes, Mama," Amanda agreed, knowing she promised the impossible. Still, she dutifully turned onto her side, punched down her pillow, and settled into it with a sigh. She needed to clear her mind, or else she would be *dreaming* of Langley next.

Closing her eyes, she pictured the swift, clear river sweeping her unruly thoughts out to sea.…

She awoke to a light-filled room and the sounds of children's laughter. *Her* children's. When she twisted her head on the pillow, she discovered herself alone in the bed. The very notion that Mama had already risen, and quietly enough not to disturb Amanda, made her certain that the hour must be late indeed. Tossing back the covers, she slid from the mattress and hurried to the window to investigate.

On the green stood Jamie and Philip, Langley facing them. Evidently, he had been leading them through a series of fencing maneuvers, though the boys wielded long sticks, tree branches by the looks of it, instead of their foils. Doubtless they had gone overlooked in the flurry of packing.

Langley had no weapon, but like yesterday morning, he had shed his coat for ease of movement. It lay draped over a low stone wall, and by the glint of sunlight against some object there, she could guess his spectacles must rest on top of it. Nothing particularly remarkable about the scene.

Except the laughter.

Philip was doubled over with it. Jamie's whole face was drawn up in an almost unrecognizable grin, no hint of the adolescent cynicism with which such an expression—already rare—was usually marred. And as for Langley…

When he was stern and serious, it did something strange and wonderful to her insides. But she was entirely unprepared for what happened when he smiled. Nothing sly or sardonic. Just curved lips, a glimpse of white teeth, crinkles at the corners of his eyes. Yet his face, handsome in its severity, was transformed utterly by it.

Amanda brought her hand to her chest, hardly certain which to blame for its sudden, spreading ache. Pleasure at seeing her sons' happiness. Attraction, no matter how unwise, to Langley. Pain in the knowledge this moment could not last—for any of them.

But they had today. This perfect, sunny summer day, far from the heat and noise and odors of London.

She vowed to make the most of it.

Turning away from the window, she went to the bell and rang for hot water. The maid who brought it helped her dress. Langley had insisted that none of the Bartlett House servants accompany them, rather a difficult proposition to explain to her mother, who relied on Sarah's artistry. Once the girl had gone, Amanda brushed her own hair and arranged it loosely, then made her way downstairs.

In the breakfast room, she found Mama and Rebecca, lingering over their coffee.

"Ah, there you are, my dear," she her mother, lifting her cup to her lips. "I suppose I should not wonder you slept so late, given how you tossed and turned half the night."

"Dear Mrs. West, I do apologize for the cramped accommodations." Though Rebecca rose and turned toward the sideboard as she spoke, Amanda still saw the blush of mortification that stained her cheeks. "The workmen were to have been done already, as workmen always are, it seems, or I should never have extended the invitation to Lady Kingston."

Coming downstairs, Amanda had passed all the evidence of the refurbishing being done to two of the house's four bedrooms—tools, ladders, paint and brushes, rolls of wallpaper, and bolts of fabric. No sign of the men whose trades those tools represented, however. She half wondered whether Langley or even General Scott had seen to it that there would be no strangers in the house.

Amanda's note to the Hursts had left very little room for her friends to decline, though Rebecca's answer, received just as the last boxes were being loaded onto the baggage cart, had hinted that a fortnight's delay in the visit would not be amiss. Amanda had read the note, perfectly understood her friend's dilemma, and had ushered her family into the carriage and come anyway.

What choice did she have?

"Say nothing more of it, Mrs. Hurst," Mama insisted, waving away Rebecca's apology. "You certainly cannot be held responsible for either workmen's recalcitrance or my daughter's...restlessness." She gave off her usual air of softness, clad in her favorite flowing stuff, with her hair perfectly arranged despite the absence of her maid. But she fixed Amanda with a look of pointed curiosity. "I can't think what's come over her."

Amanda gratefully accepted a cup of coffee from Rebecca and sat down. "Excitement, I suppose," she said, letting her gaze drift toward the windows and the fencing lesson beyond. "I hated to waste a minute of our visit."

"Then let's not," declared Rebecca. "Since the weather is so fine, shall I have Cook prepare a picnic lunch for us? We can enjoy it in one of the shady spots along the river." She looked eagerly between her guests.

"Oh, yes." Amanda nodded. "That sounds lovely." Then she glanced hesitantly toward her mother, who generally avoided even the sheltered garden at Bartlett House. "Don't you think, Mama?"

Before her mother could answer, Jamie and Philip burst into the room, both out of breath, their faces gleaming with perspiration and triumph. "Mama," Philip almost shouted, "Jamie's not hopeless after all!"

"Why, thank you, Pip," Jamie retorted, giving his brother a good-natured nudge with one shoulder. "And if it came from anyone but you, I'd treasure the compliment." But he was grinning with pride, nonetheless.

Amanda jumped to her feet and came toward them. At the same moment, Langley crossed the threshold of the breakfast parlor behind her sons. He drew up short and cleared his throat gruffly, all stern tutor now, properly clad once more in coat and spectacles.

But behind those spectacles, his eyes glittered with barely suppressed amusement, and there was something more than appealing in the way the knot of his cravat had worked loose. "Remember," he said, fixing the boys with a firm look, "gentlemen do not boast."

"Don't they?" Amanda smiled. "Then I must say, I have met very few gentlemen. Are you hungry?" she asked her sons. "Mrs. Hurst was just suggesting a picnic by the river."

"Brilliant," declared Jamie.

Philip gave an eager nod. "I'm famished."

Amanda tousled his damp hair. "Of course you are." She glanced toward the doorway. "Will you join us, Mr. Stanhope?"

The amusement in his eyes hardened into wryness as he met her gaze. "I—"

*I never eat luncheon.* She watched the words form in his thoughts before they formed on his lips. As if to ward off their blow, she turned slightly toward her chair before he could speak the rejection.

"I should be delighted, your ladyship." She spun back in time to watch him bow, first to her and then to Rebecca. "Thank you for the invitation."

The strange feeling in her chest—the one that didn't quite know whether it was pain or pleasure—swelled a bit more, forcing her to draw a sharp breath. Wanting him was one thing. But wanting his company? His companionship?

Magpies weren't meant to be kept as pets.

Less than hour later, the seven of them set out from the back terrace, the bursting hamper carried between Langley and Charles Hurst, Jamie with an armload of sturdy quilts on which they were to sit. No small army of servants to accompany them. No crates of china and silver. No furniture except the small collapsible chair Pip was struggling to keep folded as he walked along with it under one arm.

Amanda was astonished her mother had agreed to the proposal of luncheon outdoors. Even the offer of a chair hardly raised it to her notion of respectability. Mama did not look displeased, however, as she walked along arm in arm with Rebecca, the afternoon light filtering through her parasol and bathing both ladies in a warm glow.

When they reached their destination, Amanda helped Jamie unfold the quilts and spread them in the shade of a willow tree. Pip set up his grandmother's chair, muttering to himself and sucking on a pinched thumb. Meanwhile Langley and Mr. Hurst unpacked the hamper: hand pies and cheese and fresh-picked strawberries; bottles of white wine and lemonade.

Amanda chose a place and arranged her skirts about her before accepting a glass of wine from Mr. Hurst. Soon, they were all seated together. Langley lounged easily with one knee drawn up to his chest, one leg outstretched, near enough to her that she caught an occasional whiff of his shaving soap. Her traitorous body urged her to lean closer still to him, to draw in a deep lungful of that spicy scent, which conjured powerful memories of...oh, heavens. Had it really only been the night before last?

Though the food was excellent, the real attraction of the outing for most of the group was the river, here hardly more than a tranquil stream. Soon enough, the boys were declaring the day unbearably hot, a condition that could be remedied best through dipping their bare feet in the Thames. Even Mama and Rebecca expressed a desire to stroll down to the water. A few moments later they rose and left, one on either of Mr. Hurst's arms.

"Shall we join them?" Langley asked.

"Do you wish to?"

He appeared to think seriously about his reply. "No."

Uncertain what to make of the response, Amanda took refuge behind closed eyes, leaning back and tipping up her face to the blue sky mostly hidden behind willow branches. "It's lovely here."

"An excellent reprieve for Jamie and Philip," he agreed. "In my experience, growing boys are better off away from the London air."

As the leaves shifted in the breeze, sunlight dappled her eyelids and painted her face with splotches of warmth. "Not just growing boys."

When he did not reply, she finally worked up the courage to look at him. He held a juicy strawberry, the green hull pinched between forefinger and thumb. When he offered it to her, he did so in a manner that suggested he expected her to nibble it from his fingers.

A newly familiar hunger pulsed deep inside her—nothing at all to do with fruit.

"I shouldn't," she whispered.

"I know."

Then, with a wicked smile, he popped the berry into his own mouth, his even, white teeth separating the fruit from its stem as precisely as any knife. After flicking the hull beyond the edge of the blanket on which they sat, he held out that same hand to her. "Walk with me, Lady Kingston."

His fingertips were stained pink with juice. Instead of pressing her lips to their sweetness, as she longed quite desperately to do, she did something still less wise. She laid her palm across his and accepted his assistance to rise.

"Should we tell the others where we're going?"

His warm gaze hardly left her face as he darted a glance toward the river. "I hinted to your friend Mrs. Hurst that I hoped to find a moment today to discuss your intentions for the boys' lessons while we're on holiday. If anyone notices we're gone," he said as he turned her back toward the house, "she'll say that's what we must be up to."

"And are we going to discuss the boys' lessons?" she asked a few moments later, blaming her slight breathlessness on the upward slope of the path leading to the house.

A hint of a smile curved at the corner of his mouth. "No."

To her surprise, they did not go inside when they reached the terrace, but skirted the eastern corner of the red brick house and walked on, up the drive and toward the road. "I do seem to find myself asking this question with distressing regularity of late, but…where are you taking me?"

"There's something I want to show you."

She sent a glance over her shoulder, though the river was long out of sight. "And you're certain Jamie and Philip are safe?"

"Are you worried about the water? Or something else?"

"I—I don't—"

Good heavens, she was being as overprotective as her own mother.

"Three adults ought to be able to keep two smart lads from falling into trouble in a river that's hardly knee deep," he said, when she could not find words for her fears. "And as for the rest..." He patted her hand where it lay on his arm, and then did not take his away. The gentle pressure of his fingertips grounded her, tamped down her anxiety. "Hurst is a sensible fellow and suspects, I think, that you are not here just because you took a sudden liking to the idea of a holiday. He'll have his guard up. I've spoken with every servant in the household. All trustworthy sorts, employed here for more than a year. And General Scott was right: in this part of the country, any outsider will attract notice."

"Why do I have the feeling you aren't speaking generally about life in small towns and villages?" She recalled his expression yesterday morning, in the general's office, when she'd named where the Hursts lived. "Do you have some particular familiarity with this one?"

They had walked perhaps a quarter of a mile down the road—hardly more than a lane—and were only now coming in sight of another house, this one slightly larger than the Hursts' and fashioned of stone.

"As luck would have it, I do," Langley said, pausing at the end of its curving drive. "This was Benjamin Stanhope's house."

She dared an upward glance. His eyes were narrowed, staring toward the house, but not at it. Staring into the past, as he had the night he'd told her the story of his youth.

The fingertips of her free hand flew to her lips, stifling a thousand questions. Just one managed to escape on a trembling breath. *"Was?"*

He did not hear it, or pretended not to, at any rate. "Will we have a look around?"

All was quiet, as if even the house awaited her answer. "The present owner will not mind?"

"The present owner will be greatly troubled, I expect. Nonetheless..." He reached into his breast pocket and withdrew something in a clenched fist. "I'm asking you to take yet another risk. With me."

Then he uncurled his fingers, revealing an iron key.

# Chapter 15

From the moment in Scott's office when Amanda had pronounced the word *Richmond* and Scott had declared it an *interesting suggestion*, Langley had been steeling himself against the experience of swinging open this door and ushering her across this threshold.

He might have said nothing, of course. Let the Hursts' proximity to the Stanhopes' house go unremarked.

He had dismissed that possibility almost as soon as it crossed his mind. He couldn't be so close and not pay his respects to the home that had sheltered him—even when the very notion of shelter had seemed abhorrent.

But he also knew he could not make the visit alone.

Paintings and furniture, shrouded in coarse holland cloth, pressed on his vision like so many ghosts. He strode to a window in the sitting room and thrust open the draperies, let a wide stripe of sunlight drive a few of those spirits away. "The caretakers, Mr. and Mrs. Morris, do not live in. No need to keep the house at the ready. I—I never visit."

Amanda was making a slow circle, taking in everything. More than she had expected? Less? He watched her trail her fingertips over the dusty slopes and valleys of cloth that covered a camelback sofa, where he had first sat thirty years before and looked about himself with greedy-eyed wonder.

"I understand. I too prefer London to the country." She untied the ribbons of her bonnet and laid it aside on an empty table. "Or think that I do. Until I'm actually…in the country."

By any measure, it was a strange reply to make. But stranger still was the fact that he understood what she meant. The way one could persuade herself—or himself—that the memories of a place were too painful to bear, until one was forced to confront them and discovered those memories

were themselves a sort of balm. The way the hustle and bustle of town got
into his blood, made it race, until he was convinced that dull country life
would be the death of him, only to get there and discover…peace.

The way the heady danger he craved had begun to look far less like
rushing down a dark alleyway in pursuit of a fellow spy, and more and
more like standing in a half-lit room bearing his soul, his very self, to
this woman.

"Come." He turned back toward the entry hall. "Let me give you a little
tour of the place."

Every room was its own chapter of the story of his youth here. The
dining room, where Sophia Stanhope had once picked up a bowl of soup
and drunk from its brim, when she'd seen him struggling with his spoon.
The library, where Benjamin had been wise enough simply to sit and
read to himself, until Langley had demanded to know the secrets of those
marks on paper, how they could produce laughter or tears. The drawing
room where the pair of them had taught him to walk and sit and bow and
even dance like a gentleman—all the knowledge he'd hoarded, like the
magpie he was, until he was no longer sure what was truly his and what
he'd managed to steal from right beneath their noses.

Amanda laid her slender fingers on yet another door. "And this?"

"My bedchamber."

The words lit a blush across her cheekbones. He expected her hand to
fall away, for them to continue down the corridor.

Instead, she made a little noise of interest in her throat and reached for
the doorknob. "I should like to see where you slept," she said, opening the
door. "Or did you lie awake nights, even then?"

"Sometimes," he confessed.

Sometimes he had laid on his back and tears had leaked from the
corners of his eyes until his pillow was damp. Had that bewildered boy
been weeping for what he'd lost, or what he'd found?

That was a question for which he still had no answer.

Once inside, he walked to the window and sent yet another pair of dusty
draperies scooting merrily along their rod, driving out the darkness. If he
ever came back to this house to live, he supposed he would be expected
to occupy the master's chamber. It was what Benjamin and Sophia had
intended. What they would have wanted. Doubtless Amanda would find
that room more to her taste, with its elegant furnishings and larger windows
overlooking the river.

But when he turned away from the window, she was standing beside
his bed, one hand resting on a sturdy, carved bedpost, watching him. Dust

motes danced in the beam of sunshine he'd let in, a path of light leading, improbably, from him to her.

He forgot to think about the past. Or the future.

He simply followed that path.

The sunlight picked out the threads of gold in her brown hair, along with a scattering of most unladylike freckles across the bridge of her pert nose. Her dark eyes glittered. She was so perfectly, breathtakingly lovely to him, so bright and shining. No wonder his greedy soul had been drawn to her from the first.

With the unhurried smoothness of a practiced thief, he raised his hand to cup her cheek, brushing his thumb over her velvety skin. She nestled easily into his palm.

"Amanda." Would her ear catch that breathless note, incredulity at his own good fortune? "I swear when I brought you here, I had no intentions—well, no real expectation of…" He let his gaze wander to the bed behind her.

"Oh?" Her brows rose, then settled again, giving her warm regard a seductive cast. "I did."

She released the bedpost and laid her palm on his chest, slipping between his coat and waistcoat, sliding upward to his shoulder, curling her fingers around his neck. Then she lifted herself onto her toes and brought her mouth to his, the touch impossibly soft, more the suggestion of a kiss than a kiss itself.

He held himself still, savoring those little brushes of strawberry sweetness as she traced his lips with hers. Just this once, he would not waste the present moment in looking ahead to future dangers. No longer a starving, scrounging boy, but a wealthy man settling in to a feast, secure in the knowledge that the banquet would not be swept away before he'd had his fill.

When her other hand came to grip his waist, tugging him even closer, he wrapped his arms around her and returned her kiss with one of his own. A leisurely exploration of every dip and curve. A sweep of just the tip of his tongue across the seam of her lips, no deeper. Every tempting, teasing trick his mouth knew—without leaving hers, at least—until she gave up what he sought: that little groan of pleasure, of surrender, that made him instantly, achingly hard.

He rewarded her with a string of nibbled kisses along her jaw, a whisper in her sensitive ear. "So which is it to be today, my lady? The gentleman, or the rogue?"

He'd made his peace with what she wanted from him—or told himself he had.

But her answer stole his breath.

"You." Her throat rippled beneath his lips as she swallowed and said it again. "You."

Smiling to himself, he lifted his mouth to her temple, pressed it with a kiss. *You.* So simple.

So impossible.

Or was it? After all, the Countess of Kingston had seen through his every disguise.

His fingers rose to the fastenings of her gown as he murmured against her hair. "I want to see every inch of you, too, Amanda."

"Yes." She nudged his coat over his shoulders, until he had to pause and shed it. "But first you must tell me whether any of your assignments have ever involved you playing lady's maid. Under the circumstances, it would seem I chose poorly when I dressed this morning. Are you prepared to be the one to do up everything you undo?"

"I'll manage." He laid his spectacles on the bedside table, then tossed his coat onto a nearby chair, sending up a little cloud of dust. "Turn around."

Dress, petticoat, stays, shift—he made quick work of every layer, pausing to admire, first with his eyes and then with his touch, every bit of skin he revealed. Her slender arms, the sharp jut of her shoulder blades, the dip of her waist, the curve of her backside, and finally, the damp hollow at the joining of her thighs. When he slipped a fingertip into her wetness, she moaned and set her legs ever so slightly apart. "Yes," she hissed, leaning forward to grip the coarse covering of the bed in her fists, inviting him to plunder her.

"Not yet," he murmured against her shoulder, keeping his touch light and teasing. "You must undress me first."

When he slid his fingers from her sheath, she whimpered in protest but turned to face him nonetheless. The sun fell across her small, high breasts, and their rosy-brown tips made his mouth water. But she was intent on unbuttoning his waistcoat and unknotting his cravat, a charming notch of concentration in her brow.

Once she'd tugged his shirt free, he stepped back enough to strip it off over his head and sent it to join his coat. "Shall I help you with the boots, too?" he offered, lovely as it would be to watch her straddle his thigh, bend over, and pull them off, one by one.

And then it was down to his breeches. No disguising his arousal tenting the light wool. Her hand went eagerly to the buttons of his fall, then paused.

"I've never..." She was watching her fingertip circle one button. He wished he could see her eyes. "At least, not by daylight."

He waited a moment for her to say more, his mind hurriedly filling in the missing words with increasingly alarming possibilities.

*I've never* seen a naked man. *At least, not by daylight.*

*I've never* touched a man. *At least, not by daylight.*

*I've never* lain with a man. *At least, not by daylight.*

Before he could reassure her, stay her hand, offer to take his pleasure only in hers, she had slipped that first button free, then the next, and the next. "Can we…can we move just a little closer to the window, so I can see properly?"

A breath shuddered from him. "As you wish, my lady."

She took his hand, stepped lightly from the puddle of her skirts, and turned him to face the sun. Then her clever fingers made quick work of the remaining buttons. His cock jutted forward, impossibly hard and dark with need, as his breeches slid down his legs.

Amanda dropped to her knees. "Oh." That breath of sound whispered coolly over his heated flesh, followed in another moment by her curious, too gentle touch. "It really looks nothing like those marble statues would have one believe."

"It does look like that *sometimes*," he managed to grind out, willing himself not to lose control as her exploration grew more sure. "Though generally not when a lady is so, uh, close."

"And what would happen if I"—one fingertip circled the head—"kissed you, just here?"

"Christ, Amanda." It was his turn to grip the bedpost. "I'd spend—and far quicker than a man ought."

Their conversation alone had brought him perilously near it.

"Oh." Now disappointment edged her voice. "And I suppose that would be the end of our fun."

He curled the fingers of his free hand around the back of her head, fighting with every fiber of his being the instinct to urge her closer. "It most assuredly would not. Because I'd like nothing better than the chance to return the favor, and there's nothing like a woman's cry of ecstasy to rouse a man to life again."

"Return the favor?" Her gaze darted upward, surprise and delight mingled in her dark eyes. "Surely you don't mean…?"

"Oh, I do."

The tip of her tongue darted out, to wet her lips, he thought. Then he felt its comparative coolness against his hot skin. He tightened his fingers against her scalp, drawing her back the merest fraction of an inch. "Only if you're certain, my dear. And only as long as it pleases you, too."

At her eager nod, he relaxed his hand just enough that she could have her way with him—soft kisses at first, then experimental flicks of her tongue, and at last drawing half his length right into the heat of her mouth. She hadn't the faintest notion of what she was doing…and he wished it would go on forever.

But too soon—though not, thank God, quite as quickly as he'd feared—his climax was upon him. He tried to coax her to stop. Gentleman or rogue, he couldn't bring himself to believe that a lady, particularly one of no experience, would thank him for finishing in such a fashion. She refused to heed his warning, however. Her hands, which had been splayed on his thighs, slid around his legs, her fingertips gripping the tightly clenched muscles of his buttocks as he came with a shout.

Afterward, she rocked back onto her heels, a satisfied grin on her faces as she dabbed at one corner of her mouth with her discarded shift. "That was exhilarating."

"God, love." He gave a breathless laugh, the air sawing in and out of his burning lungs. "I'm delighted to hear it. But you've quite wrung me out."

In a single, fluid motion, she rose, tipped her head to the side, and fixed him with a look. "Are you going back on your promise, Major Stanhope?"

"Not on your life, Lady Kingston."

Turning to the bed, he flipped back the coarse dust cover to reveal a dark blue coverlet, and beneath that, bed linens that bore no sign of mustiness. As if, despite his admonitions, Mrs. Morris kept the house ever ready for his return.

A lump of something—guilt, affection—rose in his throat. He didn't deserve that mark of confidence in him, any more than he deserved this house. And he certainly did not deserve the adventurous, beautiful woman who at that moment was running her hands over his shoulders.

But perhaps love was not simply a reward parceled out only to the deserving?

Battling down a surge of emotion, he twisted and caught Amanda in his arms. She giggled as he scooped her up and deposited her on the bed. Then, suddenly shy, she reached for the sheet to cover herself as he pressed his knee into the mattress, preparing to join her.

He laid two fingers on her hand. "Only if you're certain," he reminded her. "And only as long as it pleases you, too."

She nodded, a trifle uncertainly. "Is there—is there such a thing as too much pleasure, I wonder?"

Smiling, he brushed his fingertips over the delicate skin on the back of her hand. "Shall we risk it?"

Her lips quirked and she nodded again, this time with eagerness.

As he climbed onto the bed and prowled toward her, she shifted her hips lower, reaching up and pulling him down to her. He claimed her mouth first, then kissed his way down her throat, over her collarbone to her pert, perfect breasts, laving and sucking each nipple in turn until she began to whimper and squirm beneath him. Moving lower, he darted his tongue into her navel, pressed his lips to the curve of her belly.

"Open your legs."

The words sounded gruffer than he'd intended, his voice rough with desire. But she did not hesitate, her knees parting to make a space for him as he dipped his head to nip her inner thigh.

And then, return the favor he did, teasing her just as she had done, with warm breath and soft kisses, the brush of fingertips over her crisp, dark curls, until her hips were lifting from the mattress in a silent plea. He slid his fingers deeper, parted those curls, and set his mouth to her at last, lapping at her spicy wetness and flicking his tongue over her nub. Gently, so gently—at first, because he did not want to startle her with the intensity of the sensation, and then to prolong the sweet agony of it. Her fingers curled in the bedsheets and a keening cry rose in her throat, making his cock leap.

Then her hand left the bed to tangle in his hair, boldly urging him closer as he had been so tempted to urge her. He needed no second invitation, sliding one palm beneath her bottom to lift her pelvis to his mouth, licking and sucking until she shattered.

Afterward, he crawled back up the bed and stretched along her side, one arm wrapped lightly around her body until she drifted back to earth, murmuring, "That was…"

"Exhilarating?" he teased. "Speaking only for myself, of course."

She smiled. "I think that must be a trick only rogues know. Not gentlemen."

"You, my dear, have met all the wrong gentlemen. The sort who think the only respectable sort of sex happens in a bed, with the woman lying on her back and the man on top." As he spoke, he levered himself over her, parting her knees with his thigh. He suddenly needed, quite desperately, to be inside her.

"Not up against a door?" she asked, encircling his ribs with her hands.

He caught her ankle, raised her knee almost to her chest as he sank into her with one deep thrust. "Certainly not." Holding her gaze, he tilted his hips and watched her eyes widen with the discovery of what that perfect angle could do. "And never in broad daylight."

Before she could offer another retort, he began to move in her, slowly, steadily, alternating shallow strokes with deeper ones, until she was panting beneath him, her nails sharp against his back. She hooked her other leg around his hip and met him, nudge for nudge, thrust for thrust. When the pulse of her orgasm called forth his, he jerked from her body at the last possible moment, spilling his seed against the sheets.

Exhaling deeply, he collapsed beside her, and she snugged drowsily against his shoulder, like a cat curled up in a beam of sunshine.

Never in his past exploits could he have imagined the particular pleasures of sex in his own house, his own bed. He'd never thought anything that smacked of cozy domesticity could appeal to him.

Now, he found himself fighting sleep, just for the chance to watch Amanda doze.

Perhaps this was what people meant when they spoke of making love? Oh, the bitter irony of reveling in such a moment with a woman who thought of him only as an opportunity to escape her own domestic prison, and temporarily at that.

*You haven't the first idea how dull my life is.*

Bending, he pressed a kiss to her hair. "I think, my dear, we'd best get back to the Hursts."

She jerked awake, blinked up at him for a moment as the words sank through the haze of sleep and sex, then scrambled upright in the bed. "How long have we been here? What will Mama think?"

"Simply tell them, we decided on a stroll so as not to waste the lovely afternoon." As spoke, he reluctantly extracted himself from the bed and began to dress. "On the matter of lessons, we discussed tongues, primarily," he said with a wink.

"Oh." The prettiest blush stained her cheeks. "Yes, of course."

"And I've concluded that your sons need additional work in Greek."

"I'm not surprised." She slid to the edge of the mattress and fished for her stockings with her toes. "Mrs. Plinkton's Academy did not offer it, you see."

"But they did offer Latin?"

She shook her head. "I used my pin money to pay a curate for extra lessons," she explained as she came forward clad only in her shift and expertly knotted his cravat. "In mathematics, so everyone at the school thought, though in truth it was always my best subject. But sadly I could find no one willing to teach a lady Greek."

*I'll teach you,* he nearly said.

But what a ridiculous offer. As if he were really a tutor, and not an intelligence officer. An intelligence officer in danger of forgetting his mission.

"Now," she said, dangling her corset from her fingers. "Let's see how clever you really are."

Though every part of him rebelled against the unnatural act, he managed somehow to lace up the corset and then fasten her dress—in short, he made himself hide from view everything he knew he'd never tire of looking at.

When he was done, she ran a hand down her side, gave a satisfied nod at the job he'd done, then lifted that same hand to her hair. "I'll need even more help for this."

Wordlessly, he stepped toward the shapeless mound of holland cloth draped over the wash stand and caught the corner of yet another covering between his fingers, looping it back to reveal a pier glass. She hurried forward, investigated her reflection with a frown, and began to pluck the pins from her hair. He held out one palm to collect them, which earned him a grateful smile. Watching her, knowing he was responsible for that well-tumbled look she was struggling to disguise, was yet another of the day's unexpected pleasures.

"That will have to do, I guess," she said at last. "Thankfully, my bonnet will—oh, what did I do with my bonnet?"

"Downstairs," he reminded her as he let the cloth drop and turned to make a cursory attempt at straightening the bed, while uttering a silent apology to Mrs. Morris. "We'll pick it up on our way out."

In the sitting room, he handed the bonnet to her, wanting to sneak one last kiss before she donned it and its wide brim put her lips quite out of reach. But he settled for tying the bow beneath her chin at a jaunty angle. "There. No one need suspect a thing."

He'd hidden away so many parts of himself, he hadn't expected that speaking of concealment could be painful. Or that his last look around the house would be infused with new memories—of where she had stood, the places her hands had rested. He hadn't felt this confused in thirty years.

"Amanda," he said quietly as he turned the key in the lock, uncertain what his next words would be.

But she was already down the steps, too far away to hear them anyway.

No more than a quarter of an hour later, they were crossing the Hursts' threshold, and Mrs. West was coming toward them.

"We decided to discuss the boys' lessons while taking a stroll." Amanda offered the explanation without prompting. He suspected she had been rehearsing it in her head, as they'd walked all the way home in silence. "So as not to waste the lovely afternoon."

Mrs. West nodded. "Did you pass the boys on your way back?"

Instinct, experience—he hardly knew to what he ought to attribute the shock of sudden awareness that passed down his spine. "The boys?" he echoed.

Now Hurst stepped into the entry hall, an open book in his hands. "Ah, there you are," he said, hardly looking up. "Mrs. West has told you, I suppose, that Lord Dulsworthy called not an hour ago, asking to take the boys for a drive."

Familiar guilt slammed into him like a well-aimed punch, and he had to struggle to right himself in time to catch Amanda as she slumped to the floor in a faint.

# Chapter 16

Someone was shaking Amanda's shoulder, rousing her. Was she to be allowed no rest at all? She couldn't quite remember *why* she didn't want to wake up—something hovered at the edge of her consciousness, something she couldn't bear to examine. *No, no.* That was just Mama, leaning over her, saying something about the heat, the sun. Muttering under her breath about the tutor presuming to give orders to her and to Mr. Hurst.

The tutor…

"Jamie! Pip!" Amanda sat bolt upright and almost fell back again when the blood rushed to her head.

Mama was fanning her with the brim of her own bonnet—when had it been removed? And there was Rebecca hurrying toward her with a pillow in one hand and a glass of something in the other.

"A cordial," she explained, pressing the little glass into Amanda's hand. "To help revive you. You must've walked quite a long way. This heat is extraordinary."

"It's not—it's not the heat." She struggled free of their hands and tried to rise. Just a few yards away, Langley stood speaking to Mr. Hurst in a low but urgent voice; Mr. Hurst was shaking his head in disbelief. "They're gone. I should never have left them."

"The boys are with their guardian, my dear," her mother reminded her patiently. "Everything's fine. I don't see any need for worry.…"

"Drink this," Rebecca pleaded.

At first, Amanda refused. Her head was muddled enough already. If everyone would just be quiet, so she could hear what Langley was saying. But then she thought of Jamie and Philip, George, a codebook so valuable another man might already be dead because of it.…

She snatched the glass from Rebecca's fingers and tossed the sweet liquid down her throat, wishing it were brandy.

Her sputtering cough drew Langley's notice, though he avoided her gaze. "I'll be after them as soon as a horse is brought round, Lady Kingston."

"After them?" Mama frowned, first at him, then at her. "Why on earth—?"

Amanda returned the glass to Rebecca, scrambled to her feet, and took her mother's hand. "The boys may be in danger."

"Danger? Surely you don't mean to suggest that Lord Dulsworthy—?"

"I can't explain right now, Mama," she interrupted with a squeeze of her fingers. "There's too much. You'll just have to trust that Mr. Stanhope knows what he's talking about—more than he can say."

Langley turned back to Mr. Hurst. "I would not ask if it were not of vital importance."

Charles glanced downward. He was holding a closed book in one hand, and pinned to its cover by his thumb was a small, cream-colored rectangular card on which something had been written. Amanda would have been willing to wager most anything that on the reverse of that card was an etching of a bird.

"Yes, Mr. Stanhope," Charles agreed with a nod. "But it's a part of town into which I've never traveled—a place in which I have no wish to be seen. You understand, I think, my hesitation?"

Disgust etched hard lines on Langley's face. "Lives are at stake, Mr. Hurst. Surely a man of sense, such as yourself, values life above reputation?"

Rebecca rushed to her husband's side. "Oh, Charles!"

"I'm going too." Amanda released her mother's hand and stepped into the fray on feet that were not quite steady.

"Forgive my bluntness, Lady Kingston." Langley still would not meet her eye. "But you most certainly are not."

"You would rather waste time trying to stop me? They're my *sons*. And this—all of this—is my fault."

"How can you—?" He bit off the next words, though Amanda suspected she knew what they would have been.

*How can you be so obstinate?*

And if Langley wasn't thinking it, then Mama certainly was. "Amanda," she scolded. "I won't hear of you putting yourself in danger—neither to life nor reputation."

"Well, Mama," Amanda snapped, "at least my gowns will be safe."

Mama closed the distance Amanda had put between them, one hand extended, worry notching her brow. "You're...you're not well, dear. I think it would be best if you lie down for a bit. Some cool spot. If you would help us, Mrs. Hurst…"

At just that moment, a servant stepped into the hall. "Your horse is ready, sir."

Rather than move toward the door, Langley's dark gaze darted among Amanda, her mother, and the Hursts. Why was he hesitating?

"Have the horses put to Lady Kingston's carriage, quick as you can," he told the servant, who nodded and was gone in an instant. "You," he said, turning toward Mr. Hurst, "take the horse and deliver this message instead, to General Scott at the Horse Guards—and only to him. Explain that while Lady Kingston was out for a walk, Lord Dulsworthy collected her sons and we do not know where he's taken them. Tell him—tell him the Magpie sent you." He nodded to the card. "Show him that, if you perceive he has any doubts." Charles nodded and was off.

Amanda shook herself free of her mother's clinging hands. "And you?" she demanded of Langley. "What do you mean to do?"

He looked her up and down, still never meeting her eye, and shook his head. "It seems I'll be in the carriage. With you."

An eternity later, as they stood beneath the portico, Rebecca and Mama murmuring together, Langley pacing off to one side, Amanda heard the crunch of gravel that announced the arrival of her carriage.

She could hardly wait for the groomsman to put down the step before she clambered inside. Langley sprang in afterward, thumping the side of his fist against the ceiling to urge the driver into motion. With fingers she could hardly make work, Amanda managed to lower the window and called out a parting reassurance to her mother and her dear friend. "Don't worry. The boys and I will be fine. Mr. Stanhope will see to it." Then she collapsed against the squab, watching her mother wave them down the road with an already tear-stained handkerchief.

"You oughtn't to make promises on my behalf." Langley was sitting across from her in the rear-facing seat, staring out the opposite window as the greens of early summer sped past. "Particularly not ones I'm not certain I can keep, my lady."

She could not help but note the distant, formal address, even though they were alone. Even though, an hour before, they had…

"I mean to see that you keep this one, Major Stanhope," she said. "At least with respect to my sons."

He made no reply. Given his rigid posture, it seemed entirely possible the words had bounced off without penetrating.

With nervous fingers, she pleated the fabric of her skirt, then swallowed and jutted her chin forward, feigning bravery. "I would give my life for my children. That is no platitude, sir." She blinked back the tears that stung her eyes and swallowed again to stave off the sob rising in her throat. How long could she keep her terror at bay through sheer force of will? "I have no fear for myself."

Still without turning toward her, he whispered, "I do."

Two simple words. Easy to imbue them with a great deal of meaning— perhaps a great deal more than she ought. Nevertheless, they broke the floodgates. Tears streamed steadily, silently down her face.

And then, she wasn't quite sure how, he was beside her, enfolding her in his arms as the carriage rattled on. He tossed her bonnet on the seat where he'd been and drew her head down to his chest. She let herself take comfort in the steady drumbeat of his heart.

"This is *my* fault," he said. "I knew better. Or ought to have done. I let myself be distracted once during a mission, and it cost a man his life. Even knowing the weight of that guilt, I...I let myself be distracted once again. I still—"

"Don't," she sobbed, raising a fingertip to his lips to put a stop to further self-recrimination.

Those lips. Thin, with a sharp bow. Rarely soft or smiling, yet surprisingly sensual. How well she had come to know them. How well they had come to know her. Heat flared in her cheeks at the memory of the pleasure that mouth had given her....

*Oh, God.* How could she even think of such things at a time like this? He spoke of being distracted, but she had provided the distraction. If anyone was to blame for what had happened to the boys, it was she.

Langley seemed to read her thoughts. He caught her hand in his, stroked the center of her palm with the pad of his thumb, then kissed her fingertip and drew it away from his mouth. "Whatever happens," he insisted, "you mustn't blame yourself."

"Then who?" she choked out past a fresh wave of tears.

"Put the blame squarely where it belongs," he said, squeezing her fingers.

She dragged in a steadying breath. "All right, then. I blame George."

Even as she said it, she could hardly believe it. *Lord Dulsworthy* and *codebook* and *kidnapping* were not words that belonged in the same sentence—in the same conversation!

"It doesn't quite seem possible, does it?" he agreed. "Or probable, at least. I confess I've had a difficult time persuading myself to be as suspicious of him as I obviously ought to have been. I should at least have warned the boys…"

She shook her head. "None of that, now. *He's* responsible. In fact, I wonder…" The suggestion that rose to her lips was so ridiculous, she could barely bring herself to utter it. "If you don't have a better plan, I think we should go to Lord Dulsworthy's. If we find him at home, we can confront him and force him to tell us what he knows."

"Confront him? Tell us?" Langley stared down at her, as if seeking assistance in untangling the meaning of what she'd said. "What sort of kidnapper would be daft enough to return to his own home immediately after the crime and then reveal what he's done?"

Laying a hand on his chest, she pushed herself upright, favoring him with raised eyebrows and a patient, prompting expression.

His disbelief was palpable. "No, surely not. Not even Dulsworthy could be so…"

Amanda quirked her lips and lifted one shoulder.

With a heavy sigh and a shake of his head, Langley extracted himself and leaned forward to slide open the little door that allowed passengers to communicate with the coach's driver. "Brook Street," he ordered. "And can't you make those horses go any faster? A fool's errand," he then declared to her, as the coachman cracked his whip and the carriage jolted, tossing Langley back onto the seat beside Amanda.

"Let us pray Lord Dulsworthy is just such a fool."

* * * *

Even as the coach swayed to a stop before Dulsworthy's town house, Langley had his doubts about whether he'd made the right decision. No, that wasn't true. He knew very well he'd made quite a number of wrong decisions.

The only problem was where to begin tallying them.

He never should have brought Amanda along on what was, at best, a wild goose chase. If Dulsworthy's plan was to hold Jamie and Philip hostage, to exchange them for the codebook, how could he expect her to calmly accept the inevitable conclusion that the codebook—the security of the nation—must be preserved…at all costs?

And when asked to choose between her and his duty to the Crown, what would he do?

Absent the carpet and awning that had been erected for the night of the ball, Dulsworthy's house looked comparatively plain for Mayfair, its only adornment the large stone urn at the top of the steps, from which spilled some flowering vine. Langley stepped down from the coach, then held up a hand to Amanda, marveling at her outward calm. Her bonnet once more hid her eyes from his view as he helped her out of the carriage and up the steps.

Mr. Evans, the butler, opened to his knock. "Why, Lady Kingston. I did not know you were expected," he said, bowing them over the threshold, hardly sparing Langley a glance.

"I wasn't. But I need to speak with Lord Dulsworthy at once."

Evans's eyes shifted toward the stairs. "I do not know if his lordship is home to callers this afternoon, my lady."

"But he's here?" Langley demanded. "That'll do." He shifted his grip to Amanda's elbow and steered her toward the stairs as the butler gawked after them. "No need to trouble yourself. We'll announce ourselves."

On a hunch, he directed their steps toward the study, trying not to think of his and Amanda's last encounter in that room as he swung open the door. This time, all was not in darkness, though the draperies were partly closed. Seated behind the desk, Dulsworthy lifted his head from his hands, his elbows still propped on the desktop. The man's bleary expression made clear that the tumbler of brandy beside him was half-empty, rather than half-full.

"Well, Dulsworthy," Langley demanded, "where are they?"

But Dulsworthy had eyes only for Amanda, who stood frozen just inside the doorway. "You shouldn't be here. A lady shouldn't see a gen'leman like thish—this."

"It doesn't matter," she told him.

He heaved a wet sigh. "I s'pose you'll never marry me now?"

Her mouth was set in a thin line, as if she were trying to hold back words better left unspoken—or perhaps a scream. "I was never going to marry you anyway, George," she said after a moment. "Is that what this is about? Another of your schemes to try to force my hand?"

"No, no. I shwear it," Dulsworthy protested. "I wouldn't—oh, what's the ushe? You'll never forgive me, either."

"I daresay that will depend on the degree of forgiveness required," she answered with surprising calm. "Now, what's happened to Jamie and Philip? Where are they?"

Dulsworthy shook his head, the wobbly, drunken gesture reminiscent of a trained bear with a sore ear.

Langley did not intend to brook a denial. In three steps, he was in front of the desk. He thrust out his hand, caught Dulsworthy by the cravat, and jerked him to his feet. "You will stand. And you will answer the lady."

Dulsworthy pawed ineffectually at Langley's clenched fist, then blinked past him at Amanda. "Why, pray tell, is your tutor ordering me about?"

"Because he's not my tutor. Any more than he was the errand boy from Porter's bookshop or your footman on the night of the ball. This is Major Stanhope, George, and I really do think you'd better answer his question."

Now Dulsworthy was blinking at him, as if trying to bring his face into focus. "Footman?" he repeated, then tried to discard the idea with another shake of his head.

"Oh, this is perfectly useless." Amanda stepped forward and laid a hand on Langley's arm, as if urging him to release Dulsworthy. "You were right. We're here on a fool's errand. We'd might as well go."

Langley obliged her by shoving him back into the chair. "Something's driven him to drink. What is it, my lord?" he demanded, his eyes darting over the desktop for some clue. "What have you done with Lady Kingston's sons?"

"Why, I—I only brought them back here, just as I was supposed to. Jacobs was most particular on that point."

"Jacobs?"

"You can't mean—" Amanda gripped one corner of the desk. "Not the fencing master?"

Dulsworthy sighed. "The same."

When she glanced Langley's way, eyes flared, he nodded toward the pair of chairs facing the desk. "Let's sit down, shall we, Lady Kingston, and allow his lordship to elaborate."

Amanda shot him a doubtful look, but eventually perched on the edge of the farthest chair.

"Now, sir," Langley said, sitting down, "if you would start from the beginning..."

"The beginning?" Dulsworthy took a generous swallow of brandy. "Don't know as I can remember back that far."

"As far as you can, then," Langley prompted. "How, for example, you met Mr. Jacobs, and how he came to be young Lord Kingston's and Master Philip's fencing master."

"Oh, well, that's easy enough. He runs a sort of sporting club, you see. For gen'lemen. Boxing, fencing, and th' like. I let it slip once that I was worried about my wards, being brought up in a houseful of women, an' Jacobs was right quick to see the problem. Says to me, in that fancy way o' his, 'I offer my services in a number of aristocratic households, my lord. I should be honored to give the sons of the late Earl of Kingston instruction in the gentlemanly art of swordplay.'"

*The sons of the late Earl of Kingston.* Something about the phrase sent Langley's thoughts flitting back to his meeting with Scott. *A friend to his service,* the general had said of Kingston. Was it possible their connection had run deeper than a generous donation or two to the Widows and Orphans Fund? Did Jacobs have a particular reason for wanting to gain access to Bartlett House? Was there something else he had hoped to find?

"And may gentlemen lay wagers at Mr. Jacobs's establishment?" Langley ventured, when Dulsworthy paused.

The man heaved another brandy-soaked sigh. "Aye."

"Are you in debt to this Jacobs, my lord?"

"Oh, aye."

At that confession, Amanda bristled, seeming to sense what it might mean, the lengths to which a man might go to extract himself from money difficulties. Langley waved at her to remain silent. Dulsworthy might be hesitant to speak plainly if he remembered that a lady was present.

"But that old French cookbook was to have cleared it, you see," Dulsworthy continued. "That chap from the bookshop"—he narrowed his gaze, as if trying to bring Langley's face into focus, then shook his head in disbelief—"*you* said it was valu'ble. I didn't think much of it when I told Lady Kingston I'd return it. But then Jacobs happened to see it—he's got more'n a drop of French blood in his veins, you know—and told me he knew where I might sell it and clear enough profit to settle up my notes. He was willing to take it right then, but I didn't like to think of making her ladyship unhappy in the matter, so I set it aside to consider the matter." The man still did not seem to understand the true worth of what he'd had, however briefly, in his hands. "But needs must, you understand. Later, when he sent 'round a note with a direction on it, another bookshop I gathered, I wrapped it up and was all set to drop it off the day after the ball. The day I took the boys out for a drive," he added, with a pleading glance toward Amanda, whose eyes in the dimly lit room held all the warmth of an ice-slicked pond on a black winter's night.

"But young Lord Kingston found it instead," said Langley, before Dulsworthy withered under the force of her chilling glare.

He shrugged. "I wasn't sure which of them picked it up. Jacobs said he could winkle the truth out of them. Said he didn't think Lady Kingston had been too pleased after the last lesson, and that it might be best to meet here from now on. So I went to fetch the boys for a little visit, only to find that the family had all hied off to Richmond on a lark. Well, my horses were fresh, so off I went after 'em. Wasn't too difficult to persuade 'em to come with me. The boys always like a ride in my phaeton—she's a prime goer," he confided as an aside to Langley. "When we got back here, they were surprised to see Jacobs, o' course, full o' some tale t' me about how their new tutor had bested him in a match. Said they didn't know a thing about any old book, and couldn't I please take them back home now, and then…" Dulsworthy paused for another swallow, this one deep enough to drain the glass. "And then, Jacobs pulled out a pistol and said the boys were to come with him."

Langley understood, suddenly, why the fencing master had refused to teach the boys how to defend themselves properly.

Amanda shrieked and leaped to her feet. "A pistol?"

"Where did he take them?" Langley demanded, rising too.

Dulsworthy dropped his head into his hands again, muffling his next words. "I don't know."

This Langley readily believed. "What about that club you mentioned? Could they be there?"

Dulsworthy shook his head, and Langley was inclined to agree. Too obvious and open a place for hiding something as valuable as a nobleman's sons. Nevertheless, when Dulsworthy scratched out the address on a scrap of paper, Langley took it.

Amanda leaned over the desk, forcing Dulsworthy to look up. "How could you? Your wards? The sons of your dear friend?"

"I never thought they'd come to harm," Dulsworthy insisted, swaying as if caught in a stiff breeze as he hoisted himself from the chair.

"In answer to your earlier question, I shall *never* forgive you, George. And if even a hair on one of their heads is harmed, I shall—"

"I think," Langley interjected smoothly, laying a hand on her arm, "we have what we need. But if you'll wait downstairs," he urged her, "I would like a private word with his lordship. Between gentlemen."

She blinked up at him, her expression a mixture of resistance and confusion, but at his encouraging nod, she turned on one heel and went out.

When the door shut behind her, Langley reached for the decanter on a nearby table and refilled Dulsworthy's tumbler. "This will only take a moment, my lord."

What he was about to do was undeniably bold. Presumptuous.

In other words, perfectly in character.

He had always been a risk-taker, just as General Scott had said. And if ever there had been a risk worth taking, it was this one. Because it was for Amanda.

"If what's happened today comes out," he began, "and people learn of your involvement in it, they will no doubt be shocked at how lightly you held your duty to your wards." Though his voice was easy, the implied threat was clear: Langley had in his power the ability to ruin Dulsworthy's reputation. And reputation mattered a great deal to such a man.

Dulsworthy opened his mouth to defend himself, then gave a reluctant nod of agreement.

"I myself judge Lady Kingston perfectly capable of acting as sole guardian, making appropriate choices about her sons' future. I suspect, if the present circumstances were known, others might agree."

At those words, Dulsworthy lifted the tumbler to his lips for another deep swallow, then thumped the glass down. Brandy sloshed over the sides and onto the desktop. "What ish—is it you want?"

"It's a simple request, my lord. A letter, in which you acknowledge your errors and cede your authority to her ladyship in whatever matters she may please, pertaining to her sons. In your hand and addressed to her. For... safekeeping, shall we say? You understand, I'm sure."

In truth, Langley wasn't certain the man did understand, but Dulsworthy gave another unsteady nod, then pulled out a sheet of paper, dipped his quill, and scrawled across the paper just what Langley had asked him to write.

"Very good, my lord. Thank you. Now, if you'll just sign your name to it."

Given the man's present condition, Langley had his doubts about the legality of the document, which was now speckled with brandy from the wet desktop.

But when Dulsworthy spoke again, he sounded almost sober—shocked into clear-headedness, perhaps, by the enormity of what he had done. "I hope you find them," he said, handing over the paper.

"I intend to." Langley folded the letter and tucked it inside his coat pocket. Once the boys had been found, he would give the document to Amanda and set her free.

At the bottom of the stairs, he caught up with her, cupped her elbow in his hand, and led her out of the house. She was stiff, trembling—whether with fear or anger, he could not say. As he handed her into the waiting carriage, he gripped her fingers tightly, making her turn her head and look him square in the eye. "I meant what I said, Amanda. I'll find them."

"I want to believe you." Her red-rimmed eyes moved past his, darting up and down the bustling street, as wealthy families prepared for fashionable afternoon outings. "But how will you even know where to look?"

He urged her inside before speaking to the coachman, his voice almost too low to be heard over the clatter of passing carriages. Then he settled across from her as they rolled into motion once more. "I know where we must start."

# Chapter 17

Dazed, Amanda stared out the window but saw nothing of the streets and houses they passed, could not have said whether they were familiar or strange. Somewhere out there, in London or even beyond, her sons were in danger, held at gunpoint by a man—a criminal, perhaps even a spy—who'd been playing a part to insert himself into their lives.

She glanced toward Langley. She might have said the same things of him. He had warned her of the danger surrounding him, but she had been determined to involve herself in the matter of the codebook. To involve herself with a handsome stranger. *An adventure,* she'd called it.

Oh, what had she done?

She was not sure how far they had traveled when Langley rapped his knuckles on the ceiling of the carriage and ordered the coachman to stop. "We'll walk from here. Only a few blocks. A crested carriage will draw a great deal of attention in this neighborhood," he explained to her. "Not all of it welcome."

Swallowing what she was determined would be the last of her tears, she nodded once to show her understanding and prepared to alight when the coach rolled to a stop. Through the window she glimpsed what appeared to be ordinary houses, not quite as lavish as Grosvenor Square but certainly not the squalor she had steeled herself to expect. The street was surprisingly quiet for afternoon.

"Gaming hells," Langley explained when he saw her studying the house fronts as he handed her onto the pavement. "Brothels. Pleasure houses that cater to a range of…unusual tastes, shall we say? If it were closer to nightfall, I daresay you might see a few of your neighbors about. Even at this hour, I recommend you keep your head down. It would not do for the Countess of Kingston to be recognized here."

*Mind your step.*

She watched her toes peep from beneath her skirts as they hurried along, a part of her as desperate as Lot's wife to take one last curious look around. But the rest of her was lost in the memory of Jamie and Pip, tearing off their shoes and stockings and racing into the cool river.

Would that be the last time she saw them alive?

"I'll pay anything," she murmured, only half speaking to Langley. "Any sort of a ransom."

He gripped her hand where it lay on his arm. "I suspect they have but one form of currency in mind."

The codebook, of course. Which Langley had handed over to General Scott. She had been surprised to learn the general had no immediate plan to trade it for his captured agent. Would he be similarly reluctant to use it to buy back her sons?

She blinked furiously against a fresh surge of tears, thick enough that when Langley said, "Here we are," she could barely make out the sort of doorway through which they passed.

The warm, spicy scents of a hundred varieties of tobacco acted more effectually than smelling salts. With a little jerk of awareness, she began to look about herself, at the wood floor polished with the traffic of many years' worth of footsteps and the tall windows through which sunlight streamed, setting aglow dozens of glass jars stacked almost to the ceiling. Drawers and shelves, a long wooden counter, and behind it a portly man with brown skin and silvering hair, who was helping a pair of customers.

She recalled having noticed the faintest scent of tobacco clinging to Langley's coat, that night in the library. But she'd seen no other sign that he smoked. Why on earth were they popping into a tobacco shop, especially at a time like this?

"I—I've never been inside a tobacconist's before," she said to Langley, who was peering at a selection of enameled snuff boxes in a display cabinet.

"You still haven't, my dear," he replied without looking at her, hardly even moving his mouth. "Not exactly. Wait a moment."

"Be right with you, sir," the shopkeeper called to them, and Langley raised a finger to the brim of his hat in acknowledgment.

At long last, the other two gentlemen made their purchases and left. A bell jangled above the door as they passed through it. "Good afternoon, sir," the shopkeeper said to Langley. "Pleased to see you again." He glanced at Amanda, and she had the impression that though his dark eyes passed quickly over her, they took in a great deal. "The Kingston blend, I take it?"

Amanda started. *Kingston?* It could hardly be a coincidence.

"Aye," said Langley.

The man scanned the otherwise empty shop and the street beyond the windows, his mouth set in a strangely grim line. "I'd have thought you might find it a bit rich for the likes of you," he said with a sigh. "Ah, well," he turned and reached for a glass jar, as if fetching the tobacco Langley had requested.

At the same moment, Langley moved, lifting a hinged section of the wooden countertop that formed a pass-through and dragging her along with him, past the shopkeeper, who seemed not at all surprised to find customers on his side of the counter, then through a small door she had not noticed before. A steep set of stairs pitched downward, into darkness.

"Welcome," said Langley, "to the Underground."

She laid her palm against the cool, rough-plastered wall, feeling her way as she descended. At the bottom of the steps ran a long corridor, lighted by a single sconce, closed doors along either side.

"The nation imagines that the British army runs its intelligence operation out of an office in Whitehall. But here's where much of the real work is done," Langley explained. He opened one of the doors, which gave way to a tiny bedchamber, hardly bigger than the one in which he'd slept in the attic of Bartlett House, hardly big enough for a narrow cot and a washstand. "You can wait in here. I'm off to tell my fellow intelligence officers what's happened. And to beg their help."

She watched his jaw move as he spoke, weighed its chiseled firmness with the quiet uncertainty of his words. "Thank you, but no," she said, laying her hand on his and drawing the door closed again. "I'm coming with you."

She wasn't quite sure what to call the expression that flickered into his warm brown eyes. Surprise? Annoyance? She settled on *relief* as he pressed his lips in a disapproving line and marched her toward another door across the corridor.

The room behind it was larger, its plain whitewashed walls lighted by several lamps and decorated with maps—no, the maps weren't merely decorative, she realized with a start as she noted the colored pins in one, though she could not begin to guess what they marked. At one of two tables, a young man dressed in ordinary clothes sat in straight-backed chair, surrounded by stacks of books and paper. "Major Stanhope," he said, lifting his head his from his work, then jerking to his feet, his surprised gaze focused entirely on her.

"Would you be so good as to relieve Colonel Millrose for a few moments? I need to speak with him."

"Yes, sir," the younger man said, marking his place in the book he'd been reading.

"This is the workroom," Langley explained after he'd gone. "Code breaking, primarily. The men have been itching to get their hands on a certain French cookbook."

Amanda did not know what to say in reply. Was this all some strange dream? Had she perhaps struck her head when she'd fainted and dreamed everything that had happened since?

He pulled out a chair and gestured for her to sit down, but her legs tingled with restless energy. She needed to be doing something. She wanted to pace, despite the room's narrow compass. But perhaps that would look too much like nosiness? With a wavering sigh, she sank onto the hard chair.

A moment later, she popped to her feet again when the door opened and the shopkeeper entered. "My lady," Langley said, "may I present Colonel William Millrose. Colonel Millrose, the Countess of Kingston."

Despite the wobbliness in her knees, she managed a curtsy. He bowed and waved her back into the chair. "You must be nearly done in, my lady. I've sent for some refreshment."

"Thank you, sir."

"Well, now, Magpie," he said, turning to Langley, a rather humorless grin splitting his face, "to what do we owe this unexpected pleasure?"

"You haven't heard, then?"

"About Lady Kingston's sons? Yes, of course." He patted his breast pocket, and Amanda heard paper crinkle. "Word arrived from General Scott shortly before you did. I wonder you did not go directly to him, rather than..." He glanced toward Amanda. "Forgive me, my lady. Your presence here is most unusual."

"I do understand, sir. But we've brought some valuable information."

Colonel Millrose tilted his head and regarded her with a new appreciation. "I'm listening."

"We've just come from Lord Dulsworthy's house on Brook Street," she said. "He took the boys there at the direction of a Mr. Jacobs. Their fencing master—though it would seem that is far from his only occupation."

"He's French," Langley interjected. "At least in part. Perhaps in league with some ring of spies—maybe the ones who have Hopkins. At any rate, he's after the codebook. Thinking the boys still had it, Dulsworthy gave them up to him at gunpoint." Amanda could not contain a shiver. "No idea where Jacobs might've taken them. The fellow runs a sort of sporting club. Dulsworthy ran up some debts there." Colonel Millrose nodded his understanding, as Langley pulled out a slip of paper. "This is the direction. But I don't think it's very likely they're there—"

"I agree," said the colonel, taking the note from Langley's fingers. "Nevertheless, we'll investigate."

"I'll go," offered Langley immediately.

"No." Millrose opened the door just a crack and passed that paper to someone in the corridor, speaking only a few low words before closing it again. "In fact, I think it would be best if you removed yourself from this assignment, Magpie." He glanced at Amanda as he turned back toward the room. "I sense it's become a personal matter."

Amanda felt her face heat. "It's true that Major Stanhope cares for my sons...." *And me,* she wanted to add, but didn't dare. How easy it would be to assign the wrong meaning to the intimacies they'd shared.

Colonel Millrose, however, seemed to understand what she'd left unspoken. "And that, my lady, is precisely the problem," he said. "I fear he lacks the necessary detachment—"

Just then the door opened again, admitting a pretty, petite woman, dressed all in black, which made her very blonde hair look blonder still. Her pale blue gaze traveled among the three of them, resting longest on Langley, before she stepped to Amanda and set the tray down in front of her.

"Thank you, Mrs. Drummond," Colonel Millrose said. "Now, as I was saying, a good agent cannot afford to be distracted—"

The spout of the teapot chattered against the cup into which Mrs. Drummond was pouring. "If he is, others will pay the price." Amanda was surprised that the chill in the woman's voice didn't turn the steam rising from the cup into a flurry of snow.

"Pay the price?" Amanda echoed. "I don't—I haven't the faintest notion what you're all talking about." But didn't she? Langley had hinted at something in the carriage. What was it he'd said?

"If he'd done his duty," said Mrs. Drummond, "my husband would still be alive."

"Christ, Fanny," Langley groaned, throwing himself into a chair. "This is hardly the time to rehash—"

"Please." Amanda spoke across him, her voice soft but firm. "I want to know."

A wary glance traveled among Langley, Mrs. Drummond, and Colonel Millrose. Evidently none of them wanted to be the one to tell the story.

At last the colonel said, "About a year ago, Captain Drummond and then-Captain Stanhope were assigned to a mission together. A matter of grave importance regarding a threat to the king himself."

"One night," Langley picked up the tale, "I was late to relieve Captain Drummond. Too late. It ought—it ought to have been I who died that night. And instead, when the king heard of our efforts, he…" A muscle twitched along Langley's jaw.

"He knighted you," Amanda whispered.

Langley jerked away from the words, refusing to meet anyone's eye.

"General Scott was afraid that the men who killed Drummond would realize his wife was in possession of valuable information," Millrose continued. "So he sent her here—"

"To serve as a glorified matron in this Home for Wayward Boys," concluded Mrs. Drummond, with a disparaging glance around the cheerless room.

So Fanny had been deprived of useful occupation and forced to live with the man she blamed for the death of her husband. Amanda could imagine few things worse. Unless the situation had been exacerbated further yet…

"Earlier," she said, looking at Colonel Millrose, "you used the word *distracted*. What was it that distracted Major Stanhope that night?"

She should have asked *who* distracted him. But she already knew the answer. Fanny Drummond was very pretty. Amanda could guess that the woman was a great favorite among the officers. Or had been—before anger and grief had encased her in a layer of ice.

"I paid a call on Mrs. Drummond that evening," Langley explained, still not meeting her gaze. "I stayed longer than I ought to have done."

"You needn't worry, my lady," added Mrs. Drummond. "It was only ever an innocent flirtation. I was a happily married woman." Though the words were clearly motivated by jealousy—either what Fanny felt or what she hoped to provoke—in the woman's cool voice, Amanda also heard the telltale notes of guilt. Guilt at the role, however small, she'd played in her husband's death. Distracting Langley from his mission had upended Fanny Drummond's whole world—a feeling Amanda knew all too well.

She cared not a jot about Langley and Mrs. Drummond's flirtation—innocent or otherwise. She cared that Langley now sat, eyes screwed shut, pinching his nose beneath the bridge of his spectacles, lost in the tortures of his thoughts. Was he comparing present circumstances to past missteps? Was he now recalling with something less than pleasure the hours they had spent together before George had taken the boys?

Well, she did not intend to let him. She did not intend to be consigned in his mind to either a distraction or a flirtation.

"Surely, Colonel Millrose, you must realize that neither Major Stanhope nor Mrs. Drummond is responsible for what happened to her husband."

Just as neither she nor Langley was responsible for what had happened to Jamie and Philip. And here, if such was required, was proof of the damage misplaced blame and guilt could do. Good Lord. No wonder Langley had wanted her safely out of this mess.

"I do," Colonel Millrose readily agreed, folding his arms across his chest. "And I've told both of them as much. But I can't make them forgive one another—or themselves. Worst of all, since that night, Stanhope doesn't trust himself. And that makes it well-nigh impossible for his fellow intelligence officers to trust him."

Amanda drew a deep breath, calling up the mental image of that morning's fencing lesson on the Hurst's lawn, the smiles on Jamie's and Philip's faces. Her sons had put their faith in this man. So could she.

"I trust him," she said firmly. "And I do not want him removed from this case."

Langley spun and looked at her, blinking as though stunned, unable to believe what he'd heard. No stern schoolmaster. No devilish rogue. Just him, raw and vulnerable, utterly without disguise. His lips parted, but no words came, in any of his voices.

Amanda met that bewildered look with a steady one of her own. She could not see beyond the present moment. She did not know how they would find and rescue her sons. But she had to believe they would succeed, just as she had to believe there would be a time, afterward, when she and Langley could share another private moment. A sunny hour in which she might bare not just her body to him, but her heart.

But for now, as they sat in this secret lair, together but not alone, she would have to be content with the unexpected discovery that she wanted such a moment—wanted many other adventures with him.

"Now, Colonel Millrose," she said primly, dropping a lump of sugar into her cup before taking a fortifying sip, "about my boys…"

"I've sent agents to scout Jacobs's whereabouts." He lowered his head, looking apologetic. "Until they return, however, I'm afraid there's not much to do but wait."

His words roused Mrs. Drummond, who had been staring thoughtfully at the floor. "If you'd like, your ladyship, I'll take you to my quarters. More pleasant surroundings in which to take your tea," she said, standing and picking up the tray. "I suspect you could use a rest."

"Rest? I couldn't possibly," Amanda began. She felt no less frantic than she had when they'd set out from Richmond, yet also strangely paralyzed, uncertain how to move, what to do. "Surely there's something we can—"

Colonel Millrose broke in. "There is no *we*, my lady. Despite the involvement of your sons, this is not a civilian matter."

She had been told as much before. But this time, her pleading glance at Langley was to no avail. He had the nerve to answer her with one of those stern, knowing looks. With a huff of impatience and a frown for the colonel, she rose and followed Mrs. Drummond from the room.

Mrs. Drummond's room was far less spartan than Langley's had been, with a real bed covered by a pretty quilt and a paneled screen to divide the sleeping and dressing space from a little sitting area made up of two upholstered chairs and a round table between them. On that table, Mrs. Drummond placed the tea tray.

"Thank you," she said after Amanda had seated herself on the far side of the table. "For what you said about who's to blame. I think all this time I—I've taken a selfish sort of joy in the guilt Langley's felt." The faintest blush rose on her pale cheeks. "Because I was angry. And because I didn't want to admit my own fault in the matter."

She sat down in the other chair, poured a fresh cup of tea, and held it out to Amanda. Amanda considered taking Fanny's hand instead, offering some gesture of consolation. But the other woman's stiff, wary posture did not invite such familiarities. So she accepted the cup and said simply, "Fear and grief can make us strangers to ourselves, Mrs. Drummond. Sometimes a wound must be cleaned before it can heal."

Mrs. Drummond nodded, rose, and began bustling around the room, gathering towels and a hairbrush. "I'll put these on the washstand, behind the screen. You'll feel more yourself after you've washed your face and combed your hair."

Amanda felt positively grimy next to Mrs. Drummond, with her neat black dress and perfectly coifed blonde hair. "Thank you."

When Fanny reappeared from behind the screen, she stood and looked at Amanda for a moment, her head cocked to one side. "May I give you a piece of advice, Lady Kingston?"

"Please."

"Don't let these men persuade you against your own judgment." She cast a disparaging glance in the direction of the workroom. "They will persist in believing that women are fragile creatures with little but comfort and cakes to offer up to the cause," she said, with an embarrassed gesture toward the tea tray, "whatever I say."

Amanda knew firsthand the frustrations of feeling overprotected and undervalued. She wondered whether Mrs. Drummond might have been quicker to forgive both Langley and herself if she had been given some meaningful work to do. If she had been allowed to exercise more than her feminine charms.

"Thank you, Mrs. Drummond. I shall make certain Colonel Millrose knows I haven't any intention of being kept in the dark about matters pertaining to my sons."

At last, Fanny stepped toward the door. "I'm sure you could do with a little quiet, my lady."

Though in truth she would've been glad of the company—any sort of distraction from thoughts of Jamie and Philip, or even Mama and the Hursts, who must be worried sick and probably blaming themselves—Amanda let her go. For the second time that day, she unpinned her hair, brushed it smooth, and coiled it up again, then washed herself as best she could. Finally, she sat down again, took up the now tepid cup of tea, and tried not to think of anything at all. Especially Langley.

Tried…and failed.

She loved her mother, no matter how they got on one another's nerves. And she could not imagine a love stronger than the one she had for her sons, whose present peril was like a wild beast rending her heart, and she unable either to fight off the terror or stanch the wound.

Perhaps it was wrong, then, to fancy that what she felt for Langley was love, when it bore so little resemblance to the other. Although she was occasionally exasperated with him. Afraid for him, too, and the risks he was willing to take to protect her and her sons.

All those familiar feelings were overlaid with a quiet certainty that without him, her life would be immeasurably poorer. No quipped conversations. No scolding glances. No mischievous wink when she refused to mind her step.

But what sort of life could the pair of them—a dull, respectable lady and a daring secret agent—build together? What sort of life did she want?

She was still mulling that nebulous future when a knock came and the door opened to admit the room's rightful occupant

"I'm sorry to disturb you, Lady Kingston," Mrs. Drummond said, "but Colonel Millrose would like to see you in the workroom. He has something to report."

Amanda stood up and glanced around the windowless room, searching for a clock. "What time is it?"

"I'm not sure. Things don't go according to any schedule in the Underground."

"But how can you stand it, always in darkness, not knowing whether it's night or morning?" No wonder Langley didn't sleep properly.

"I suppose it's a bit like life, my lady. You can't always see what's in front of you." Fanny's shoulders lifted and fell as she ushered Amanda into the corridor. "Sometimes you just have to leap."

# Chapter 18

When Amanda entered the workroom, Langley leaped to his feet—not just because it was the proper thing to do, but because he found he could not do otherwise. A soldier snapping to attention in the presence of the one in command...of his heart.

Then he scowled inwardly, taken aback by his ability even to think up such sentimental nonsense. Such feelings—not just wanting her, but *needing* her—had little place in the current moment, nor in the life he had chosen to lead.

"A problem, Magpie?" Billy asked, one brow cocked in his direction.

Perhaps his scowl had not been entirely *inward*. "No, sir," he snapped, and Amanda flinched.

"Well, come in, come in, Lady Kingston. You too, Mrs. Drummond. I daresay your being here might help to put her ladyship at ease. Now, may I introduce Lieutenant Greene and Captain Abel? They have some information for us. Please, everyone, sit down."

"Gentlemen." Amanda sent Langley a glance, then chose a chair opposite, putting the breadth of the table between them. Fanny sat down beside her, a veritable phalanx of trouble. Preferring to stand, too restless really to do otherwise, Langley closed the door and propped one shoulder against it.

Greene spoke first, his gaze scanning all of them as he spoke. "I've scouted the fencing master's club on Jermyn Street. Just two rooms: a large one on the ground floor, fitted up for fencing and boxing and the like, one smaller above, where gents can read the papers and get foxed. Beggin' your pardon, my lady," he added with an embarrassed nod toward Amanda. "No public betting books, though I've no doubt but what money changes hands on occasion. A small office in the back, where a nervous little fellow with ink stains on his fingers told me he hadn't seen Jacobs for three days. Little doubt but what he was telling the truth. I don't think that can be their hideout."

Billy gave a grim nod. "I hope you had better luck, Captain Abel?"

"Well, sir, the address to which Lord Dulsworthy claimed he intended to deliver the codebook—the one written on the wrappings—took me to a shop in Lambeth."

"What sort of a shop?" Langley demanded.

Abel sent a self-conscious glance toward Amanda. "A dressmaker's shop, sir."

"A dressmaker?" Amanda's dark eyes widened. "If he meant to sell the book, why on earth take it to such a place?"

"That remains to be seen, my lady," Billy answered soothingly. "What else, Abel?"

"Either its wares aren't up to snuff, or it's not a respectable place. I saw only one person step inside in the time I watched, all done up in a long cloak despite the heat, and if it was a lady, I'll eat my hat. He never came out, neither. At least, not out the front, and the door at the back didn't look as if it's been opened this year—rust on the hinges, cobwebs in the corners."

"Any cellar?"

"Aye, sir. I think so. Saw no way in nor out, but there was a window right at ground level, all boarded up."

"What's around the shop?"

He shrugged. "Quiet street. There's a room to let above the shop—empty, from what I could see. An apothecary next door, with a note in the window that said he'd gone out and wouldn't be back until tomorrow."

Millrose weighed the information in silence, seemingly unperturbed by the fact that Amanda was tapping on the tabletop with one fingernail, a steady drumbeat of nervous impatience. Langley's pulse too was clattering in his veins. At last Billy turned toward him. "What say you, Magpie?"

"Could be the place," Langley answered with more composure than he felt. "We'll have to have a look around inside."

Billy nodded and withdrew a watch from the pocket of his waistcoat. "Nearly six. If we wait until after dark—"

"After dark?" Amanda jumped to her feet and after a startled moment, the other men rose too. "That's hours away. I can't possibly wait here, doing nothing, on the mere *hope* that—that—" With a flourish of her hands, she collapsed back into her chair.

"Captain Abel, Lieutenant Greene, thank you for your reports." Billy gave each of them a nod of dismissal. When the door had closed behind them, he sat down and sent Langley a look indicating he was to do the same. Reluctantly, Langley approached and drew back a chair.

Folding his arms on the table, Billy leaned toward Amanda. "I do understand your anxiety, Lady Kingston. This Jacobs may have one of my men too. But you must realize I can't risk more agents' lives without better information. If we rush in without a plan, it could put everyone in even more danger."

Amanda looked only slightly chastened. "But surely you agree that time is of the essence, Captain Millrose?"

After a moment's stillness, Billy gave a somber nod. "A few hours, though—"

"Send me." Rash words, Langley knew, but he had failed to act too many times—and not just on this mission. *I trust him,* Amanda had claimed, though he'd done nothing to earn her trust. Quite the opposite, in fact.

Well, he intended to earn it today. He'd sacrifice himself, if necessary, to return her sons to her side.

Billy passed a hand over his mouth, as if hiding a laugh. "Into a dress shop, during business hours? Don't you think that's carrying your penchant for disguise a bit too far?"

Before Langley could answer, Amanda cleared her throat. He glimpsed a familiar tilt to her chin, a distressingly familiar spark in her dark eyes. "I—I do not claim to have any expertise, but as it *is* a dress shop, or purports to be, why not send a woman?"

"A woman?" Billy laughed, then sobered when he realized she was serious. "I do not particularly like the idea of—"

"Amanda," Langley said warningly, forgetting for a moment the intimacy it betrayed.

Billy spun to look at him, and at the same moment, Amanda's chin—that pointed chin, that dear, defiant little chin—jutted forward. "Why not?"

"Don't—" Langley began. *Don't be ridiculous,* he had been going to say. But of course it wasn't ridiculous. She had never been ridiculous. Not even on that night in the garden when she'd babbled about birds and broken his spectacles.

As if to prove it, she continued with astonishing calm, "Haven't I the right? I certainly have as much to lose."

He couldn't deny that, of course. She might never recover from the loss of her sons. But Langley was equally certain he could not go on if he lost her.

"She means for you to send her," he explained to Billy, whose brows shot up to the middle of his forehead, an expression not of surprise but— *damn it*—interest.

"Well, now." Billy lifted his folded arms from the table to rest them on his chest, rocking back slightly in his chair as he studied Amanda. "That certainly would not be expected."

*Because it's utter madness!* Langley almost shouted. "You cannot possibly be considering—"

Amanda sent him a glance that might have matched one of his own for sternness, then turned to Billy. "I have to save my sons." Her voice was uncharacteristically firm—which was how he knew she was terrified. It reminded him of the way she had spoken to Dulsworthy, on the day he had tried to get her to exchange control over her sons' future for her hand in marriage.

"They may not even be inside, Lady Kingston," Billy explained in a gentle voice. "The safer route is for all of us to wait here until Jacobs makes his demands known."

Langley could have told him that Amanda wasn't interested in *safe*.

"He wants the codebook." She sounded impatient at being forced to state the obvious. "Is General Scott likely to offer it in exchange for either Lieutenant Hopkins or my boys?"

Neither he nor Billy answered. Fanny gnawed at her lower lip as her blue eyes flooded with sympathetic tears. But Amanda gave a self-satisfied nod. "I didn't think so. In which case, if Jamie and Philip are to be rescued, I'm going to have to be the one to do it."

Fanny reached for her hand. Billy's chair came crashing down onto all four legs as he parted his lips to say something reassuring.

But Langley spoke first: "Not alone."

A moment later, Fanny added, "I'll go with you."

While he and Billy spoke over one another in protest, Amanda said only, "Thank you. I'd hoped you would offer."

"Well, it wouldn't be proper for a lady to go out without a maid," Fanny explained, though privately Langley wondered whether such rules applied outside of Mayfair. "I'd loan you a different gown, if we were of a size, my lady." Amanda was several inches taller. "But perhaps a veil?"

"An excellent notion," Amanda agreed.

"Say something, Billy." Langley looked at Millrose, who shrugged helplessly. "Surely you don't mean to countenance this scheme?"

"I suspect it won't matter what I say," he said, with something like a smile of admiration for Amanda. "I don't like the degree of danger, especially not with women and possibly children involved. But the plan gets full marks for ingenuity. So"—his gaze flicked between the two—"what happens once you're inside?"

"Mrs. Drummond and I will pretend to be demanding customers. While we create a scene in the front part of the shop, someone else"—here, she had the grace to glance toward Langley—"can investigate the back door and the boarded-up window."

Billy appeared to think over her plan. "Let's say we do that. Let's say Jacobs is inside—he's unlikely to be alone. We'll have men on the streets, before and behind the house, of course. Armed men. Nevertheless, you will both be taking a grave risk. It could all go wrong too quickly for anyone to come to your aid."

"Then we will have to be resourceful, Colonel Millrose. I certainly do not want Mrs. Drummond to come to harm. If things start to take an unfortunate turn, I'll say I've forgotten something and send my 'maid' back to my carriage." She managed a slight smile for Fanny. "But if my sons are inside that shop, I won't leave without them."

To Langley's utter shock, Billy appeared to be considering the scheme. After a moment, he gave a crisp nod. "All right."

Langley swore—not under his breath, and without any apology.

No one paid him the least mind.

"I'll go and get a few things together," Fanny said, rising. Billy stood too, leaving Amanda alone at the table, her dark eyes wide, as if she were only now realizing the enormity of what she had proposed.

Fanny stepped to the door. "Pardon me." In place of her usual brittle expression, he glimpsed strength—strength he hadn't suspected her of possessing.

Or perhaps he hadn't wanted to see.

"Fan," he whispered, as she reached past him for the door. "Don't do this." If she refused to go along, then perhaps Amanda would come to her senses.

"If you have something to say to me, Major Stanhope," she said, glancing once over her shoulder, "it might better be said elsewhere."

He'd been avoiding this conversation for over a year, and a part of him longed desperately to avoid it a little longer, even as he knew he couldn't. The words exchanged in the workroom earlier that afternoon had felt like having a plaster ripped off. Now it was time to see what scars remained. Exhaling sharply, unable to bring himself to look at Amanda, he opened the door. "All right."

In the semi-darkness of the empty corridor, Fanny's pale eyes searched his. "Does she know? How much you love her?"

"I—" Heat flushed into his face. "Is it so obvious, then?"

"Some of us have learned to look past that public face—those public faces—you put on. When I walked into that room earlier today, I realized I had never before seen you truly afraid. But there was no doubt in my mind that you were afraid now…and for her." Fanny's voice was still cool, but not cold. "Once, I thought it might make me feel better—to know that you, too, were susceptible to these petty, human emotions." Her ice-blue gaze faltered. "It turns out, I was wrong. It's really quite a wretched sight." Something wry quirked at the corner of her mouth, then was quickly smoothed away. "Tell her. That's my advice. Tell her before you lose your nerve, or you'll never be any good to anyone here again."

"Fanny," he chided, then caught her hand. "We were friends once. I don't deserve your forgiveness, but nevertheless, I am sorry. Sorry I couldn't save him, and sorry it's taken me all this time to say as much."

She withdrew her fingers from his grip and smoothed her palm down the front of her dress. "I know."

"And you're still determined to go with her?" he asked, swallowing past the knot of emotions in his throat.

"I am. Because it's time for me to start earning my keep around here." Then she laid her hand on his arm and favored him with the first genuine smile he'd seen on her face in a twelvemonth. "I promise I'll do my best to keep her out of trouble, Magpie."

\* \* \* \*

Amanda's knees shook beneath her skirts as she and Fanny approached the supposed dress shop. She paused for a moment and closed her eyes, wishing she had the ability to sense whether her sons were inside.

"Oh, dear," Fanny clucked. "The sign on the door says *closed*."

"What?" Amanda's eyes popped open. "Well, we're going inside, regardless. If we have to, we'll pound on the door until they open it, and we'll tell them we have an emergency."

Fanny's head tilted to the side as she fixed Amanda with a skeptical look. Her bonnet covered up every strand of her distinctive blonde hair. "An emergency that requires a dressmaker?"

Amanda darted her gaze around, searching for inspiration, and found it in a rusty nail sticking out from the wooden handrail leading up to the apothecary's shop. What was one more casualty of her wardrobe? Tugging off one glove, she used her trembling fingertips to pry the nail loose. Then she handed it to Fanny and turned her back to the woman, speaking to her over her shoulder. "Tear my dress. Jagged strips. Right down to the petticoat. We'll—we'll say a stray dog attacked me, had me right in its jaws. I only just managed to get away, but I'm overcome. I need somewhere to sit down and something which with to make myself decent."

Fanny took the nail and her blue eyes swept Amanda from head to toe. "You're certain, my lady?"

"Please."

Gripping the rusty implement, Fanny reached out for a tentative swipe, at first snagging the figured yellow muslin, but not tearing it. Then, drawing a determined breath, she switched her hold on the nail, the better to control its movement, speared its point through the delicate fabric, and dragged it downward. One long strip, then another, until most of the back of Amanda's skirt was in tatters and the unmentionables beneath were on full display.

Amanda gave a satisfied nod, and Fanny tossed the nail into the gutter. Dropping her makeshift veil over her face, Amanda then drew a deep breath, and shrieked. "Bad dog! Oh, bad dog! Down! No!" Fanny soon joined in the scolding of the imaginary animal, until Amanda nodded toward the door and mouthed, "Now."

Fanny first knocked with her knuckles, then hammered against the door with the side of her fist. "I'm not sure they're going to answer, my lady."

"Keep trying," Amanda urged. "I can see a light burning within."

Fanny kept up the fierce battery, and after what seemed an eternity, a man who looked entirely too unkempt to be a shop clerk, particularly one at an establishment catering to ladies, came to the door and opened it a crack. "Closed," he said in a heavy accent, pointing to the sign.

"Can't you see my lady has had a mishap?" Fanny demanded in turn, directing the man's attention to Amanda's unfortunate appearance, even as she wedged the toe of her sturdy walking boots into the narrow opening of the door. "Was it your mangy cur that had the nerve to grab hold of her dress and run off? Let us in, man, let us in. My lady can't stand in the street in the all-together."

With a show of fearlessness, they forced their way into the dressmaker's shop, driving the befuddled man backward. He said nothing more, making Amanda wonder whether he spoke more than a few words of English.

Fanny must have reached a similar conclusion. "Now, fetch some pins and a bolt of whatever you've got that's fine, so I can mend her dress," she said, miming each object as she cast a skeptical glance around the little shop.

It must never have served a particularly elegant clientele, and did not appear to have served any customers at all for some time. A moldering odor hung heavy on the air, and everything was coated in a layer of dust.

Ribbons and trimming dangled limply from mostly empty spools, and the pattern books lying on a nearby table were years out of fashion.

"Well, sirrah? Don't just stand there," Fanny ordered the man, who had retreated behind the counter.

"M-moment," he said before darting into the back.

"What next?" Fanny asked quietly, although he was out of earshot.

"I'm not certain," Amanda confessed.

He returned a moment later with a bolt of coarse cloth tucked under his arm and proffering a dish of straight pins in one hand.

Amanda stepped forward, ostensibly to investigate what he'd brought but really to discover if she could see anything past the tattered curtain through which he'd disappeared. "Could I trouble you for a cup of tea?" she asked hoarsely, leaning on Fanny's arm. "That horrible beast..."

"Goodness gracious, my lady. You look as if you might faint. Here, let me help you to a seat," she said, taking Amanda's arm and nodding toward a chair with worn upholstery. "I'll see that you get your tea if I have to step into the back and make it myself."

Amanda heard footsteps creak on hidden stairs and the curtain lifted again. "That will not be necessary," a voice declared in soft voice, lightly inflected with French. Behind her veil, she narrowed her gaze at the man who had joined them.

*Jacobs.*

For a moment, Amanda was too stunned to react. Then she fished in her reticule for an handkerchief and shook it out with a flourish—the prearranged signal, which she hoped would be visible through the grimy front window—before reaching beneath her veil to dab surreptitiously at her nose. "My good sir, will you not take pity on me? I can promise your shop a year's custom in exchange for this small assistance now." She had to prolong their exchange as long as possible, to give Langley and the others time to act.

"Why, of course we will assist you, my dear lady," insisted Jacobs. "If you will just follow me into the back, I will personally see that everything is taken care of."

For the first time, Amanda felt the danger of her situation. If she were not careful, and clever, she would succeed only in adding to Jacobs's number of hostages. *Or victims.*

A shudder passed through her. "I wouldn't wish to intrude," she said, hoping the thick veil muffled her speech past the point of familiarity.

Fanny stepped between them. "My lady is too faint to stand. I can fetch what's needed, if—"

A shout rose—from somewhere beneath their feet, if Amanda weren't mistaken. *The cellar.* Alarm sketched over the face of the supposed clerk. Jacobs's eyes narrowed. "Va voir," he ordered the other man, who dropped the bolt of fabric and the dish of pins on the counter and scurried once more behind the curtain. More shouts, and a *bang* that might've been a gunshot. "Now," Jacobs said, approaching Amanda, apparently indifferent to the noise below, "I cannot help you unless you will let me see..."

Footsteps thundered up the stairs. At once hopeful and fearful, Amanda turned her head toward the sound, and in that moment's distraction, he snatched her veil away.

"Why, Lady Kingston," he sneered into her face. "What a surprise."

At that same moment, Jamie and Philip burst into the room from behind the curtain, their faces streaked with dirt but appearing otherwise unharmed. "Mama!" They raced to her, almost knocking their former fencing master off his feet as they passed. "You should've seen it! Mr. Stanhope—"

Desperate to gather them into her arms, she instead shoved them away, to safety. "Go, boys. Out the door with Mrs. Drummond. I'll be there as soon as I can."

Jacobs snatched at Fanny, but she was too quick for him. She slipped through his grasping fingers and grabbed the boys by the hands. "Come!"

They resisted, terrified, but Amanda hadn't breath to urge them. Jacobs had her by the throat, pinning her to his body with his forearm. Something hard jabbed into the middle of her back—the barrel of a pistol, she feared. Fanny managed to drag Jamie and Philip out the front door, just as someone else raced up the back steps. Surely another of their captors, in hot pursuit. Amanda's cry of warning came out as a croak, and Jacobs jerked her into silence with a flex of his arm as a figure burst through the curtain.

*Langley.*

Deprived of breath, she could only mouth his name as he staggered into the room, gasping for air himself, with one arm hanging limply by his side. Blood seeped through his coat sleeve, staining the dark wool almost black.

"You," Jacobs muttered darkly. "I might've known."

"That's right," Langley replied, shaking sweat from his eyes. His spectacles were missing again, and Amanda saw no sign of a weapon in his hands.

"I cannot say I am disappointed." Jacobs prodded her forward with his knee until they were face to face. "It was clear days ago that the threat of losing Lieutenant Hopkins was insufficient to get me what I wanted. I had thought that the boys...but alas," he said with a Gallic shrug and a glance toward the door to the street. "Surely, however, you will not sacrifice a lady—this lady," he said, shaking her, "for an old cookbook?"

"Let her go," Langley calmly ordered. "You can't win."

"Perhaps not," Jacobs agreed with a mirthless laugh, turning her body just enough to reveal the gun. "But either way, you will lose."

That slight motion put the counter within Amanda's reach. Closest at hand sat a little box that had once been filled with pieces of chalk, the sort dressmakers used to mark patterns on fabric before cutting. Scrunching shut her eyes and mouth, she reached for it and tossed its contents over her shoulder, into Jacobs's face.

It wasn't much, but the dust made him sputter and relax his hold on her throat enough for her to reach the dish of rusty straight pins. When she sent them flying, he swore and released her, throwing up a hand to shield his eyes from a hundred tiny darts.

With one hand, Langley seized the bolt of fabric and gave Jacobs a wallop across his torso, knocking the pistol from his hand and sending it skittering across the dirty floor as he doubled over to catch his breath.

As the two men scrambled for the gun, Amanda's hands met with the final item within reach: a heavy pattern book, with gold lettering curling across the cover. When *Ladies' Best Fashions for Winter 1802* met the back of Jacobs's skull, he slumped forward, groaned, and lay still at last.

She collapsed on hands and knees and crawled toward Langley, who was trying to scoot himself up against the wall one-handed. Colonel Millrose appeared in the curtained doorway and bent to snatch up the gun.

"Lieutenant Hopkins is below," Langley said, his breathing labored. "He needs medical attention."

"So do you," Amanda told him, cradling him against her body and laying gentle fingertips on the sticky, spreading stain that covered his arm.

"Just a scratch," he insisted. "I'll be fine."

Hoping for confirmation, she darted a glance toward Colonel Millrose, whose mouth was set in a grave line. But her attention was quickly drawn back to Langley when he murmured, "We made a good team, Amanda."

And with that, his eyes drifted closed.

# Chapter 19

Langley groaned as Fanny squared the tray in front of him. "Not more beef tea?"

"It's strengthening," she replied with a smile, reaching to fluff up the pillow between his back and the wall.

"It's also damned hard to eat soup with one arm in a sling," he grumbled, gesturing with his injured arm and promptly wishing he hadn't.

When she straightened, he could see the scold etched into her brow, although the smile still curved her lips, warmer and more genuine than he had seen in a long time. "Well, after what happened earlier, I won't presume to try to help."

"Sorry about that. I never have been an especially good patient."

"And thank God for that," declared Colonel Millrose as he entered and made Langley's small quarters at the Underground officially crowded. "Means you've never been too badly hurt. I'd like a word with the Magpie, Mrs. Drummond, if you don't mind."

"Of course not, sir. I'll go back to my studies."

"Studies?" Langley asked when the door closed behind her.

"She's familiarizing herself with varieties of tobacco," Millrose explained, easing into the only chair. The room was so narrow, his bent knees nearly brushed the edge of the bed. "When we returned from Lambeth, she proposed being allowed to take on some of the shop duties, to free up my time. We'll still want to make her less recognizable, do something about that hair, of course. But after her performance at the dressmaker's, I'd say she's earned a new assignment. Wouldn't you agree?"

Langley nodded. He wasn't surprised by Fanny's determination or her bravery.

"And speaking of new assignments," Millrose continued, "I've had a message from General Scott."

"Oh?" Langley picked up his spoon and managed to slurp in a mouthful of broth rather than ask the question that had been eating at him since he'd awakened.

*What about Amanda?*

His memory of events at the shop were mostly clear, but choppy. He knew, for instance, that the boys had been rescued and Amanda had escaped Jacobs's clutches unharmed. But what had happened afterward, where she and her sons were now, was a mystery to him. One he could have solved with a simple inquiry, true. But should he?

That mission was over.

Millrose nodded, as if to confirm it. "He has a new assignment for you, when you're ready. Though I'm not sure you're going to like it."

Which meant Langley was going to hate it. Irritation prickled along his skin. Surely he'd done enough to renew his status as Scott's best agent?

"He wants you to leave the Underground."

Rather than meet the other man's eyes, Langley glanced around the windowless room, smaller than some prison cells. The wretched rope cot. The lack of privacy.

He knew full well it could be worse.

"And do what, may I ask?"

"Well, that's rather, er, complicated...." Billy shifted uncomfortably in the unforgiving wooden chair. "I think the situation with Lord Kingston put it into his mind."

Langley almost choked on his second spoonful of beef tea. "Kingston?"

"Yes. Under interrogation, Jacobs confessed that he'd been hoping to have an opportunity to search Bartlett House. Seems the late earl was rumored to have a few hidey-holes about the place. For secreting away important papers and the like." Langley's thoughts were immediately drawn to that night in the library, and Amanda's seductive disclosure of her husband's stash of illicit brandy.

"Is the general—?" Langley had to stop and clear his throat so that the words didn't sound rough with eagerness. "Is he sending me back to Bartlett House?"

Millrose didn't answer. "Scott says he doubts the story is true, but it reminded him of the usefulness of his prior connection to Lord Kingston and those West End types. It's good to have...*friends* in such circles, according to him. And he thinks"—Billy's pinched expression clearly revealed his reluctance to disclose the details of the new assignment—"Sir Langley Stanhope might fit the bill nicely."

"He wants me to resign my commission?"

"I don't think so, no. Not officially, at any rate. I suspect that he... he thought you might want a change. Something a little less dangerous. Thought you might have grown tired of being the Magpie."

"I *am* the—" Langley began, then stopped himself. *Had* it always been a role, a part he played? A disguise?

Was *Sir Langley* any more real? Not now, no...but could he be? Would he be welcomed in the hallowed halls of Mayfair, a person of interest in which delicate secrets could be confided, as General Scott evidently hoped?

Moving in the circles of the late Lord Kingston would also mean seeing Amanda now and again. Langley's wayward mind called up the image of her in that red dress, the night of Dulsworthy's ball. How would it feel to watch her laugh and dance with other gentlemen?

Unless, of course, she'd had enough of excitement and adventure and was determined never again to leave the house.

"How is she?"

That quiet question ought to have made no sense at all, unless Millrose somehow possessed the power to anticipate the direction of Langley's thoughts.

Nevertheless, he answered. "Lady Kingston is perfectly well."

"I'm glad to hear it. There was a letter meant for her. From Dulsworthy," Langley recalled. "In my coat. The day of—the day—" His spoon clattered back into his bowl as he freed his hand to gesture at his injured arm. "What happened to it?"

"The coat was ruined, I'm afraid. The surgeon had to cut it away to get at your arm and dig out the bullet. But Fanny herself placed the contents of your pockets in here," Millrose said, tapping the top of the little bedside table, with its single drawer.

Relief sighed from Langley's aching chest. "Good." At least he could give Amanda that much.

"There's more to General Scott's orders," Millrose said after a moment's silence. "But first, I was curious..." Though the size of the room gave a man's eye very little opportunity to roam, Billy was doing an excellent job of avoiding his gaze.

"Go on."

"I've been wondering about the, ah...that is, whether you..." A sharp exhalation puffed his lips, as if he were trying to force out the question.

"What exactly is the nature of the relationship between you and the countess?"

It was Langley's turn to shift awkwardly, and the movement nearly upset the tray Fanny had placed over his lap. "As I'm to be a gentleman now, I suppose the only proper reply I can give is that the lady must be the one to answer such a question."

Millrose gave an impatient wave of his hand, brushing off Langley's words like an irritating gnat. "Yes, of course." Then he reached that same hand into his breast pocket and withdrew a stack of folded notes. "But I think, in her way, she already has. She's written four times to enquire after your health, you see."

"But we were in Lambeth together only—

"Yesterday. Yes."

Hope flared in Langley's chest, but he ruthlessly tamped it out. A secret liaison had been one thing, but the terms of this new assignment would make its continuation impossible. For all her professed love of adventure, public exposure of an affair was not a risk a lady, even a wealthy widow, could afford to take. And she had made clear she didn't want anything more.

Unless her thoughts on the matter had changed?

Millrose wasn't finished, however. "General Scott himself suggested that your connection to Lady Kingston might prove valuable in your efforts to infiltrate the beau monde."

"Did he?" Evidently, he had not given up on his matchmaking.

"Furthermore," and here, Billy's voice grew more hesitant still, "he hinted that he's written to her to say as much."

When Langley tried to picture Amanda's face at the receipt of such a letter, his limbs felt heavy. He must have lost even more blood that he'd realized.

"And then, of course, there's the matter of what you told her in the dressmaker's shop."

"What *I* told her?" Langley strained to remember, but the closing events of the day had gone gray around the edges.

"You said that the two of you made a good team."

"I did?"

"Aye," Millrose said, tapping the stack of folded notes on the corner of Langley's tray before jumping to his feet, as nervous as Langley had ever seen him. "This may be the most dangerous assignment I'll ever send you on, Stanhope. But then, you're one of the bravest men I've ever known. Brave enough to tell her how you feel."

Langley's heart pounded, making his injured arm throb. "Is that an order, sir?"

"If it'll help things along, yes."

Those words required more than the usual amount of time to penetrate Langley's thoughts, crowded as they were with images of Amanda writing and sending four notes in less than a day. Surely they suggested a deeper degree of concern than one might expect her to lavish on a mere passing amusement?

"Well, then, don't just stand there, man," he shouted when he finally understood what Millrose had said. "Where is she?"

"Bartlett House." Obligingly, Billy lifted the tray pinning him to the bed. "The whole family's there."

*Less than a mile away.*

Langley swung his legs over the side, then sagged against the wall as the little room spun. "Christ." That single mile might as well be a hundred.

"Take it easy, Magpie." Millrose extended an arm, and Langley gratefully accepted his assistance as he struggled to stand on alarmingly weak legs. "This isn't the time for any, er, strenuous declarations." A flicker of amusement frayed the edges of the man's frown of concern. "But if you *are* determined to go down on one knee, at least we can be sure Lady Kingston possesses both the strength and resourcefulness to get you back on your feet."

\* \* \* \*

"Happy birthday, Jamie." As she spoke, Amanda reached out a hand to brush the hair from his brow, then stopped herself. First, because the shadow falling across his face disguised the purple smudge of a bruise beneath his eye, the visible remnants of the terrible hours he and his brother had spent in the company of Jacobs and his associates. And second because her first born was a young man now, not a child, and could decide how to style his own hair.

With a flash of a grin, he tossed his head, momentarily sending the hair back where it belonged. "Thank you, Mama. You didn't have to go to the trouble of a party."

Her answering smile was considerably weaker. Had she sheltered her sons so thoroughly that they could use the word *party* to speak of a few extra flowers in the morning room, and a slice of cake with their grandmother?

"It seems to me we have a great deal to celebrate," she said.

But when she tried to force her smile wider, it wobbled. Yesterday's horrors were still too fresh for her to be able to recall them without thinking of how much worse things could have been. They might have found the dressmaker's shop empty. Jacobs, in his desperation, could have harmed her boys to get what he wanted. The blood stains on the tattered dress presently tucked away upstairs might be the last bit of Langley she would ever see again.

The rest were only horrors of the imagination. But the part about losing Langley might yet prove to be true. Despite Colonel Millrose's reassurances about his injuries and the strange letter from General Scott that had arrived that morning, it was too easy to think the Magpie might fly away and be gone from her forever.

"Oh, bother," she said, surreptitiously dashing tears from corners of her eyes. "I forgot your present upstairs." On her bedside table, still wrapped in brown shop paper, lay the thin geometry book. "I'll just—I'd best go fetch it, hadn't I?"

"Let me," her mother offered.

Amanda shook her head. No matter how foolish, she wanted one last, private chance to clutch that parcel, the one that had brought Langley into her life, close to her heart.

But before she could frame her refusal into words, her mother laid a hand on her shoulder and nodded toward the garden. "Don't you think you should see to your guest first?"

"Guest?"

Amanda followed her mother's gaze, through the windows of the morning room, past the flowerbeds, to the wrought-iron gate. In the alleyway beyond, disguised by the unkempt branches of the hedge, she glimpsed a figure. A man in a red coat.

"It's Mr. Stanhope," said Pip, moving toward the door.

"*Major* Stanhope," Jamie corrected, following him.

"*Sir Langley*," their grandmother declared with a note of finality as she released Amanda's shoulder to catch the boys by their elbows. "And I'll wager he's here to speak to your mama about something important, so you stay here."

Dazed, Amanda descended the three broad steps and crossed the garden, fearful every moment that he would prove to be just another specter conjured by her tortured mind. At the gate she stopped and wrapped one hand around a sun-warmed metal post. "Why didn't you come to the front door?"

He lifted one shoulder, though the movement made him wince with pain. His uniform otherwise disguised his injuries admirably, the scarlet wool reflecting color onto his pale face, the drape of one sleeve almost hiding the sling in which his injured arm rested. "This seems...more fitting, somehow."

"Well, either way, I'm glad you're here," she said.

At the same time he told her, "Billy sent me to talk with you." Then for a long moment, he said nothing more.

"About General Scott's letter?" she prompted.

"In a manner of speaking." Another pause, and he refused to meet her eye. "What did you make of it?"

"Well, I was certainly surprised to discover that my husband was a—well, an associate of General Scott's, should I say? I wish he had confided in me. I might have been some help to him, more than a hostess. But I suppose he must've thought me too much of an empty-headed rattle," she concluded with a forced laugh.

"If the late Lord Kingston believed any such thing," Langley said, "he would have been a fool. And in my experience, General Scott does not suffer fools."

She did not know which was stranger: the tenor of his reassurance, or the fact that she was reassured by it. "Thank you. I am flattered that General Scott believes I could be of assistance now—"

"But I daresay you've had enough excitement for one lifetime." His narrowed gaze darted toward the garden, to where the boys and her mother were no doubt watching them with interest. "You're under no obligation to go along with Scott's schemes, you know."

Every time he spoke, his voice sounded more gruff, pricklier than the hedge between them. Always before when he had acted and sounded thus, she had imagined him determined to ward her off from danger.

For the first time, she wondered whether he might not be trying to goad her. Had he hoped—did he *want* her to agree to General Scott's idea of a partnership between them?

"Whereas you are obligated to follow orders, Major Stanhope?" she asked.

He gave a curt nod, his jaw set in a familiar, stubborn line.

"Well, I suspect the ladies of the *ton* will be only too happy to pour their secrets—and anyone else's they may happen to learn—into the ear of the dashing Sir Langley. And when you and I cross paths at these society events," she went on, "I shall try not to let my jealousy interfere with your mission."

"J-jealousy?"

She had heard him speak in half a dozen different voices. But she had never before heard him stammer. Something devilish and delightful flickered to life in her chest. "Mm, yes. I confess that when I read General Scott's letter, I was disappointed. Oh, not in the overall idea, of course—I'm happy to use my connections to help gather information on behalf of the Crown. It's just that, well…lately, I had found myself wondering about the possibility of another sort of partnership between you and me. Perhaps foolishly, I had been hoping for a different kind of proposal altogether."

His hand rose to encircle the post next to the one where her hand rested. Almost, but not quite, touching her. "Oh?"

At just that moment, a shadow of wings fluttered over them. She glanced up as the bird found its perch on the top of one of the fence posts. Its striking black and white feathers gleamed in the afternoon sun.

"A magpie," she said, surprise making her voice sharp.

A sign of something, surely?

"But alone." His knuckles had turned white where they griped the black iron. "One for sorrow," he said, quoting the familiar rhyme.

Releasing the post, she reached through the gap to lay her palm against his chest. "Not alone," she whispered. "Two for mirth."

Beneath her hand, his heart beat a little faster. "*Marriage*, as I always heard it."

"Oh?" She curled her fingers against his coat. "Those sorts of variations are fascinating, aren't they? For instance, as a young woman—and certainly as a widow—it would never have been evident to me that *mirth* and *marriage* could have anything at all to do with one another. But recently, I—"

"Amanda."

She spoke over him, ready, quite ready, to take the greatest risk of all. "I—I began to ask myself whether—whether it might not be possible to—if, for instance, a marriage had some…*spark* behind it, if it were what people call a—a…love match, then perhaps—"

"Amanda." He took a step forward, and the brass buttons on his coat clanged as he pressed his chest against the iron bars.

Silently she mirrored his movement, closing the narrow gap between them. "Yes?"

"Do you always talk this much when a man's trying to tell you he loves you?"

"Oh. Well, I can't honestly say, you know, because no one has ever—"

With a quirk of one dark brow that turned her insides to custard, he leaned in and silenced her with a kiss, sweet and hot, filled with the promise of passionate adventures yet to come.

"I think," she said, when her breath was mostly her own again, "I should probably invite you in." With her other hand, she turned the key in the lock and opened the gate. "Matthews told me just this morning that the smith came while we were in Richmond."

Langley laughed as he stepped into the garden and put his good arm around her waist. "It's just as well. I doubt you'd find it terribly—*dashing*, was that your word?—if I tried to scale that fence just now. Though Colonel Millrose did say he thought you'd be willing to pick me up if I fell flat on my face."

"I like him." She tipped her head against his shoulder. "And he's right, you know."

His gaze flickered toward the morning room. "I also wasn't expecting to declare myself in front of an audience."

"We were just having a little celebration," she explained as she urged him along the curving path. "It's Jamie's birthday today."

"I won't be intruding?"

"I know how much you dislike sentimental turns of phrase. But I rather suspect you'll be the best present of all." She glanced up at him with a wry smile. "After all, *I* only got him a book."

The boys poured out of the morning room and raced toward them. "Major Stanhope! Major Stanhope!"

"Sir Langley," her mother said from the top step and sketched a curtsy.

Langley released Amanda and bowed. "Mrs. West."

"I take it the two of you have something to tell us?"

Amanda could not decide whether her mother was displeased.

"I would be sorry to steal the spotlight from Lord Kingston on his birthday, ma'am."

"It's all right, sir," Jamie insisted.

"Well, then," Langley began, and he tightened his grip around her waist, as if he needed the support. "Your mother and I are—"

"Getting married?" inserted Pip, sounding entirely unimpressed by the revelation. "We'd guessed that much already, sir. Oh, I meant to tell you"—he came to Langley's other side as he spoke—"I used the parry-thrust to get away from those chaps, just like you taught me."

"That's very good…Pip," Langley said, venturing the familiar name.

Jamie's dark eyes glittered. "Imagine how impressive it would've been if you'd had a sword and not a dressmaker's yardstick."

"Well." Mama tipped her head to one side, surveying the foursome with thinly disguised amusement as the ascended the steps. "I'd say this calls for cake."

While Jamie cut thick slabs of Mrs. Trout's excellent orange sponge and Mama poured tea, Amanda slipped away to retrieve the book.

"Open it," she said when she returned and pressed the package into Jamie's sticky hands. Then she sent a shy glance toward Langley. "I suppose you could say it's from both of us."

"Ah," Jamie cried as he tore away the paper, "*De l'Esprit géométrique.* Thank you, Mama." He pressed an even stickier kiss on her cheek. "And thank you, sir."

"You know," Langley said, accepting an awkward left-handed handshake, "Pascal's work has been instrumental in the science of encryption."

Pip snatched the book from his brother's hand. "You mean codes and such? Like spies use?"

Langley's lips quirked. "The very same."

Her younger son's eyes flared with a heretofore undreamt-of expression of interest in mathematics. "Will you teach us, sir?"

A catch rose in Amanda's throat. The boys' attachment to Langley overjoyed her, of course. But for just a moment, she had forgotten that a part of their future together still lay in shadow.

Langley, however, only smiled and nodded at the request. "I'd be delighted. And you've just reminded me that I do have a little gift of my own." He reached into his breast pocket, grimacing a little as he shifted his sling to do it, and withdrew a folded paper. "Though I admit I was thinking of your mother when I got it," he said as he held it out to her.

It was a curiously stained piece of parchment, and when she unfolded it, she could have sworn she caught a whiff of brandy. She had to read through the scrawled words twice to make sure she understood what they said. And who had written them.

"What is it?" Jamie demanded.

"A letter, from Lord Dulsworthy, about your going to school—"

Disappointment flickered in Jamie's dark eyes. "You mean, *not* going."

The words seared her. It had taken her too long to realize her own overprotectiveness. Despite a lifetime of resentment at being told to mind her own step, she'd very nearly clipped her sons' wings. But it was not too late to watch them soar. "I admit, I have my reservations. It's only natural for mamas to worry," she added with a glance at her mother, both seeking and offering forgiveness for years of misunderstanding. "And after your father died, I wanted to be the one to make all the decisions about your education. But that was wrong of me. Lord Dulsworthy's letter means that when you boys are ready"—she looked at each of her sons in turn, and finally at Langley, wondering what he'd done to procure George's cooperation—"it will be a *family* decision."

"I can go to Harrow?" Jamie's face lit up as he came to throw his arms around her neck. "Thank you, Mama. And thank you, too," he added, turning toward Langley. "Say, what are we to call you after you marry Mama?"

"Major Stanhope?" Pip was eyeing his uniform.

"Perhaps Sir Langley?" suggested their grandmother.

Jamie straightened and looked from Langley to Amanda and back again. "Would it be all right to call you Papa?"

Langley started. "Yes. I suppose it would. If you wish it. Someday." Each little statement was punctuated by a noise in his throat. Once she might have misunderstood that gruff sound, but now she recognized it as a mask for his embarrassment. And his surprise. And his pleasure. "I would be honored, Jamie."

Anyone who came upon them, enjoying tea and cake in the morning room—Pip trying out fencing maneuvers with an icing-covered knife while his grandmama laughingly reprimanded him, Langley and Jamie with their heads bent together over a treatise on mathematics—doubtless would have taken it for a sketch of ordinary family life. Perhaps even a trifle dull.

Amanda, however, knew that beneath the surface of those everyday moments lay passion and adventure enough for a lifetime. And love, too. Because the man beside her might hide behind a number of disguises and go by a laundry list of different names.

But to her, he would always be the Magpie.

# Epilogue

Pausing in his perusal of the message that had just been delivered, Langley watched Amanda arrange the last of the summer roses in a vase on the hall table. Such a simple, ordinary thing. Just as cozy and domestic as he'd imagined the first time he'd brought her to this house. The day he'd first begun to consider whether this place could once more be a home. Whether it might be possible to build a future with her.

And now, that future was here.

Folding the note behind his back, he stepped closer, laid his free hand on her hip, pressed a kiss to the curve of her shoulder. "You know, your mother and the boys won't be here for at least another hour."

For the past few weeks, Mrs. West had stayed with her grandsons in London, while Langley and Amanda had enjoyed a honeymoon of sorts in Richmond. He had missed Jamie and Philip and looked forward to the reunion of their family, but their arrival was certainly going to put a damper on his project to make love to his wife in every room of the house.

"Only an hour?" Amanda exclaimed, even as she turned toward his embrace. "I should make sure that Mrs. Morris has—"

"She has."

"And check on the—"

"Already done."

"Well, what about the—"

"Sorted, I'm sure."

"You don't even know what I was going to say," she protested with a delightful pout.

"Don't I?" He shot a stern glance over the top rim of his spectacles, knowing the effect such a look usually had.

This time, however, she met that seductive, commanding stare with pursed lips and wry amusement. Carefully, she reached up and adjusted his spectacles, forcing him to look through the lenses. "What did the messenger bring?"

The pair of them had come from different worlds, and in marrying they'd vowed not to forget those different lives, but to fuse them. Could it be done?

The answer to her question would be their first test.

"A letter from General Scott," he said.

Despite Langley's newfound appreciation for domestic life, word of an assignment had sent a familiar anticipation tingling through him, mingling in interesting and exciting ways with his desire to share every moment with his wife.

But how would the news make Amanda feel?

Her brows curved upward. "Oh?"

He tried to sort the meaning from her expression and her tone, but could not. When he did not immediately present the letter, she fished behind his back to retrieve it. He watched as her dark eyes scanned the contents.

"A house party," she read.

He nodded. The intimacy that grew between the guests at a house party always exposed something interesting. He'd attended such events before, but never as Sir Langley Stanhope.

And always before, he'd been alone.

Carefully, she refolded the note. "He wants us to host a house party. Here."

"Yes."

"Will people come, do you suppose?"

"Oh, yes."

Their wedding had been a quiet affair, attended just by her family and a few of Langley's fellow officers. Nevertheless, the announcement of the marriage in the London papers had garnered a great deal of interest and speculation, according to Mrs. West's accounts of the gossip. People were fascinated by Langley's mysterious past and heroic exploits, and frequently expressed a desire to see the new Lady Stanhope take up her proper place as a scion of fashion and elegance.

Given how expertly Langley had been disguising himself for most of his life, he found it more than a little unsettling to be the object of attention. But it was a role his clever wife had been born to play.

Having anticipated society's reaction to their marriage, General Scott now intended for them to put that interest to use: Sir Langley and Lady Stanhope would be his secret agents, moving in the first ranks of society. Spying occasionally on the spies themselves, just as Millrose had once hinted.

"We'll have to ask Mr. Morris to see to the east chimney," she said, laying aside the note, "or half the guest rooms will be filled with smoke." Once more, she began to fidget with the roses, undoing what she'd so painstakingly done.

He caught her fingers in his, sensing her nervousness. "If you've changed your mind, love, we can tell Scott no."

When she looked up at him, he saw clearly the eager sparkle in her eyes. "No, I haven't changed my mind. But I can't help feeling...well, *guilty*, I suppose. I have everything a woman is supposed to want—and more. I love my children. I love you. Shouldn't all this"—one hand fluttered free, taking in the roses, the furniture, the quiet house, before coming to rest against his chest—"be enough?"

He pressed her palm against his heart. "The world tries to make us choose between what's expected and what's exciting, between who we are and what we love. But family is an adventure. Love is an adventure. And this"—he tipped his chin toward the table, where the letter lay—"will be an adventure."

"Mama would say that a lady should mind her step..."

"A mother's desire to protect her children is both admirable and understandable, wouldn't you agree?" he said. She gave a rueful laugh and her cheeks pinked at that gentle reminder of a trait she and Mrs. West shared. "But sometimes we have to leap, you know. Even if we don't know where we're going to land."

"Do you know, that's exactly what Mrs. Drummond told me." She tilted her head to one side, and a beam of sunlight made her dark eyes glitter mischievously. "But I rather thought magpies flew."

"Then let's fly, my love," he said, swooping in for a swift kiss. "Together."

\* \* \* \*

General Zebadiah Scott gave a satisfied smile as he tipped back in his chair and tossed the morning paper onto the otherwise-empty desktop. Gossip columnists were as important as the officers in his service when it came to gathering information. Perhaps *more* important—too few spies were attuned to the value of the latest on-dits, even when they concerned Sir Langley and Lady Stanhope's house party.

He had not long to bask in his triumph, however. The new angle of his chair to the desk, combined with a shaft of sunlight slanting over the newspaper, forced a previously-overlooked item into his line of vision. He leaned forward again, the front legs of his chair dropping softly onto the carpet.

*Pandemonium! Sly Lady Sterling has struck again, this time*

*vexing a visit to Vauxhall Gardens for the ordinarily penurious*
*Lord P—, a plump pigeon plucked before he could play.*

For good measure, Scott removed his spectacles, polished them against his waistcoat, and settled them carefully on his face again before reading the lines a second time. But the words remained as opaque—or clear—as they had ever been:

Lord P— (Penhurst, presumably) had been robbed by London's most notorious—and fascinating—thief.

Pandemonium was a high-stakes hell. A man of Penhurst's reputation would never have been permitted to gamble there on credit, so Lady Sterling, whoever she was, must have pocketed a weighty purse indeed. One wondered where he had acquired the funds—and how she had discovered they were in his possession.

As Scott added Penhurst's name to his mental list of the Lady Sterling's victims, something clicked quietly into place. Over the past few months, a surprising number of aristocrats had found themselves in a similar predicament. He knew each to be a man with a personal weakness, some past misdeed that made him potentially easy prey.

Lord Dulsworthy's recent treachery—Scott hardly knew if someone so dull-witted could rightly be accused of treason—was a pointed reminder of a how a weak man could be exploited by the enemies of the Crown.

Some speculated Lady Sterling was no mere thief, but an avenging angel acting on behalf of individuals who had been wronged by the men in question. Scott rather hoped than knew it to be so. But if it *were* true, then she was in possession not just of these men's valuables, but also their secrets, worth far more than mere pounds and pence. What scandalous stories could the Lady Sterling tell? And what might the subjects of those tales be willing to pay, or do, to ensure her silence?

A good many Englishmen had cause to regard such a clever woman as an enemy.

Scott wanted her as an ally.

"Collins!"

He called for his aide before remembering that he was not in his Whitehall office but at home in his study, hiding from Mrs. Scott as she put the finishing touches on her preparations for their trip to Brighton. He pushed to his feet and stepped toward the bell, but before he could ring it, Highsmith, his redoubtable butler, stepped to the doorway, unfazed at having been summoned by the wrong name and in such a fashion.

"Yes, sir?"

"Has—er, has Mrs. Scott finished packing, Highsmith?"

"The footmen brought down Mrs. Scott's trunks earlier this morning," he reported, then hesitated. "But she's at work on yours again, I'm afraid."

"Good, good," said Scott absently, grateful for his wife's distraction. As best he could, he tried to keep his domestic life untroubled by his work.

At that unlooked-for reaction to what should have been unfortunate news, something like surprise flickered into the butler's eyes. Ignoring it, Scott returned to his desk and scrawled a few words across a piece of paper, then folded and sealed it. "I need you to deliver this message to—to my tobacconist's. An urgent matter."

Highsmith's eyebrows rose fractionally higher, though their movement was almost lost in the vast expanse of his forehead, undifferentiated from the dome of his bald pate. "Of course, sir," he said, taking the note.

"And see to it that my trunks are locked and brought down at noon sharp. Empty or full." His wife had packed and unpacked them half a dozen times at least. But come morning, he meant to be on his way to enjoying the refreshing sea air, with or without luggage.

"Very good, sir."

Not an hour later, Captain Jeremy Addison was standing before his desk, his dark head bowed over the same item in the same newspaper. When he looked up, he wore an expression somewhere between nonplussed and annoyed.

At the sight of it, Scott battled back a smile. "Ah. I take it you have heard of the Lady Sterling?"

"My sister Julia finds the woman's exploits amusing and takes it upon herself to keep me apprised."

Scott could well imagine the teasing. "An interesting choice of alias for a thief, is it not? *Sterling.* Hints at excellence, trustworthiness. Purity—of motive, perhaps, if not of method."

Addison looked up, fixing him with a pair of shockingly blue eyes. "I trust you didn't call me here over a trivial coincidence. Sir."

Scott, who did not believe in coincidences, sat down behind his desk and motioned the other man toward a chair.

From time to time, he saw an opportunity to shift one of his agents to a position that was still useful, though considerably less dangerous. Often, the change in assignment was precipitated by a change in responsibilities at home: a man might come into a piece of property, as had happened recently with Lieutenant Sutherland, the Earl of Magnus. Though it was certainly not official policy, Scott generally did what he could to make sure the officers in his service seized such a chance to step into a quieter life, settle down, start a family. The war could and would get along without them.

Of course, many of those officers were not inclined to leave his service and required a little nudge. Some, like Major Laurens, now the Duke of Raynham, had been reluctant to return to claim an inheritance they did not want. Others, like the Magpie, fancied themselves in love with danger.

But none of that experience could help Scott now. Jeremy Addison needed not a nudge but a shove, and not toward a quiet life, but away from it.

Though a viscount, he never flaunted his title; he'd offered his skills to the army as a codebreaker instead. Though he was handsome and intelligent enough to attract any lady's notice, the only women he ever mentioned were his mother and sister, tucked away in a rented cottage in Hammersmith. Though he might have made a reasonably comfortable home with them, he chose to quarter in the Underground. Scott felt sure his message had found the man alone in the dank, dimly-lit workroom there, bent over a book.

Embarrassment over an inherited debt—that was all the explanation Captain Addison had ever given for relegating himself to the shadows. Beyond preposterous to believe that the search for a mysterious and morally ambiguous woman was just the thing to entice him back into the light.

Nevertheless, Scott intended to test the case.

He steepled his fingers as he contemplated how best to begin. "Like your sister, I've been following the Lady Sterling's career with interest. She targets men whom I would call…vulnerable, in some way. Men with secrets they would like to keep. And while money may be one motivation for her exploits, I suspect it is not all she takes from these men."

Perhaps in spite of himself, interest flickered in Addison's bright eyes. "She's gathering information, you mean?"

"Yes. Information that can be used for blackmail. Indeed, she may already be in possession of secrets capable of doing real damage—to the war effort, the King, even the nation. I need to know whose side she is on." He slid his fingers together and laid his folded hands before him on his desk. "So I'm sending *you* to find her."

Addison, who had been obligingly nodding along with his commanding officer until the last, jerked to his feet. "*I?* But I—I don't—" His throat bobbed in a hard swallow. "What am I to do with her if I succeed?"

"*When*," Scott corrected, handing the newspaper across his desk to Captain Addison as he would a set of orders. "And I should think the answer would be obvious, *Lord Sterling.* I want you to marry her."

Can't get enough of these spies and the women who love them?

Be sure to read

**WHO'S THAT EARL**

And stay tuned

For more from the Love & Let Spy series

Coming soon from

**Susanna Craig**

And

**Lyrical Books**

Printed in the United States
by Baker & Taylor Publisher Services